The Epic Mahabharata   Book I

The
CHILDREN
of
MIDNIGHT

The CHILDREN *of* MIDNIGHT

ASHOK K. BANKER

JAICO PUBLISHING HOUSE

Ahmedabad Bangalore Bhopal Bhubaneswar Chennai
Delhi Hyderabad Kolkata Lucknow Mumbai

Published by Jaico Publishing House
A-2 Jash Chambers, 7-A Sir Phirozshah Mehta Road
Fort, Mumbai - 400 001
jaicopub@jaicobooks.com
www.jaicobooks.com

THE EPIC MAHABHARATA - BOOK 1:
THE CHILDREN OF MIDNIGHT
ISBN 978-81-8495-658-0

First Jaico Impression: 2017

Page design and layout: Inosoft Systems, Delhi

Printed by
Replika Press Pvt. Ltd.

|| ॐ ||

We bow first to Nara-Narayana
and Devi Saraswati
before uttering the first word
of this great endeavor…

Jaya!

|| invocation ||

|| om ganesha namaha ||

invoking the power of the infinite om,
with the tip of your ink-dipped tusk
you first recorded this tale of tales
as dictated by the venerable krishna-dweipayana vyasa.

may this scribe's humble attempt
to traverse again that great ocean of stories
please you, lord.

|| idam na mana ||

|| dedication ||

for yashka, who said, 'awesome.'
and is an awesome daughter.
for ayush, who said, 'do it.'
ayushmaanbhavya, my son.
for bithika, who said, 'write.'
and is always right, dearest wife.

this gift of words and swords,
this ocean of endless wonders,
this forest of stories.

|| kshamapana ||

to every person i have ever known,
i join my hands in humility,
and beg forgiveness,
for any error i committed,
knowing or unknowing.

even though you and i
are two distinct individuals,
separated
by walled-in compartments of self,
yet when you lose,
i don't win.

the path to true and lasting peace
begins with unconditional forgiveness.

to end the war without
let us first end the war within.

|| michhami dukkadam ||

‖ to the gentle reader ‖

the song belongs
to they who listen

we had a pact,
you and i,
that I would transport you
on wings of song
from ayodhya to lanka
and back again.

now that journey is done.
and we prepare anew
to embark on another
far greater voyage
across the ocean of itihasa.

listen now, my friend,
for like the first tale,
this new song I begin,
is not just mine to sing,

it is her story,
his story,
your story,
our story.

‖ jaidev jaidev satyamev jaitey ‖

|| contents ||

|| prarambha ||

The Road Already Travelled

The Kuru race descended from the line of Bharata, he who was born of Shakuntala, the hermit's daughter, and Raja Dushyanta, who failed to recognize his own progeny at first but later acknowledged his lapse and embraced both his neglected wife and son. Bharata and his descendants then ruled over the rich alluvial plains in the land of the Five Rivers, lending his name to their lineage as well as the sub-continent inhabited by the Kuru race.

In time, Raja Shantanu, a descendant of Bharata, came to love a woman of ethereal beauty, never realizing that she was in fact the river goddess Ganga cursed to take mortal form for a period. Shantanu and Ganga's time together was a torrid melding, as fierce as the river herself in spate, but eventually, it was doomed to end. The terms of her curse and exile from her true home having been fulfilled, Ganga had to return home to her watery course, taking with her the sole surviving son of her union with Shantanu. That illustrious son of Ganga and Shantanu, named Devavrata, was raised by his mother and great-forebear Himavat, lord of the great mountain ranges, and was imbued with godlike talents and abilities.

Shantanu's grief at losing the love of his life was mitigated to some degree by the joy of having regained a son so illustrious; he had no rival in any world. For Devavrata was the epitome of dharma in his deeds and words and in every conceivable way. He was a demigod in power and spirit, capable of besting the most formidable mortal armies single-handedly, indestructible in pitched battle or single combat, and was in fact blessed with the gift of immortality until the day he voluntarily chose to end his own existence. He could have possessed any woman he desired, and was desired by all women, yet he surrendered his own conjugal pleasures and abdicated his own claim to the Kuru throne in order to satisfy the demand of the fisher king father of of the ferry-woman Satyavati. For through the manipulation of the river goddess, Shantanu had rediscovered love, a love as epic almost as the one he had shared with Ganga herself.

Meeting the fisher king's daughter on her boat as he was ferried across the river, Shantanu was overwhelmed by desire for the young girl. But so different was their station from that of the Kurus that her father feared that with a son like Devavrata in line to inherit, no son of Satyavati would ever have claim to the throne of Hastinapura.

And without a scion on the throne, Satyavati would be no better than a concubine: people would say that Shantanu had married a lowly fisher girl only to fulfill his own lust. Devavrata, the ideal son in every respect, could not bear to see his father's heartbreak at being denied his chance at love yet again. Mindful of his own mother's part in orchestrating this union, and knowing that she felt responsible for ensuring that Shantanu found joy again in life, he prepared to undertake a great and terrible sacrifice.

Devavrata saw that the only way to ensure his pater's claim to love and joy was to sacrifice his own. And so he undertook the terrible vow for which he earned the name *Bhishma*. Swearing he would never enjoy conjugal relations with any woman throughout his mortal existence, and never lay claim to the Kuru throne himself, Bhishma then urged his father to marry Satyavati and rediscover love again. Reluctant at first, Shantanu eventually caved in and married the fisher king's daughter.

For a while, all was well. Shantanu and Satyavati lived in conjugal bliss and in due course, were blessed with fine and righteous male heirs while Bhishma's administration expanded the kingdom to an empire the likes of which had never been seen before in the sub-continent. But eventually, through a series of misfortunes the sons of Satyavati both died, leaving behind childless widows. The Kuru throne lay empty, for owing to his terrible vow, Bhishma was only a regent; he could never rule the kingdom in his own right. Satyavati argued that he should release himself from his vow but he refused flatly, saying that the earth could stop turning and the sky may fall, but he would never rescind his vow. She then attempted to persuade him to father sons upon her daughters-in-law as was the custom under the circumstances. Yet once again he refused, displaying the adherence to dharma that had made him a legendary name among men.

At her wit's end, the Dowager Queen finally resolved to send for her own illegitimate son by a prior union, the Sage Krishna-Dweipayana, now gaining fame as the collator of the Vedas and hence titled Vyasa. Laying the problem of progeny before her son, she requested him to cover her daughters-in-law and sire heirs to the Kuru throne. Vyasa agreed that what she asked was permissible under dharma in these circumstances. He agreed to do as she asked but cautioned her to ensure that the princesses were completely receptive and agreeable to the union too, for it was they who would bear his seed to fruition. Eager to see the Kuru throne occupied by a legitimate heir, Satyavati agreed.

But the princesses Ambika and Ambalika were unwilling and uncooperative during their respective acts of coition. Their behavior greatly displeased the great sage Vyasa, earning his displeasure and his curses as a brahmin. Hence, although he had seeded their wombs, one son was destined to be born blind, the other abnormal in appearance. A third son, the only one that would be born whole and possessed of all faculties as befitted a king, was unfortunately sired upon the princesses' maid and could never claim the throne.

Such mishaps, as the great sage Vyasa eloquently phrased it, could well be the seeds of future conflict. He then vanished with the potent power he wielded as a result of his meditative strength, leaving the Dowager Queen Satyavati to ponder on the future of the Kuru race.

‖ paksha eka ‖

|| 1 ||

An air of anticipation hung over the great metropolis like a cloud of hemp smoke.

The capital city of the Kuru nation, equally well known as Nagapura, City of Snakes, and Hastinapura, City of Elephants, waited with bated breath.

The royal criers had gone about the city the night before, calling out the news that Dowager Queen Satyavati, Widow of Raja Shantanu, late King of Hastinapura and Lord of the Kuru Bharata nation, would appear before the royal assembly at the auspicious hour recommended by the preceptors to issue an important announcement. One that they had all been waiting to hear for over a year.

The citizenry lined the avenues and roadways, sat atop rooftops and under catchments, filling up every dusty field, every mud-tracked roadway and every byway. Children sat on their father's shoulders or on their mother's hips, merchants and traders, hunters and farmers, brahmins and soldiers, all stood jostling one another. Hundreds of thousands of souls waited eagerly to hear the royal proclamation. Runners awaited, the reins of their mounts held in hand, ready to ride for their own capitol cities; for the news and its implications would change not only the course of their tribe's history but their nation's politics as well.

Inside the magnificent palace stronghold, the great Sabha hall was thronged from wall to wall with kings, princes, ministers and merchant lords, preceptors and traders, as well as ambassadors from a score of distant foreign lands. Even the sentries posted at each of the hundred and eight pillars of the great hall were pressed back against the cold stone by the immense crowd. The influence of the Kuru Bharata kingdom extended across the nations of the world. Traders and priests crossed oceans and deserts, mountain ranges and war-torn regions to travel here to the heart of the great Land of Five Rivers, known to many still by its ancient name of *Jambudwipa*, land of the Jambun Tree.

The dark blue fruit with its sticky sweet juice was only one of the many exotic items of produce, craft and manufacture that were found in this great sub-continent and nowhere else in the known world.

There were ambassadors with complexions darker than Satyavati herself; there were pale-skinned foreigners with yellow hair with strange garb and tongues; men from the Cathay lands with long mustaches and drooping eyelids; and allies, tributes and even royal visitors from distant foreign lands. Some of these foreigners were of dubious loyalty. A few had warred, allied against or otherwise opposed the expansion and growth of the Kuru Bharata race. At least one or more had ancestors who had perished in the legendary battle of Ten Kings on the Parusni plain where King Sudas of the Trtsu Bharatas had won a great victory against a far superior force led by ten rival kings. Former enemies or past rivals, all present now saw fit to bow their coiffured heads to the power and might of the Kuru throne. There were no hidden daggers tipped with poison for the descendants of Bharata Sudas. Only rich tributes and priceless treasures waiting to be gifted as tokens of humility and acknowledgement to the sovereignty of the Kuru dynasty.

For while the house of Bharata had grown and prospered greatly these past generations, in the past decade or two under the legendary steward Bhishma, it was no longer merely a kingdom, or even a nation. It had now become a formidable empire. The sheer mass of power and wealth and influence centered upon this single keep rivaled the greatest empires of distant continents. What happened here affected the world. The problem of progeny that had plagued the ruling dynasty was well known to all who followed the politics of kingship. If talk of amorous activity is a favorite pastime of all men and women, then talk of the amorous activities of royalty occupies a special position. For in an age where all news and learning was through spoken words, the whispered accounts of what royals did in private – and how they did it – was a great source of entertainment. And as the wisest bards demonstrated daily, entertainment was the best form of passing on information. Even the great Vedas, annals of the greatest wisdom known to civilized mortal kind, were told in the form of *katha* or story. And the story of the problem of progeny faced by the house of Kuru Bharatas was one that had been told and retold infinite times by infinite retellers across the known world, for by such means was information conveyed in ages past, news related, itihasa scribed, and history recorded.

It was the thirst for knowing which brought this vast gathering here today to throng the streets and rooftops and bridges and culverts and riverbanks and raj-margs and avenues and alleyways of Hastinapura City, and which crowded hundreds of over-dressed over-jeweled and overweight nobles and diplomats into that Sabha hall.

The crowds had grown restless, the gossip more spirited, when the tall, dark and stately form of Queen Satyavati appeared upon the dais of the Sabha hall. Her appearance was met with instant silence as every pair of eyes turned to her, lips silenced themselves, and ears awaited her proclamation.

She began with the customary homilies, made the usual ritual declarations and honored the ancestors, gods and all those required to be acknowledged by tradition. When all the formalities were over, she came to the nub of the matter. Not one to waste breath, knowing she already had a captive audience eager to receive her words, she glanced once, briefly but notably, at the towering form of Bhishma, who stood in full court armor, gleaming and resplendent, the most magnificent specimen of manhood in the entire assemblage; a symbol of the power of the entire Kuru Bharata nation and pillar of the very structure that held her aloft. He acknowledged her with a glance that revealed nothing but a son's respect and a younger's humility, though he was almost as young as she, and far far more powerful than she could ever be in a thousand lifetimes. Yet, his subtle gesture was significant, intended as a message to all who observed them, this unlikely duo of step-mother and step-son. For it was by Bhishma's leave that she ruled Hastinapura and through Bhishma's power and influence and reach that she maintained that post. That brief exchange of glances had been sufficient to convey to the world at large that all was well between the Dowager Queen Widow and her step-son, the Steward and Regent of the Kuru Empire. All was well and as it had been since Shantanu's demise. Nothing had changed in the power equation here.

A thousand wagers collapsed on that look alone.

A thousand fortunes were won and a thousand lost because of that sideward glance and subtle nod of acknowledgement.

A dozen national histories would be rewritten because of the strength and unity displayed in that casual look.

Kurujangala was unchanged and immutable. Let no one doubt or question that status quo, even on pain of death.

Her message conveyed, Satyavati came directly to the proclamation that all were waiting to receive.

'It is a great day for the Kuru dynasty, a great day for Hastinapura and Kurujangala, the dawn of a new epoch,' she said with a regal tone and manner that belied her origins as a fisherman's daughter who had spent her youth ferrying pilgrims across the Ganga, clad in scanty garb and stinking of fish. Now, as she stood before the awe-struck eyes of the nobility, dignitaries and commoners, she was the very image of what a queen should be— proud and dignified, the gold *mukut* on her head and gold sceptre in her hand leaving no doubt about her authority.

Her proud, slender form and beautiful dark complexion evoked envious glances from the ladies of the court as she scanned the sea of faces before her and her manner befitted the Queen of the greatest kingdom in the Arya world. 'The Kuru dynasty has two male heirs,' she said. 'The princesses Ambika and Ambalika have each given birth to a son. Both boys are healthy and well.'

The cheer that exploded from a million throats buffeted the air and carried for yojanas in every direction. The celebration that followed, enhanced by a royal edict granting free access to the granary reserves and soma stores of the palace to one and all for the entire duration of the traditional feasting period, was as epic as befitted the greatest dynasty of the sub-continent. Runners leaped aboard their wagons and carriages and mounts to carry the news to the farthest ends of the earth. Champions dueled one another for prizes. Gamblers won or lost fortunes. Men conjoined with their wives in the hopes of fathering princes themselves. The wives countered, mischievously, that they had better, or else Ved Vyasa would have to come and do it for them!

Few stayed to hear the shocking afterword to that proclamation, delivered by Satyavati to a select inner group of trusted familiars after the main assemblage had departed. These select few could be depended upon to spread the news cautiously, with care and empathy, among the people at large, down-playing the unfortunate afflictions of both new born sons and emphasizing the fact that they were still, nonetheless, heirs to the Kuru empire and destined to sit upon its throne. A throne still defended and protected by none other than Bhishma. Satyavati was a wise enough stateswoman not to harp on the specific limitations both boys had been born with, mentioning them in passing as if it was quite natural for a son to be born blind and the other son to be born white-skinned in a race of dark skinned people.

What she did emphasize, in that iron tone that had made her a formidable figure in Aryavarta politics, was that Bhishma remained firmly in control of the kingdom itself and would continue to steward it for as long as he was alive. The same held true of her, maintaining her position and influence over the governance of the kingdom for as long as was foreseeable. She was at pains to ensure that everyone understood and spread the message clearly – nothing had changed in the balance of power in the sub-continent and regardless of the infirmities of the two newborn heirs, Hastinapura itself remained as powerful as ever. Let none challenge that power or they would face the wrath of Bhishma Devavrata himself.

The message was understood and passed on, through the circuitous routes that political messages traveled, reaching the bejeweled ears of every king, emperor, tribal chieftain, bandit lord and horse master in distant continents.

Hastinapura had two newborn sons that day, both destined to follow the line of succession.

One was born blind.

The other was malformed in appearance.

It was questionable whether either one would be fit to ascend the throne and even if he did, whether he would be capable of staying seated on it.

Yet the essential balance of power had not changed.

The reins of power still remained firmly in the hands of the son of Shantanu, Bhishma. The seat of power was still occupied by Satyavati, Shantanu's wife.

Nothing had changed that day in Hastinapura, she insisted. And yet, as those who knew politics well understood, everything had changed.

The public celebration nothwithstanding, this was the real news of the day.

|| 3 ||

At first, all seemed well in Kurujangala.

A new age had dawned. The empire was already prosperous, powerful and growing by leaps and bounds. The arrival of two new sons invigorated it. Too many chieftains, traders, kings, farmlords and other ambitious allies had doubted the dynasty at crucial times, thinking that without a king, it was a leaderless team of horse that would go astray or tumble over a cliff. 'Gajasahrya is an elephant without a head!' some said and plotted to secede, cheat, deceive, steal from, deny, or otherwise dupe the dynasty of the Kurus. Some thought that without a king upon the Kuru throne, a few years failure to pay tribute would not be noticed; others presumed that they could use the excuse to raid their neighbor's grazing pastures and steal their water and horse and kine at will. Some chose the opportunity to declare themselves *rajan*, kings in their own right. An astonishing variety of transgressions were committed in those early years after Shantanu's demise, believing that the power of the dynasty had waned and they could now do as they pleased.

They were all proven wrong, bitterly wrong.

Even in his youth, Devavrata was a formidable prince and administrator. He was no young spoiled scion, seeking pleasure in wine, women and princely pursuits. He considered the kingdom's welfare to be his dharma, and put all his entire energy into upholding it.

After he became Bhishma, he continued to do so with the single-minded determination of a demigod on a mission of dharma.

There was a popular saying:

> *'Greatest of mothers, Kashi.*
> *Greatest of nations, Kurujangala.*
> *Greatest of cities, Hastinapura.*
> *Master of dharma, Bhishma.'*

Even Brahmins feared his austere vows, for while Brahmins were sworn to celibacy, they were permitted to make exceptions to sire fathers upon childless Kshatriya women. Some, like the Rishi Kandaka, even took the form of other creatures in order to perpetuate species: in his case, he took the form of a deer to balance the population depleted by the growing human density in the Khandava forest. His own half-brother Vyasa had emerged from his decades of solitary meditation to further the Kuru lineage. But for Bhishma, the word was the law. His interpretation of dharma was literal and uncompromising. When he had sworn himself to lifelong celibacy, he had meant it. Such unwavering adherence to a vow only added to his legend. Some believed, incorrectly, that it was the source of his indomitable prowess in war.

Celibacy had nothing to do with Bhishma's prowess as a warrior and general.

However, the fierce nature that had caused him to take that vow and, more importantly, adhere to it without once straying, his iron resolve did in fact reflect the ferocity of his will.

Bhishma was a force of nature unto himself.

He rode down cattle thieves, trampling them into the very dung of the cows they had stolen. Land thieves were buried alive in the soil they had presumed to encroach upon. Water polluters were treated the worst: for to Devavrata Bhishma water was the mother of life itself. They were fed, piece by living piece, to the giant turtles and crocodiles and gharials, while their kinsmen watched. Terrible was his vow, and terrible were his punishments. No wrongdoer escaped punishment. No transgressor received mercy. No relief was given to the law-breaker. No excuse accepted for the very rich, the powerful, or even the pious. He treated all equally. And punished them equally.

Those who had assumed that the young prince who had been away with his mother for all his childhood and youth, would surely be as soft and relenting as the very water of the Ganga river which he worshipped daily, learned the truth the hardest way. Even as young Devavrata, he was formidable. But after Shantanu was gone, and the foolish ones began to presume that the demise of their king was an opportunity for personal gains, Bhishma soon corrected any misimpression about the kingdom being kingless.

As immovable as Himavat, his grandfather, and as

relentless as his mother Ganga, he soon demonstrated that he was like no king anyone had ever known. A king would at least take time to tarry with his queen or his concubines, go hunting every now and then, travel for pleasure or to accept social engagements in other kingdoms; at the very least he would fall ill every once in a while, or require a respite from kingly affairs. Bhishma Devavrata seemed never to rest. His vow was upheld so strictly, no woman was permitted to come within reach of him: even serving girls scurried to move out of his way when he strode the long vaulting marble-floored corridors of Hastinapura palace. The question of dallying never arose. He took no holidays, went on no hunts for pleasure, never accepted social engagements unless they were combined with Kuru business. He never once fell ill and remained in robust virile health, taking barely any time to recover even from the most grievous wounds taken in battle, to the consternation of the royal vaids. He seemed to require hardly any sleep, or rest, or nourishment. Like a relentless juggernaut of justice, he roved the kingdom, unstoppable and incorruptible, dispensing terrible unmitigated punishments to the transgressors of dharma.

Thereafter, Kurujangala became renowned as the kingdom which had virtually no crime or transgressions. For no matter where a crime was committed or what manner of transgression it might be, the terrible Bhishma would somehow arrive there and ensure that justice was meted out without mercy or delay. Yet, to those who committed no crimes and applied themselves to concerted efforts for growth, he was magnanimous to a fault. For those whose conduct proved them loyal to the Kuru dynasty, he would reward with lenient taxes and a share of any new bounty they assisted in procuring, whether by means of invading of other kingdoms, or the exploitation of natural resources.

By the time the two sons were born to the princesses Ambika and Ambalika, every caucus of power in Kurujangala was unambiguous in its loyalty. Every last denizen of the land, even those sworn allies in far-flung corners of the empire, raised a voice in celebration and joy. For the greater prosperity of the Kurus meant the greater prosperity of them all. Such was the promise of Bhishma's regency and administration. Having two additional heirs to the throne could only mean that this prosperity was now guaranteed even after Bhishma's eventual demise, if and when such an event ever occurred.

Even those who secretly resented the power of the Kuru throne and wished and hoped for their downfall were effectively shut up by Satyavati's announcement. The last vestige of hope for the naysayers and dissenters was crushed.

So they all did as any sensible player in the game of thrones and kings must do: they bowed down to the Kuru dynasty, celebrated its continuance with the birth of the two new male heirs, and occupied themselves in building their own fortunes, setting aside for now, all thought of secession or rebellion.

The period that followed the birth of the two boys – three sons, to be precise, since in many ways the maid's son was the most blessed of the three – was a golden one in Kuru history.

The kingdom of Kurujangala, the district of Kurukshetra,

the dynasty of the Kurus, all grew in prosperity and repute. Indra showered his blessings, spawning bountiful crops and rich harvests. Flowers and fruit colored the landscape, providing fragrant garlands and sweet nectar. Beasts of burden undertook their labor without complaint; animals mated and littered and were content; birds filled the air with cheer. Traders prospered; artisans found ample work; bards were rewarded well enough that they composed odes of joy. Prosperity, gainful employment and the absence of local unrest changed the character of the citizenry. Even the commonfolk of the kingdom gained a reputation as being honest, fair-minded and jovial. Soldiers were brave; gurus more learned than ever; students better behaved and eager to gain knowledge. People respected one another and upheld dharma. Rites were performed as prescribed; charity was given without complaint; robbers and thieves found more opportunities to earn lawfully than through criminal acts. Pride receded, anger quelled, greed was shunned: when all was plentiful, no man had reason to covet another's wealth, possessions or stature. People aided one another in their rise to success. What use was competition when partnership benefitted both parties more profitably? Across the country, it seemed as Krita Yuga had dawned anew. It was as if the sun of history had traveled backwards in time and the world was young and fresh and full of hope once more.

It was only as the boys grew old enough to be seen and heard by one and all, once the public ecstasy at the royal issue had faded, once they stepped out into the public view, that the kingdom and the world realized to their shock that the rumors were true after all.

|| ४ ||

Yuvraj Dritarashtra, the elder of the two princes by a few days, was as blind as a stone. He was, however, gifted from the outset by an extraordinary number of compensatory abilities. He could hear, smell, sense, and feel far more sensitively than any normal man. With the help of the Guru Kripacharya, he learned from a nascent age to develop these abilities and use them to cast a kind of sensory net around his body, moving and manoeuvring with astonishing grace and agility in the trickiest of settings. He was even able to fight in this fashion against sighted warriors, and often offered worthy opposition. But his opponents soon learned that while his senses and training could over-compensate for his disability, his mind itself was afflicted of a weakness. This was his own self-conscious awareness of being handicapped. Wholeness begins and ends in the mind, and has nothing to do with possession of all bodily faculties. Because Dritarashtra believed himself inferior in some way, because he yearned and regretted the absence of sight, therefore he was over-sensitised to this lack. All an opponent had to do was whisper the word 'Blind' in any combination of insults – 'blind fool', 'eyeless wonder', 'owl prince' were among the less offensive epithets – and

Dritarashtra was lost. Overcome by anger at first, later by frustration, then by despair, and finally by a crushing, debilitating paralysis of the mind, will and body, he would lose the bout. This weakness grew into a canker which in turn blossomed into a condition in its own right. One day, the blind prince threw his weapon aside with a clanging finality and went to his chambers, from whence he did not emerge for either food, water or conversation for a whole seven-day. After that, he was never the same, reduced to a rail-thin dark-souled shadow of his former self. He never touched a weapon again, or tolerated being asked, however kindly, to consider taking up arms again.

|| 5 ||

Yuvraj Panduranga was, just as his name suggested, 'White Colored'. An albino with milky pale skin and colorless eyes that could not withstand bright light. The light of the sun was so tortuous to him that from a tender age, he fell into the practice of sleeping by day and emerging by sundown. This in itself was regarded as scandalous, even against dharma. Yet he was a prince of Kuru. And no one dared speak ill of this or any other habit of the Princes of Kuru. By night, his milk-pale complexion seemed to glow in pitch darkness, frightening many a soul that glimpsed him in the hours of the owl watch. His condition rendered him able to see sufficiently even in pitch darkness, like a predatory animal, and so he trained as a Kshatriya by cover of darkness, requiring only the faint gleam of shielded lamps for the benefit of his instructors and sparring partners. In time, this disadvantage turned into his keenest advantage, enabling him to fight when no Kshatriya could. Even so, the stricture against raising weapons after sundown rendered even this unusual skill a fault, and armed the bows of his detractors who spoke ominously of Kshatriya dharma being violated. The fact that the stricture against fighting after sundown was intended for those who could not see by darkness meant nothing at such a time; the letter of the law was more important than the intent of the law.

In a world which scrutinized every facet of a royal heir mercilessly, accepting nothing less than the most rigorous standard of genetic perfection, neither was fit to rule. How could a blind king face an attacker, leave alone lead an army into battle? How could a paleskin command respect from his opponents? Even though he was strong and sound of body and mind, the very sight of him would undermine his regal stature – and also, how could he fight effectively when even the bright light of morning was unbearable to his sensitive eyes? A weakness or deformity of any kind was unacceptable. Both princes were deemed unfit to rule by Bharata standards.

And yet, they were Kuru princes. Sons of Vichitravirya and Chitrangada in every legal respect, regardless of the fact that they had been surrogate-fathered by Vyasa – who was, after all, Satyavati's son and a renowned maharishi. They were conceived, carried to term and successfully birthed by the late kings' wives, Ambika and Ambalika, in the presence of hundreds of palace faithfuls and preceptors, who monitored every stage of the process as custom demanded, confirming the biological lineage beyond the shadow of a doubt. Nobody could dispute their legitimacy or their lineage.

It was a quandary. And one that would lead to a dangerous spiral of events.

If the seeds of war had been sown when Vyasa fathered progeny upon the princesses Ambalika and Ambika, and also, incidentally, upon their maid, then the coming of age of the princes Dritarashtra and Panduranga represented the first green shoots of that seed, poking their way up thornily to emerge from the rich soil of Five Rivers into the gloam of the northern sun.

The seeds of war were about to sprout a great tree of violence, one that would tower above hundreds of millions of lives in the land of Jambudwipa. And the fruit of that great tree, would be a terrible dark and cankerous thing, bitter as heart's blood.

|| paksha dvi ||

|| 1 ||

Dritarashtra's earliest memories from boyhood were of a voice and a hand. His brother's voice and hand.

He did not recall the specific details of the first time, but he recalled one particular time when he, as a toddler, had stumbled and fallen.

Born without the gift of sight, falling was something he did often back then. Skinned knees and bruised elbows were such frequent occurences that his were always scabbed. But there were falls and there were *falls*. Some falls resulted in more than skinned knees and bruised elbows. He suffered a string of injuries, none too serious, but each sufficient to deliver more lasting damage than mere bodily harm alone.

In most cases, it was his self-confidence that was really hurt. To be able to run, to play, to gambol, or even to simply walk, without constantly falling or colliding, was something even the most ordinary of children enjoyed. Yet he, a prince of Hastinapura, heir to the great Kuru Empire, could not take more than a few dozen paces without injury. Could not play with the other children he heard laughing and squealing and running about with such abandon. Could not do as his growing, energetic little body desired. There was no outlet to his boundless energy. No panacea for his problem.

The royal household did everything possible to ensure his safety and comfort. There were daiimaas and maids everywhere. But he was a child, a strong, robust boy with a growing body and eager, questing mind. He wanted to cut loose, to run, play, yell, jump, tumble, to unleash the dog of youth.

These luxuries were denied him.

He had to sit and listen, merely listen, as other children did all those things. When he tried, as he often tried, to join them, it would always end the same way, with him falling, or colliding, injuring himself, bleeding and cut, or bruised and battered. And each time, his self-confidence diminished along with his zest for life.

A bitterness took root in his heart.

Questions arose: Why me? Why deny me this most basic of abilities? Why punish me in this manner — it is a punishment, is it not? For what crime? What was my karma in past lives that I need suffer so in this life?

Though everyone assured him that it was neither karma nor punishment, simply an accident of nature, he could not believe it. A daiimaa, the very one who had nursed him from birth, kept telling him that he had been handicapped because he was too strong, too brave, too intelligent, too powerful. *The devas feared your might,* she told him as she dressed his injuries and wiped his tears, *they feared that you would come to swarga one day and challenge them in their own abodes, so they took away your sight that you might never find the way.*

I don't want to challenge the devas, he cried, *I don't want to go to swarga, I just want to* see.

His mother said nothing. She was barely present in his life. A shadow, a presence, a physical body that offered no warmth, comfort or affection, she only saw him at night when he was brought to her after his bath, after he had been cleaned and dressed and made presentable, to bid him a good night. Even then, she did so absently, with strange formality and a sense of distance. Even when he hugged her tightly she would pat him on the back lightly, as if admonishing him for something he had done and then, if he continued holding on too tightly or too long—which was almost every night at first – she would speak to daiimaa and daiimaa would gently untangle his little hands from around her neck and separate them.

He could not recall a time his mother had fed him, dressed him, bathed, washed his cuts, dressed his wounds, or bandaged his injuries. Telling her about the day's accidents only seemed to elicit the same response from her: a stiff silence followed by a curt, 'I see'. No offer of sympathy, no words of reassurance, no gentle caress or any other show of support. Simply that vaguely disapproving 'I see'. Even the choice of phrase seemed designed to belittle him. *I see...and you don't, you silly little blind boy.*

She never said anything so hurtful. She simply never said anything that showed affection, or love.

He heard other children with their mothers, the way they spoke, laughed together, played together, ate together. He heard babes suckling at their mother's breast. Heard the

33

female voices cry out with alarm when they saw their child about to come to harm or after he or she had hurt himself, heard the distress and concern in their maternal voices. He never heard such emotions in his mother's voice.

And on that day, the day when he fell, and a hand reached out and took hold of him, a voice spoke and strengthened him, it was not his mother's hand or voice.

It was his brother's.

'Dri!' Pandu cried.

Dritarashtra gasped as he felt his feet swing out over emptiness.

He scrambled backwards, trying to find his footing on the edge of the river bank. The heels of his feet slipped on the loamy mud, slipping. He felt himself falling, heard the roar of the water below, and absurdly thought: 'At least I can't scrape my knees or elbows on water.'

Then his brother's strong hands were grasping him tightly beneath his armpits, surrounding his chest like a vice. Pandu's breath was hot on his left ear, grunting and exclaiming as he too seemed to struggle with the wet muddy ground, then he yanked back hard on Dritarashtra and both of them fell on their backs on the ground.

They lay there a moment, the mud soft and cool underneath.

Dritarashtra could feel the soft evening sunshine on his face, arms and legs. He knew his special silk anga vastra and dhoti must be soiled from falling in the mud, perhaps torn. He could hear the voices of daiimaa and the younger maids from behind, calling out his name, then the sound of footfalls slapping the damp riverbank. A moment later, he felt the presence of people all around, helping him up, fussing over him.

'He was about to step off the edge!'

'Into the river!'

'He could have drowned!'

'The water flows so strongly here, he would have been taken downriver in a flash.'

'He would have been a mile away before we started after him.' All this and more like it. He was used to it. He had been the center of many such scares and alarms. But he knew this was different.

It was the anniversary of his naming day, for one thing. Then there was the river: he had never fallen into a river before. And of course, there was Pandu's voice, right beside him.

'Dri, are you well?'

He turned his head toward the sound of his brother's voice.

He attempted a smile.

Then, remembering what one of the children had told him—'You look like a vetala when you do that!'—he spoke aloud.

'Pandu.'

'Yes, Dri?'

'Bhraatr.'

It was all he could think of to say at that moment.

Gratitude, affection, respect, adoration, all packed into that one word. Bhraatr. *Brother.*

The daiimaas fussed over Pandu.

As did Bhishma-Pitama and Grandmother Satyavati when they were taken before their elders.

'You saved your brother's life, young Pandu.'

Dritarashtra recognized the smooth deep tones of his uncle's voice. They always reminded him of the roar of the river itself for some reason. Though that was hardly possible: for how could a man's voice resemble the voice of water?

'Had he fallen into the river, he would be drowned, or dashed against the rocks downstream.'

This was Grandmother Satyavati. Her husky sonorous tones were unmistakable.

Dritarashtra heard Pandu snort, a dismissive sound. 'That would never happen,' he heard his brother say, 'Not as long as I'm there.'

There was a brief moment of silence. Dritarashtra sensed that the elders were looking at each other in that moment, then looking at Pandu. He knew this from similar silences during conversations with other adults. People always did that if you said something unusual or unexpected. They looked at one another. He wondered why they did it. What would they see, after all? Each other's faces? Surely faces did not change from moment to moment. Only voices could convey emotion, as far as he knew. But he also knew that there was much that he did not know.

He heard in that silence their pride for his brother, and

heard that pride reflected in Pandu's reply. *Not as long as I'm there.*

He felt a surge of emotion rise in his chest, and felt tears rolling down his cheeks. That was the first time in his life he had a sense that there was someone in the world who actually cared if he lived or died, and who would risk his own life for him.

Bhraatr.

‖ 3 ‖

Pandu felt deep sympathy and love for his bhraatr.

Ever since he could run and play, he had wanted to play with his brother, run alongside him, team up with him against the other children. He felt proud to know he had a brother, a fellow heir to the great Kuru throne. It made him feel as if he was part of something bigger than himself. An empire, a dynasty, a tradition.... a family.

It had been difficult accepting that Dri was not like him, or like any of the other children.

Sight was something Pandu, like all children, took so much for granted, that he could not understand how anyone could not see, and still live. How could you not see all the colors, the shapes, the light, the people, the places, the things? It was unthinkable!

In the beginning, he had thought that maybe someday this would pass. One day Dri would wake up and be able to see. Everything would be fine then. They could play and run and play at wargames, and have so much fund together!

He even dreamed of it, happy dreams in which the two of them had wild exotic adventures together. Fighting rakshasas, battling the enemies of the Kuru empire, besieging enemy forts, quelling rebellions, squashing troublemakers. These were all things he had heard Bhishma-Pitama doing, and dreamed of doing himself some day soon, when he was old enough to fight too.

In these dreams, he, Pandu, was different too. His skin and eyes were normal, the same dark shade as other people of his race. He could see and fight and do as he pleased naked if he wished by full sunlight, instead of having to constantly clothe himself in lawyers to protect his skin and vision from the sun, or wait until sunset to roam freely. They were a formidable pair in these dreams, Dritarashtra and he. They were princes of the world. They went everywhere, did as they pleased, and no one who challenged them survived. It was so wonderful, he would wake up smiling from these dreams and jump out of bed, eager to go to his brother and tell him.

Then, as he grew a little bigger, he understood that day would never come. He did not stop hoping and dreaming—he dreamed all the more after that—but a part of him *accepted* that it was not going to happen. Dri's blindness was as permanent as the old sword guru's missing arm.

'Arms don't grow back, blind don't see,' the old man had said gruffly to Pandu, swatting him on his backside with the wooden practice sword, 'hoping won't make it so, just as dodging my sword won't make you a better swordsman. Stand and fight. You're a Kuru, act like one.'

At first he had felt bad for Dri. Then very sorry for him. He was always falling, colliding, hurting himself, getting into accidents. Always forced to sit and listen while the other children played. *Listen!* Paagh! Where was the fun in listening to other children playing? It was as if Dri was punished. Which was all wrong because Dri was the best behaved child in the entire palace complex. After all, how could a blind child ever do any mischief? Pandu felt very sad indeed for his brother.

He tried to involve Pandu, tried to make him get up and join them at play. He couldnt help it. He wanted to share the moment, the fun and the pleasure with his bhraatr. But these attempts always ended with Dri falling, or knocking heads, or colliding, or tumbling, and after a while, Pandu stopped encouraging his brother, not wanting to be the cause of him sustaining further injuries and humiliation. He missed his brother. Missed having a brother. Really having a brother who was a playmate.

But as more time passed and they both grew a little more, Pandu began to feel a different emotion.

He began to feel protective of his brother.

He began to accompany Dri around wherever he went, watching him, calling out his name to warn him if he saw Dri about to fall or trip or dash into something. The daiimaas were there for that, of course, and they did their task admirably well, but Dri took to ignoring them and deliberately walking where he pleased, as if defying their constant warnings and cautions. But when Pandu called out a warning, Dri always responded. He would stand still and wait till someone told him to step this way instead, or to walk the other way. Pandu felt pleased that Dri listened, that he was able to help his brother in some small way.

He was watching Dri the day of Dri's naming day celebration.

The family had a tradition of spending naming day celebrations on the banks of the Ganga, always at the same spot, under the great huge banyan tree. It was the place where great-grandfather Shantanu had met his first wife, great-grandmother Ganga. It was also the place where grandfather Bhishma Pitama had been reunited with his father Shantanu when he, Bhishma, returned from *his* grandfather Himavat's house. There were other things that had happened in this spot, something to do with babies and the river and great-grandmother Ganga: those were things that the daiimaas did not speak of to the children. It was for their elders to tell them once they were a little more grown up. This place had a special meaning to the family and they spent all naming day celebrations here, bringing cooks and tents and servants and throwing a grand feast for hundreds and thousands of the highest nobles and aristocrats and ministers and diplomats. There were dancers and musicians and lavish feasts and colored banners and horse riding displays and wrestling matches and all kinds of other entertainment.

All of which Dri could not see even though it was his naming day celebration.

When Dri wandered away on his own, Pandu saw him. He saw also that the daiimaas and maids were busy gossipping. It was not their fault. They assumed that Dri was sitting and listening to the music. But Pandu was sitting nearby and he could tell that Dri was *fed up* of listening. Who wouldn't be, when all you could *do* was listen!

So when Dri got up from his comfortable silk-cushioned seat and wandered away, strolling by himself, Pandu left his snack and followed him.

He saw when Dri was about to step off the edge of the riverbank and fall into the river.

He leaped forward, grabbing hold of his brother and pulling him back to safety. He banged the back of his head on a small rock when he fell, but he didn't care. He was happy he was able to save his brother from falling into the river. He couldn't have borne it if Dri had fallen and gotten drowned, or dashed on the rocks, or even hurt badly. He was his *brother,* and he was *blind*. Pandu *had* to look out for him.

They were brothers after all.

|| ५ ||

Satyavati and Bhishma watched from the terrace of the palace. It was some weeks after Dritarashtra's naming day. Ever since that day, Pandu and Dritarashtra had become inseparable. They were playing together now, Pandu teaching Dritarashtra how to wield a sword. They were using wooden practice swords and Pandu never et his swings connect with his brother's body, but Dritarashtra could not help striking Pandu occasionally. Bhishma saw Pandu wince when the side of Dritarashtra's sword caught him on his collarbone. That must have hurt. But Pandu did not lose his temper or admonish his brother. He congratulated him on a 'kill strike'!

'They love each other very much,' Satyavati said.

'Yes.'

Satyavati glanced at Bhishma. He was her foster son by marriage, but he was much older than she. It lent their relationship a curious edge. Nominally, Bhishma deferred to his foster mother, and by law, she was the Dowager Empress of the Kuru Empire. But Bhishma, as the eldest living male and son of Emperor Shantanu, was Prince Regent. Because he defended the empire, ruled and governed it, controlled and oversaw every aspect of its functing, kept it safe and prosperous, he was regarded with the same respect as she. Somehow, the balance of power worked. They had never been seen to argue or heard to disagree. The bond of mother-son between them dissuaded any political attempt to divide and conquer. They were a perfect pair and together they ran Hastinapura and the Empire as smoothly as a pair of charioteers ran a sixteen horse team.

But they were nothing alike.

Satyavati saw that now as she glanced at Bhishma. When she watched the growing bond between Pandu and Dritarashtra, it made her feel good.

She had been so disheartened when the sons of Princess Ambika and Princess Ambalika had been born blind and albino. At least Pandu had found ways to overcome his disability, by dressing to protect his sensitive skin and eyes in sunlight, and training twice as hard to overcome any questions of his talents as a prince. The boy had a big heart.

Dritarashtra was stout of heart too, but his disability was harder to overcome for the role he wished to play. With his heightened senses, he could function well enough to live comfortably the rest of his life, even perform certain princely tasks that only required listening and delivering judgement, but how could he be expected to ride to battle, to go to war, to confront enemies or suppress rebellions, survive assassinations, all the warring and marauding that was an integral part of being an heir to the most coveted throne in the world?

It did not help that Dritarashtra's mother had turned her face away from him. Since the day he was born, she had not demonstrated any affection or concern for his well being. Ironically, it was as if she had turned a blind eye to her own son's existence.

Pandu's mother was only a little better; she too clearly resented the way she had been impregnated. Her head understood that it was necessary for the kingdom and the lineage; her heart rebelled against the fact. Satyavati had seen her look at Pandu with a clear expression of distaste for his pale, colorless features, his white hair and white eyebrows, his inability to endure bright light or sunlight. But there was still some affection there underneath the distaste. Ambalika did not hate Pandu the way Ambika hated Dritarashtra. She tolerated her son at least. Satyavati knew that this was more than partly because Ambalika understood that with Dritarashtra's disability, it would most certainly be Pandu who ascended the Kuru throne. That knowledge itself made her albino son appear tolerable in her eyes. *Vain woman*, Satyavati thought, then sighed. Was she not herself vain too? Would she have reacted any differently had she been in Ambalika's place? It was easy to judge from afar, harder to be that person.

But Bhishma was definitely not like her, or any other ordinary mortal.

He was watching the two boys now with a strange expression. His striking grey eyes were looking at them but he might as well have been looking at the horizon.

'The talk among the citizenry concerns you?'

He turned that thousand-yojana gaze upon her, and she had to force herself to meet it without flinching. One did not easily match stares with Bhishma. She could not even imagine what it must be like to meet this giant of a man on the battlefield, with his enormous strength, knowledge, skill and ability to defeat any opponent. The sheer sight of him alone was known to send warriors fleeing. They had good reason.

'The citizenry always talk. It is what they do.' he replied.

She sighed. 'Nevertheless, it concerns me. Because there is some truth in their talk this time.'

He continued to stare at her. 'If it is true, then it cannot be helped. Let the people talk.'

'This kind of talk could lead to trouble. Even an uprising.'

'Uprisings can be quelled.'

'It would better if we do not have to kill our own people.' She thought for a moment then amended her statement: 'Any more than we absolutely must.'

Bhishma did not seem perturbed. 'I can find out who seeks to foment rebellion. Root them out in their nests, wipe out any uprising before it raises its hood and slithers to attack us.'

Bhishma said the words as if he were speaking of the extermination of pests. That was how he differed from other men. It was not that he was cruel or cold, but that he simply saw things as they were, harsh and dangerous, without any euphemistic softening of the jagged edges. Satyavati had never been able to regard crises with such dispassion. She felt strongly, passionately, intensely and did not hesitate to express herself in like fashion. To be alive was to feel; to live was to unleash the life force. She had not been born of a glacial river; her mother had been a hot-blooded fisher princess whose clashes with Satyavati's father than been legendary. But even she knew when to fight and when to *fight*.

'I do not doubt your ability to maintain order, son of Shantanu. But if we acted against every king, noble and warrior who talks against Hastinapura, we would soon have no one left to govern. No. Violence will not resolve this problem. We must do more than simply crush the poison tongues. We must silence them.'

Bhishma was silent for a moment before responding. 'I do not comprehend your meaning, Mother. Do you wish me to use violence to quell the unruly or not?'

'I wish you to do nothing at all,' she said. 'It is elsewhere that I seek the resolution to this dilemma.'

She gestured with a small raising of her chin, pointing to the two boys in the courtyard below. 'It is to the future generation that we must look to silence their own detractors. They are the cause of the gossip and unrest. They must answer their critics by their own actions.'

Bhishma regarded the boys below. His expression did not change but his words betrayed his lack of conviction. 'And you believe they can face do this? Bear the weight of the Kuru empire and my father's legacy on their slender shoulders?'

A blind boy and an albino was what he left unsaid.

'They are Kuru,' she said simply.

He had no answer to that.

They watched the two boys continue their swordplay long past their mealtime. By the end, she observed, Dritarashtra was actually able to parry and counter Pandu's strikes at least a third of the time. She watched thoughtfully. Bhishma was right about one thing: the fate of the empire would rest on these young shoulders, whether she liked it or not. For better or worse, they were Kuru princes. She decided then that she would not make the mistake that so many others had: she would not pre-judge them. *At least let them be blooded and then see.*

'Perhaps it is time to bring them to Guru Kripacharya,' she said.

Bhishma was silent for another long moment. This time, she expected an argument. Instead he said simply, 'I concur. It is time for boys to become men.'

‖ 5 ‖

Bhishma drove the four-horse chariot with the ease of a master sarathi.

He was driving the boys personally to the guru's ashram.

Satyavati had fussed over them endlessly, giving them a number of instructions that he was sure they would forget the instant they reached the ashram. He had merely helped them aboard the high platform of the chariot well, and started the team off with a gentle working of the reins and a few softly clucked sounds. The daiimaas had wailed and cried their hearts out as he rode away. In moments, they had left the palace complex and were leaving the city by the rear sally gate.

He had spoken nothing to them thus far. The chariot rumbled over the kingsroad as fields of crops rolled by on either side, succeeded in time by the open ranges of dairy, cattle and poultry farms. Some of it fed the bottomless appetite of Hastinapura, but the larger part was sent off to other parts of the empire by wagon trains, and even to foreign kingdoms by ship or by land across the spice route. He contemplated reeling off figures of grain harvests, cattle production, then decided that the last thing two young boys about to be separated from their homes for several years needed was a lecture on economics.

He glanced back at them.

Pandu and Dri were both standing in the well of the chariot, looking out at the passing view.

They appeared quieter than usual.

The well of the chariot was designed to shield grown men; the two boys could only just manage to look out over the edge of the well. At least they were both of a good height for their age, physically strong and well built. If only they had not been afflicted with their respective handicaps, they would have made fine warriors.

Even with their limitations, they could still be of good service. That was why he had agreed with Mother Satyavati to take them to Guru Kripacharya. It was time for them to step up and become the best possible versions of themselves they could be—or prove themselves unable to do so. Bhishma and Satyavati, as wardens of the empire, needed to know sooner rather than later if one of the two could someday serve as Emperor of Kurujangala. If not...? Well, that was a fjord he would bridge when he came to it. For now, all that concerned him was putting the heirs of his father's legacy to the test. And the best person to administer that test was Guru Kripacharya. If they were of good mettle, he would hammer them into fine swords.

They were past the farms now, and passing the lumber yards. The scents of grain and barley had given way to buffalo and fowl, and now the aroma of fresh sap and timber replaced them. Men working in the yards saw them passing and paused to watch them go by. Pandu and Dritarashtra looked back at them, taking in every scene, every sight as if their lives depended on it.

'It is a long ride,' he said, turning his head so the wind would carry his words to them. 'You may lay down and rest if you desire.'

There were rugs laid on the floor of the well. Refreshments too. That was the daiimaa's doing.

Neither Ambika nor Ambalika had come to see their sons off, as was the custom. He assumed they had said their goodbyes in chambers. He knew that neither mother doted on her son.

Bhishma did not feel human emotions the way most mortals did, but he did understand what was appropriate under certain circumstances, and what was not. It was unfortunate that the wives of Chitrangada and Vichitravirya did not love their sons as they should have. A mother's love, especially a queen mother's love for her princely son, could give a boy a great boost. Bhishma knew that he would not be the man he was today if not for his mother's strength. Ganga had a heart of ice, it was true, and felt even less emotion than he did; if he was half-mortal, she was no mortal at all, even when she assumed the physical form of one. But she loved him deeply in her own way, and he knew that he could always count on her support. Not to mention, his grandfather Himavat, Lord of the High Himalayas named after him, and every other denizen of the great mother river. He still recalled how hard it had been for him to accept that he was to leave his mother's embrace and take his place in the mortal world, by his father's side. It was a long time ago but to Bhishma the pain was as a fresh prick from a thorn.

The memory of his own separation from his mother made him empathize a little more with his two young wards.

He glanced back at them. They were still standing, leaning their chins and hands on the rim of the chariot well and watching the world go by.

The chariot had left the lumber yards far behind, crossed the first low hills, and was now rumbling through the relatively less dense woods before entering the formidable jungle for which Kurujangala was named.

It had been more half a watch since leaving Hastinapura. They ought to have desired rest now, or nourishment. Children always seemed to require one or both of those two items. They were also unusually quiet even for them. They had been quite loud and boisterous during their last sword practice, clearly enjoying their newfound activity.

It came to him late but it came nevertheless: *They are feeling anxious and scared of what lies ahead. Like minnows out of their depth, without the comforting presence of their usual caretakers.*

He could not bring them *daiimaas*, or home comforts. But he could divert their minds from their homesickness. He had an idea what he could do to remedy it. It was something that had worked for him, years ago, when he had left his mother's clasp and gone out into the world on his own. There was no reason it should not work on them.

|| 6 ||

Dri was surprised when he felt the chariot wheels slowing and heard the creaking of the taut leather reins as Bhishma-Pitama steered the horse team. He had not expected to arrive at their destination anytime soon. He sniffed warily. It smelled like forest, but it had smelt of freshly cut lumber only a few hours before. Surely Guru Kripacharya's ashram could not be within such a short distance from the city?

'We are stopping in a clearing,' Pandu's voice whispered in his ear. 'I don't know why.'

Dri felt a rush of warmth for his bhraatr. Pandu had been entertaining him since they left Hastinapura, speaking softly in his ear, informing him of the places they were driving past, sketching in details that Dri could not have guessed at merely from scent and sound clues. It had enriched the journey considerably.

Until this trip, Dri had hated travelling. It invariably meant a bewildering profusion of smells and sounds, most unrelated to one another, leaving him with disturbing mental pictures of what they might mean. Pandu's commentary was such a delight. It helped him make sense of the world.

Not just a meaningless jumble of smells and sounds, he could form a sensible image of what lay out there. Farmers harvesting crops. Grazing cattle. Clucking fowl. Timber being cut and prepared for transport downriver.

But why were they stopping now? And what place was this? Even Pandu didn't know.

'Kurus.'

Bhishma-Pitama's voice was as smooth and clear as always. Pandu's hand on his arm advised Dri that they were to disembark from the chariot.

'Jump down,' Pandu said, and Dri jumped from the chariot without hesitation. Both boys stood before their grandfather, awaiting further instruction.

Bhishma noted that they were standing close together, shoulders touching. He had observed Pandu whispering to his brother in the chariot, and dwelled momentarily on the wisdom of allowing Dritarashtra to grow up dependant on his brother's eyes and presence. He pushed the thought aside. Such concerns would be the domain of their guru soon. Bhishma had only a day or two to spend with the boys; he did not intend to use the time correcting them. Let brother lean on brother. They were bhraatr after all. If Guru Kripacharya wished to separate them, let him do so. Bhishma wanted to show them a good time today. They deserved it, in his opinion.

'We shall take a short holiday before proceeding to Guruji's ashram,' he said aloud.

The look of surprise on both brothers' faces was nearly

identical. For once, even Dritarashtra's usual slack faced expression was replaced with something akin to a happy face.

'You will both be away for a long time. As your grandsire, I wish to spend time with you pursuing activities that bring you delight. Tell me, Pandurang, Dritarashtra, what would you like to do?'

There was a brief moment of utter silence. Then the responses clambered over each other, as enthusiastically as if he were confronting a whole squad of young boys, not merely two.

'Hunt!'

'Fish!'

'Climb!'

'Dive!'

'Fight lions!'

'Stay the night in the forest!'

'In a cave!'

'Track wild boar!'

'Build a machaan!'

'Visit Kailasa!'

'The desert!'

'Spear snakes!'

'Drive the chariot!'

'Hunt rakshasas!'

'Besiege a fort!'

'Build a fort!'

'Attack a—'

Bhishma laughed.

The sound was unusual enough that it silenced both boys at once. He laughed and laughed, the rolling tones of his laughter echoing through the forest, reflected off the chariot behind them to bounce back in Dri's keen ears. Both Pandu and Dri watched and listened in astonishment. They had never seen or heard their grandfather laugh before. In all probability, nobody had.

Bhishma himself could not recall the last time he had laughed — not since he was a boy, probably. When he lived in the river, swimming and hunting with his river friends and playing underwater like any fish, truly, completely happy in his mother's embrace,. He had never been that happy since, would never be again. It was the way of life. Babes cooed, children laughed, men smiled...then they learned to smile without meaning it, and finally, death laughed at men and ended their humorless lives.

But he was laughing now. He was happy again.

He had remembered what it was to be a boy again.

To be innocent, carefree, the whole world before you, all of life lying ahead, unexplored, undiscovered, filled with wonders and treasures, adventures and secrets.

He came forward, spreading his arms as he crouched down, startling Pandu who nevertheless stood his ground bravely, startling Dritarashtra when he felt his grandfather's large hands and cool breath, and he put his hands around both of them and swept them up in a great, happy bone-crushing hug.

The boys were surprised at first, then understanding came over them, their grandsire's action speaking more eloquently than his words. Giving themselves over to him, both of them broke out laughing as well.

Bhishma stood up, still hugging the boys, carrying them as easily as a crane lifting a pair of young salmon, and laughed on. The forest filled with the sound of the three Kurus laughing.

‖ 7 ‖

The next few days were a blur of activity.

Pandu and Dri learned more in those days than in their short lives until then. They learned to track, to hunt and kill, to fish, to skin and clean and cook, to start a fire, to keep it going, to bank it so as to reduce telltale smoke emissions. They cut sapling boughs, carved them into bows and shafts, strung together vines to string the bows, then learned to use the weapons.

They hunted deer, and Dritarashtra learned how to still his body and senses and breathe till he became one with the jungle and its patterns, to distinguish the soft sounds of the deer breathing, snorting, yanking grass, chewing, to aim and loose by these sounds alone, and by the end of the trip, to actually hit his target.

Pandu learned to stalk the deadly but very delicious wild boar stage, to corner and kill it without risking it ripping open his abdomen and spilling out his bowels – though it tried mightily, and came close enough to leave Pandu with a small crescent-shaped scar for life – and then to skin and clean and cut and cook the animal, wasting no part of it.

They ate what they caught, and they ate very well indeed.

Bhishma Pitama did no hunting himself, restricting his role to that of a mentor. It was terrifying at first to the boys, but also exhilerating. To be given such responsibility, thrust into such an adventure, face to face with snorting, smelly, whiskery-faced death, yet knowing that if it came down to it, their grandsire would surely step in and protect them.

Or would he?

He said he would not, and they took him at his word, which made them try harder, and perhaps that was what made the difference in the outcome. To play at hunting while Grandsire watched over them was a challenge. To actually hunt while Bhishma Pitama watched – but did not intervene – was a responsibility. They learned the difference in those days in the jungle.

Pandu found it even more exhilerating because the dense jungle afforded him cover from the cruel sun that tormented his sensitive skin. Unlike in the open environs of Hastinapura, here he could roam and range at will under the shady canopy of the woods. He was overjoyed when he realized this at first. The sense of liberation from the tyranny of sunlight was exhilerating. Even in the chariot, he had had to keep a burlap cloth over his head to protect his skin. Back home, he always dressed in attire that kept his entire body covered, even in the hot season. Now, for the first time in his young life, he could be free of such encumbrances. He could swim and play in a pool fed by a waterfall by day, the dappled patches of sunlight robbed of their intensity by the time they reached him, he could hunt and run and practice and play all day without having to wait for sundown. And when sundown did come, he could lay down to sleep like other people did, as people were supposed to do.

The nights were a different matter. Accustomed to the soft silk cushions, army of servants, their every need catered to on demand, the two heirs of Hastinapura had never experienced true hardship. That first night, both were unable to sleep for hours. Their straw pallets were pokey and uncomfortable. The darkness was absolute, a living thing that pressed in around them, squeezing, throttling, suffocating. And the jungle was alive. It was on that night they realized that the jungle was in fact a city.

Inhabited by countless denizens, each of whom had their own business, cuthroat ambitions, goals and targets, occupations and duties, all going about their work under cover of darkness. Not merely selling, trading, buying, serving, as in Hastinapura. Killing, hunting, raiding, attacking, fighting, squealing, screaming, roaring, growling, sniffing.

Oddly enough, Dri suffered more than Pandu. He had been born in darkness, it was his natural state of being. He did not fear it in itself. But the living jungle that enveloped him and its inhabitants were all the more terrifying because he could not see any of them, and was compelled to imagine their nature from their sounds and smells alone. To him, they were all monsters. He slept with his hand-made rough hewn bow clutched tightly in both fists and he did not sleep deeply or long.

Pandu was unnerved at first, but as the first watch passed and he grew more accustomed to the sounds, he became intrigued, and then fascinated by the savagery of the life and death game being played out all around him. He knew what several animals looked like, and what their sounds were, and so he could form mental images of what was transpiring most of the time, or guess at it. A lion bringing down a deer. Two wild boars tangling horns. A herd of deer passing through on their way to the pond. The mental pictures that formed in his mind were informed by the sights he had seen.

What he 'saw' when he heard the jungle sounds that night was wholly different from what his brother 'saw'.

He slept eventually, and dreamed of the animal city going about its business while he slept, taking strange pleasure in the inevitablity and unending cycle of life and death. To him, the jungle was a city of animals. Was that not why they called the animal kingdom? He felt more at home here than in his own princely apartments in Hastinapura. The jungle awakened some ancient powerful impulse within him, a race memory of a time when all creatures lived together in the forest, and the forest was their world.

He slept and dreamed of a world where he roamed as freely as a lion, a tiger, a bear, a wolf and ruled his own ranging ground using only his wits and brute force.

In contrast, Dri tossed uneasily all night, unable to break free of the nightmare world where teeth, fangs, claws surrounded him, and only pain and agony lay in wait. He wanted nothing more than to go back home, to the seclusion and safety of his apartments in Hastinapura, to be able to call for daiimaa, and embrace her large, warm, soft maternal self. The jungle was one brother's nightmare, another brother's paradise.

By day, they were as one being. Both did everything together, as a team. Pandu communicating with his brother as much by deft touches, a whispered word or a combination of sound and touch; Dri moving confidently, secure in his bhraatr's presence and support, allowing his instincts to guide him, catching sounds that Pandu could not even hear if he tried, his acute hearing a tool that enabled him to 'see' without seeing.

Pandu's hand was impressively steady, his ability to draw back a bow-string and loose in a single fluid motion markedly superior to Dri. By the eve of the third day, he could, if he desired, stalk, hunt and down game entirely on his own. He had an instinctive understanding of the jungle that Bhishma found intriguing. It was like Bhishma's own symbiotic relationship to water bodies: to Bhishma a river was a living highway filled with teeming life. He knew every creature, plant and rock that inhabited that bustling intercourse and could traverse that watery world as easily as any finned denizen. Pandu was like that in the jungle: it was as if he was home, had been born and brought up here, and knew it like the back of his hand. He knew things without being told: like the side of a tree upon which moss grew in a season, the fact that a doe that grazed in a certain pattern was heavy with child, or that the claw marks on a sala trunk were not from a sloth bear but from an aging half-blind lion that used it to clean and sharpen his claws. The speed and efficiency with which he picked up the essentials then graduated directly to far more advanced skills was astonishing even to Bhishma, for he was accustomed to the normal abilities of most mortal children. He had brought his half-brothers Chitrangada and Vichitravirya to the forest at around this same age, and while they had been fearless and eager to learn, they were not in the same league as Panduranga. This young boy was born to the hunt. He was not merely good: he was a prodigy.

Bhishma took pride at first in the thought that his father's son by Satyavati could not be anything but a prodigy. By the second day, he acknowledged that this was beyond mortal ability. As the son of a mortal man and a goddess himself, Bhishma knew he possessed senses and knowledge and abilities that were not within the reach of other mortals. Pandu was not in his league and would never be, of course, but he was definitely a notch or three above mortal talents. The how and why of this extraordinary superiority furrowed his brow for a while. It came to him late in the morning of the third day:

Pandu was seeded by Satyavati's first-born son, Vyasa. The sage was a child of the forest himself, a being greater than mortal but less than divine. Born of a union between Sage Parashara and Satyavati years before she met and married Raja Shantanu, Vyasa grew to adulthood within hours of birth, and after taking his mother's blessings, departed for unknown destinations. From his mother and his river relatives, Bhishma knew that Vyasa had gone into the deep woods, into the heart of the heart of the jungle, to a place where even the most self-flagellatory tapasvi sadhu would not venture.

There, in a place where the jungle itself did not permit mortal intrusion, Vyasa abided, subsisting on infinitessimal molecules of nutrition derived from air alone, inserting vines into his veins and merging sap with blood, inhaling the color of leaves and the dark energy of moonlight, the sinews of the wind, the songs of birds, and storms stirred by insect wings. From water drawn up through the soles of his feet he slaked his thirst. From the whispering of butterflies he came to know the intimate secrets of the forest. The jungle fed him as one of her own, and in return he fed the jungle with his own energies and fluids forming a symbiotic bond that was beyond the capacity of human understanding or belief.

Pandu had inherited his father's intimate relationship with the jungle. The forest herself recognized her brethren and welcome him, opening her secrets to his mind and senses. That explained it.

But it did not explain why Dri lacked the same bond.

Where Pandu was completely at home in this verdant environment almost at once, Dri appeared uncomfortable, anxious, even afraid. At crucial moments, he would err and fail to loose the arrow which would have downed his prey, or to follow through on an easy kill. His senses were no less acute than his brother's. He possessed the same uncanny level of intimacy with the jungle as Pandu. But where Pandu thrived and revelled in this habitat, Dritarashtra did not want to be here at all. Bhishma saw the signs the very first night; while Pandu slept peacefully, all but purring in his sleep, Dri thrashed about, started at sounds, and was drawn into the clasp of nightmares that sucked his energy dry. So long as Pandu was beside him, guiding and encouraging him, Dri was in fine form. He did his part exceedingly well, capable of matching any sighted boy his age. But time and again he sabotaged himself, hesitating, drawing back at a crucial moment, failing, pulling back, or otherwise disengaging when it came to the nub.

Bhishma felt sympathy for the boy. He was clearly afraid of the jungle; even though he could have been as much at home as Pandu, he *chose* not to let himself trust the mother forest.

Why or how was something Bhishma could not quite fathom. They were both birthed from the seed of Vyasa after all, possessed of similar skills and abilities. Yet they were developing in very different ways. Was it the lack of sight, he wondered? No, he sensed, it was something more.

He recalled that their mothers had reacted differently when Vyasa had come into their respective chambers to sire heirs for the dynasty upon the princesses. Pandu's mother had been horrified by the sage's wild appearance and had turned ashen white. That would result in Pandu's lack of skin color, Vyasa had prophesied. But after her initial fright, she had kept her eyes open and undergone the seeding. That showed great courage on her part: to have seen a man who physically repulsed her and still consented to take him to her bed. On the other hand, Dritarashtra's mother had shut her eyes from the start, unwilling to even look at the man copulating with her. Perhaps that accounted for Dri's weakness: not the blindness itself, which did not diminish his ability, but his imagination. Like his mother at that crucial moment of conception, Dri feared the unseen, and because it was unseen and therefore unknown, it loomed as something far more terrible than the reality. That was it, Bhishma decided. Dritarashtra suffered from his mother's flaw: a last-minute failing of will. It was a dangerous flaw in any man, but a fatal one in a warrior or a king.

It meant, Bhishma mused sadly, that Dritarashtra could never rule as king. To be emperor of Kurujangala required epic fortitude. A king who hesitated at a crucial moment could cause the downfall of the empire.

As the holiday drew to an end and he began preparing to resume their journey to Guru Kripacharya's ashram, Bhishma decided he would not judge them both just yet. They were still young and about to be delivered into the tutelage of a great master teacher. He would belay judgement until they had graduated from the ashram and achieved manhood. A great deal could transpire in that period. Boys would become men. Princes could become kings. And life could surprise you.

But in his heart of hearts, he knew the die was cast already.

Of the two brothers, only Pandu was fit to rule. All that remained was for time, and the guru, to prove his assessment right—or wrong. It was with this thought on his mind that he finally delivered his two wards to the guru's ashram.

|| 8 ||

Pandu felt a flash of excitement as they came within sight
of the ashram. Guru Kripacharya's gurukul was nestled
in a clearing deep within a forest even denser and lusher
than the one in which they had spent the past few days
with Bhishma Pitamah. Here, the trees were so tall, he could
not see the top of them, however hard he craned his neck.
Their branches formed a canopy so dense that the only light
that filtered through was greenish in hue. Not a single bar of
direct sunlight passed through here, except in the clearing,
where, from the angle of the light, he guessed that the sun
would shine down for a few hours each morning, that was
all. Even a brook they passed by was nestled between stands
of trees that only gave a few yards of space, reluctantly,
for the water to pass. He felt a thrill of anticipation at the
thought of all the animals that must drink here all day and
night long, of the wealth of game for the taking. And this
was further north and higher up the foothills, which meant
there would be bigger game here, larger predators, much
bigger leaf-eaters. Bhishma Pitamah had told them stories
of past hunts with his own father, of sighting a Nilgiri blue
stag the size of an elephant cow. Surely there would be
some Nilgiri here in the mountains. And tiger, bear, lion,

panter, leopard and wolf too. The jungle pressed in from all sides, like a crowd of spectators eager to touch the hem of the two great princes of Kurujangala. The sound of birds, insects, small game, the babbling brook, the shirring of wind, all rose like a symphony of music and voices raised in a hosanna to greet their arrival. He imagined spending days and nights in this wilderness. Years. The prospect thrilled him beyond words. He felt as if the jungle had been waiting here all his life, waiting for him to come to it. And now he was here at last, he was home. His heart sang and resonated in chorus with the song of the forest.

Dritarashtra felt raw panic as Bhishma Pitama released his hand and began speaking with the other adults who had joined them from the ashram. He had heard and smelled the jungle and the overwhelming sensations he felt were despair and terror. The past few days had been tolerable, even enjoyable at times, because of his grandsire's and bhraatr's presence. True, Pandu would still be here with him at the ashram for the duration, but he already sensed that Pandu did not share his fear and loathing of the wilderness. If anything, he heard and sensed joy in his brother's voice and words when he spoke of it. Pandu loved the forest. Dri did not. And though grandfather had said he would not intervene to help if they were in trouble, he had already seen that was not true. On at least two occasions, he had either aided Dri or prevented him from harming himself.

Now, in a few moments, Dri would be left here in this desolate, forsaken wilderness, and the last adult protector in his life, his grandsire, would leave. Leave and go back to the city, to the palace, where he would reside in comfort and security. While Dri stayed here, in the stark savage clutches of the jungle, this living, breathing thing that pressed in on all sides around him, like a herd of wild fanged beasts wanting a closer sniff to gauge the weaknesses of this blind little two-legged prey. A moment of utter despair washed over him.

He turned to Bhishma Pitama, sensing his grandsire prepare himself for departure, and said with a voice half-choked with fear and desperation: 'Please, grandsire, please, take me home to daiimaa. Don't leave me here. I want to go home with you. Please take me.'

He heard the startled silence that followed his pleas, the sharp intake of breath from his side, and knew that everyone, including Pandu, was surprised and disappointed at his outburst. Most of all Bhishma Pitama, who had repeatedly urged them to always show restraint of emotions and reactions, as a warrior and a king always kept his true feelings to himself lest they be used as weapons against him. But he couldn't help it. He couldn't bear the thought of staying here for days, nights, months... *Years*? Impossible!

'Dri...' he heard the patient tone in his grandsire's voice and knew that he was supposed to understand from that single syllable that this was no way for a prince to behave, that he was a Kuru, heir to the great dynasty of Kurujangala, great-grandson of Shantanu, inheritor of a great legacy and responsibility, ruler of the civilized world, an emblem of dharma. The world looked to him for guidance and governance. He could not burst out begging and crying thus.

And yet, for the next several moments, that was all he could do.

He begged, he cried, he screamed, he howled, and finally, when Bhishma Pitama reluctantly but firmly tore him loose from the leg he had latched onto, he heard the pain and sorrow in his grandsire's voice as he said, not without sympathy: 'Be strong, my child. All things are hard in the beginning. Give it time. You will adapt.'

And then, with a strong stride and without a backward glance back (Dri sensed, for he could sense such things without the benefit of sight), his grandsire was gone. Back to the pathway several miles away where they had left the chariot to negotiate the densest part of the forest on foot, and thence back to Hastinapura, a good three full days and nights ride from here. Five hundred miles? A thousand? Two thousand? He did not know. It did not matter. He was far enough away from home that he may as well be in the netherworld, among the Nagas, or in the lower realms, where Asuras roamed like mad demons eternally. His family had left him here. He was forsaken.

'Dri,' said his brother's voice in his ear as he stood, desolate and bitter of heart. 'Dri, do not fear. I am with you, bhraatr.'

But in that moment of black despair, bitterhearted at being abandoned in this desolate forest against his will, Dri felt a sudden surge of anger at even his beloved bhraatr.

Without even thinking about it, he shoved Pandu away with a fierce push.

'I don't want you! I want to go home!'

He regretted the action and the words as soon as they were committed. But he knew that there was truth in them too, heart's pure naked truth. He did not want a brother's help. He wanted his home, his family, his protection and security. He wanted his mother. But she had abandoned him long ago. She had let go of his little hand even before he could walk on his own. She no more cared what happened to him than she cared about what happened to a deer roaming these jungles. She was the first to forsake him. Grandsire Bhishma Pitama was the next. Panduranga would forsake him too. In time, everyone would forsake him. It was what people did. They made you want them, need them. Made you trust them, love them. And then, when you needed them most, they turned and walked away, shaking off your hand.

In that moment, Dritarashtra's handsome face coiled and twisted, his tears stopped, his sobbing ceased, his heart drank its own bitter juices, and he vowed that if the world could be this cruel to you, if even those whom you loved most, the woman who had birthed you herself, could forsake you, then he would learn to be cruel as well.

He would show them. He would show them all someday. He let the rishis lead him into the ashram without another word of protest.

|| paksha triya ||

The beautiful young girl executed a perfect swan dive
from the top of the rock, her graceful body hanging
suspended in the air before slicing the surface of the lake
with barely a splash. She emerged more than a dozen yards
away, her pretty face smiling. Her companions laughed and
applauded. 'Another perfect dive as always, Princess!'

Kunti tossed back her lustrous dark hair and swam
strongly across to the far bank. It was a good fifty yards
away and even the strongest swimmers in her company did
not dare try to race her. Kunti was in the habit of swimming
one hundred breadths daily, and could still race them all
home to the palace afterward. They contented themselves
with playing at swimming on the shady side of the lake, the
more boisterous ones splashing water at one another and
squealing, the vainer ones braiding flowers into each other's
hair to make the merchant's sons in the marketplace turn
their heads as they passed.

It was a lazy afternoon, the sun slipping to the western
sky, songbirds calling in the trees, flocks of geese and ducks
and pheasants flying overhead; butterflies flitted over the
flowers, deer grazed on the soft kusa grass nearby, and
at one point in the slow indolent afternoon, a young lion

crept down to the lake on the far side of the glen and drank his fill, keeping a wary but unafraid eye on the laughing cavorting maidens, before slinking back into the shadowy depths of the jungle.

Kunti was on her eighty-ninth lap when she felt the change. She paused in mid-stroke, treading water. Something was different.

The lake was quiet. The songbirds were silent, the bees had ceased buzzing, and the dragonflies that had been humming over the water were no longer to be seen. The ducks had ceased their quacking in the rushes. Even the birds flying overhead did so silently, the angled shadow of their passing the only indication of their presence.

Across the lake, she could hear the faint sounds of her companions playing and laughing, but they too seemed to sense something was wrong, and hushed one another. From the forest, a lion emitted a single dismayed roar, as if protesting, then he fell silent too. Kunti turned in the water, frowning as she tried to understand the cause of this change.

A shadow began to grow in the center of the lake.

The sky was clear blue, the sun dipping in the west but still half a watch from sunset. There was not a cloud in the sky to cause the shadow. Yet, as Kunti watched with puzzlement, the center of the lake began to grow darker and darker.

Could it be fish? No. The shadow was circular and concentrated in the center of the lake, not moving the way a school of fish might move.

As Kunti watched, the shadow began to darken, turning the sallow surface of the water black as pitch. The water then began to swirl.

Kunti was closer to the far bank of the lake than to the center. But even here, a good dozen yards or more from the edge of the dark water, she could feel its pull.

The swirling black water began to turn round on itself, spinning faster and faster.

In moments, it became a churning, the water breaking and producing waves that should have been white-tipped but were dark instead. Now, Kunti could feel herself being drawn in by the force of the churning, pulled towards the center of that swirling vortex.

Strong swimmer though she was, she had to strain to pull herself back. Grabbing hold of a willow root that dipped into the water, she wrapped the tendril firmly around her arm, standing on the muddy floor of the bank in waist-deep water, as she watched with rising alarm.

The center of the lake had turned into a whirlpool.

The whirlpool churned and spun faster and faster, like no vortex Kunti had ever seen or heard of.

It was as frenzied as a whitewater rapid, roaring now with great force.

Across the lake, she could see her companions standing on the shore of the lake, backing away in fright, as they watched this freakish display. Kunti could not believe this was a natural phenomenon.

She had been swimming in this lake with her friends

since she was old enough to swim, which was not longer after she was able to walk. She was a young woman now, all of fourteen summers of age, and she no longer needed nurses to accompany her. The kingdom of Kuntibhoja was at peace and had been at peace for decades. The nearest neighbors, Avanti and Mahishmati, were not at war with Kuntibhoja or with each other. She had no need of bodyguards and could handle herself if need be. But for the first time in her life she wished she had both bodyguards and a sword with her.

What good would a sword do against a water demon?

Nothing, probably. But it was all she could think of. That, and the realization that she should do as her companions had done and get away from the lake at once. Even if she was on the wrong side, and would have to walk all the way around the bank to get back to her companions and the pathway that led back to the palace. She should get away from this thing, whatever it was. This was some unnatural phenomenon.

Yet some part of her resisted.

She could not bring herself to turn and climb up on the bank, to run away from the churning maelstorm that was now roaring and spinning in a dervish frenzy, sending water spraying across the tops of the trees that hemmed the lake.

She watched, compelled by a fascination she could not explain.

The whirlpool swirled now in a descending cone, the dark water of the lake foaming white. The roar of the water drowned out all other sounds but at the edges of vision, she glimpsed birds flying, animals fleeing, and underfoot, she felt creatures of the under-earth scurrying away from the waterside.

Something began to rise from the center of the maelstorm.

Not a demon. A man.

A rishi, clad in the red ochre garb of the forest hermits, hair matted and piled overhead, possessed of the aging, withered limbs and wasted body of the lifelong penitent engaged in bhor tapasya.

There was nothing withered or aging about his eyes.

They shone with a ferocity that was unnerving. Large, bulging eyes in a bony angular face, their pupils were a unsettling grey. The penetrating gaze from those eyes scanned the shore of the lake, as if searching for something. Kunti had the sense that he was searching for landmarks, to ascertain his exact location.

Had he come from the underworld? How did a man emerge from a whirlpool in a lake? What force was raising him up now above the water, into thin air?

As she watched with open amazement, the old rishi lowered the point of his raised staff, pointing at the whirlpool.

At once, the maelstorm subsided, settling suddenly into a calm unbroken surface. The wind that had howled a moment earlier died away. The ripples and waves caused by the disturbance ceased. The lake was now as calm and still as it had been before. The cries of the agitated birds, the sounds of animals in the forest, the scurrying of insects, all subsided.

The rishi stood on the surface of the lake, as comfortably as a man standing on solid ground. As Kunti watched, he began to walk across the lake, the soles of his feet dipping into the water lightly, merely breaking the skin of the water, hardly disturbing it otherwise. He was headed directly for Kunti's side of the lake. As he neared the bank, he caught sight of Kunti, and registered her presence.

Kunti felt a sudden chill in her heart. All at once, the balmy summer sunshine felt icy cold. She wrapped her arms around herself, realizing how wet her garments were, and how scantily clad she was. Her outer garments lay on the other side of the lake, where her companions and she had discarded them. She wished she were there right now, surrounded by her playful friends. They would have been screaming by now, but Kunti was not given to outbursts of emotion. She stood her ground, remaining calm. The rishi was almost at the shore anyway.

He was staring straight at her now, his piercing gaze taking in her lack of proper attire, her dishevelled and damp condition, her shivering posture... What must he think her to be? She looked far from a princess right now. As she glanced up anxiously, she saw his eyes darken visibly, turning from grey to jet black. A darkness swirled around him like a cowl, exactly like the water of the lake had turned dark and swirled. A miasma enveloped his face and head. She saw his dark eyes shining from inside the miasma, directed only at her as he reached the bank and stepped ashore.

For a moment, the thought struck her that could be a Naga, one of those denizens of the nether realms who were said to rise to the surface of the world and assume any form they pleased. The man who emerged from the lake could well be a snake in a man's body. He had emerged from a lake. His eyes were as fierce as any snake's venomous gaze. The darkness of the water could be caused by his venom. And this human form could just be a disguise to enable him to approach unsuspecting humans.

Like me! She thought, on the verge of panic now. The rishi stood mere yards from her. He stared at her with those piercing dark eyes, his concentration intense, his hand gripping the wildwood staff hard enough to cause his knuckles to turn white, every aspect of his posture suggesting a predator about to attack.

Remember who you are, she told herself firmly. *You are no ordinary young girl. You are Pritha of the Yadavas, daughter of Surasena, sister to Vasudeva, adopted daughter of Kuntibhoja of the Bhojas, princess and heir to the Bhoja kingdom. You will not let yourself be intimidated by anyone—or any*thing.

She released the breath she had been holding. Gathering her errant emotions, Kunti bundled them together, tied them in a tight knot, then tucked them away. With perfect self-control, she joined her palms in a namaskaram, bowed her head low, and intoned: 'Vanakum, Swami. Welcome to our humble kingdom of Kuntibhoja.'

|| 2 ||

The rishi stood glaring at her. The intensity of his gaze seemed not to lessen even when she greeted him. His bony face and penetrating eyes remained as fierce, his posture still one of attack.

'Who might you be, young doe?' The voice was surprisingly pleasant, a startling contrast to the fierce appearance.

Kunti inclined her head. 'May it please your holiness, I am daughter of Kuntibhoja, king of the Bhoja nation. I go by the name of Kunti, after my father.'

He continued to regard her with the same severe scrutiny. She waited, unnerved inwardly but determined not to let it show. He raised his staff, and strode towards her. She resisted the urge to flinch, cry out, back away, or run, though all these presented themselves as desirable actions.

The rishi reached the spot where she stood, still dripping from the lake, and passed her by without pausing, working his way up the path.

And then he was gone.

She could see him, striding away through the glade, his tall bony form moving through the trees. Away from the lake, away from her.

She heaved a giant sigh of relief and all but collapsed to the ground. She sat there, just breathing for several moments as she collected her wits. From across the lake, she heard the faint sound of voices calling.

She looked up and saw her companions on the far bank, shouting and gesturing frantically.

She raised an arm, acknowledging them. They gestured to her, calling to her to come across the lake.

Kunti thought she had never been so glad to see her friends, silly though they could be at times, and overly obsessed with clothes and jewellery, and appearances, and most of all, men.

She got to her feet, still amazed to be alive.

When that old rishi had come striding towards her with his staff raised, she had been certain he was going to attack her.

Now, of course, it seemed silly to have thought it. Why would an old hermit attack a helpless young girl?

Then again, the old hermit had emerged from a maelstorm in a lake, a maelstorm that he seemed to have caused, then walked on water. He was no ordinary hermit, that was for sure. Who knew what else he was capable of?

She shook her head, trying to shake off the sense of dread that lingered after the rishi's passing. She took two steps into the lake, then stopped in ankle-deep water. Suddenly, she had no desire to swim. Not right now. Not today. Perhaps not for a while. And perhaps never in this particular lake.

She waved and gestured to her companions on the far side, pointing to the west. They waved back, acknowledging that they understood.

She turned and ran around the lake, through the trees. Not the way the old hermit had gone, the other way. The long way around. She didn't mind running an extra mile or two, so long as she did not have to face that scary face again. She covered the distance in record time, startling a pair of weasels back into their holes. The forest was slowly returning to its normal sounds and ambiance after the unnatural event at the lake.

She saw her friends through the trees and sprinted to meet them. They met in a clamour of cries and embraces and tears.

'–saw you in the lake and then that *thing–*'

'–thought you were sucked in–'

'–what would we tell your father–'

'–the King would have our heads for–'

'–what was that *thing* that came out of the lake?'

'It was a Nagdevta, wasn't it?'

This last came from Ramyakumari, a sweet but simplistic daughter of a cowherding family. Ramya was terrified of snakes and prayed daily to Garuda, Lord of Birds and arch enemy of all serpents.

'It was an old rishi, that's all,' Kunti told them. 'He asked me who I was, then walked off down the path.'

'Did you tell him you're the queen of this realm?' asked Jaggatpuri indignantly.

'I'm not the queen, Jaggi,' Kunti replied.

'You might as well be, since Raja Kuntibhoja doesn't have any sons.'

'Did he say who he was? I bet it's Brahmarishi Narada!'

'He didn't say and I didn't ask.' Didn't *dare* ask. She gestured back in the direction they had come. 'Let's go back. I have to collect my clothes.'

'Oh, I have them!' Sunidhi said, producing a bunched bundle she had been squeezing with both hands anxiously.

'Thanks for keeping them unwrinkled,' Kunti said, as she shook out the crumpled garments. She slipped them on quickly. 'Now, let's go home. This lake makes me nervous. That old rishi could come back anytime.'

They chattered excitedly as they walked. Most of their speculation was about the rishi's spectacular arrival. Kunti, having seen the event up close, had a theory.

'I think he used the water of the lake to travel from another loka to our one. The water is sacred Yamuna runoff after all. These old rishis have the power to ask the sacred River Goddesses to transport them through worlds, don't they?'

'But why come here? There are no gods here to visit. What possible business could he have in our kingdom?'

They were still exclaiming and speculating over the rishi's identity and mission when a man slipped through the trees behind them and began to follow. He stalked them for a while, staying close enough to hear what they were saying but avoiding being seen. His attention was rooted on Kunti most particularly. He watched her every move, took in her every gesture and word, admired the way she shook her wet hair, bumped her hip against a friend's to make a point, laughed with her head thrown back and hand raised to her chin. More than desiring her, he was hopelessly besotted. His longing was evident in his look, the way he smiled at her laughter, the wry shakes of his head he gave when she said something tart to her companions, and they squealed in delight.

This man was head over heels in love with the princess of Bhoja. He finally made his move a mile outside the city. Coming upon them from behind, he fell into step barely a yard aft of Kunti herself, matching pace with them.

The other girls noticed him first, their eyes widening as they saw him, then relaxing and smiling as he touched his finger to his lips to shush them. They kept his secret, but their own amusement at his presence undid them. Kunti noticed their unprovoked giggling and frequent glances behind and stopped suddenly, spinning around with her hands on her hips.

‖ 3 ‖

'You scoundrel!' she said indignantly.

He all but collided with her. Her stoppage was so sudden, he barely had time to stop himself. His hands went out before him instinctively, and came to rest on her shoulders. She lost her footing and fell backwards, landing on her behind on the ground, and he tumbled on top of her, half-attempting to catch her and stop her from falling, half-trying to stop himself from falling with her. He half-succeeded: she ended up on her back on the ground, but he managed to stay on his feet. He had hold of her shoulders and helped her back to an upright position.

She shoved his hands off her shoulders. 'What do you think you're doing?'

'I thought I was coming to the lake to bathe with you,' he said in a soft, affectionate voice, 'but you were already gone by the time I reached. So I was coming to visit you at your father's house.'

She cocked her head. 'And what would you have done there? March into his court and asked him for permission to visit with his daughter?'

'Perhaps I would have asked him for permission to do

more than visit?' he replied with a grin. Her friends gasped in mock outrage at this comment.

He glanced at them with an innocent expression. 'I meant I would have asked him for her hand in marriage. What were you girls thinking?' They laughed and flapped their hands at him.

Kunti relented and let her face relax in a smile. She glanced over her shoulder. 'You girls go on ahead. I'll catch up with you.'

'Don't be late or we'll tell your father!' they called out, then ran away laughing.

'We had a rendezvous on the north side of the lake under the ashoka tree after you finished your swim,' he said as they walked leisurely together through the woods in the late afternoon light.

'I never finished my swim today,' she replied. 'Something very strange happened.' She told him about the maelstorm and the strange snake-eyed rishi.

He stared at her. 'You aren't making fun of me, are you? This really happened?'

'I swear to you on my ancestor Yadu's name,' she said, reaching up to touch the lower boughs of apple trees as they walked. The apples were still tiny and green at this time, and she was careful not to jostle or break them free.

He whistled. 'Who does that? I mean, who comes out of a lake like a Takshak rising from the Naga kingdom?'

She turned to him with a gleam. 'That's what I thought too! He even looked like a Naga, his eyes dark and so intense, I thought he was going to open his mouth and show a forked tongue and then–' She crooked her forearm at the elbow and thrust her hand forward like a cobra striking. 'He was scary!'

'Probably just some old rishi-muni on an urgent mission to save the world,' he said, 'You'll probably never see him again. It was a good thing you didn't get sucked into that maelstorm yourself.'

'Would you have jumped in to save me if you were there?' she asked coyly.

He grinned. 'Of course. I have to protect the future mother of my future children, don't I?'

She giggled, covering her mouth with her hand held upright. 'First you joked about asking my father for my hand in marriage, now you're talking about motherhood and children. Aren't you forgetting one important thing before either of those things can happen?'

'What's that?' he asked, pretending to be genuinely curious.

'I have to decide if I'm ready to get married,' she said, ticking off the first point on her finger, 'then I have to decide *who* I'm going to marry.'

'Oh, is that all?' he asked, 'Well, the second point is already moot. As for the first, how about this summer? If you could decide by then, we could be married late autumn, the perfect time of year.' He gestured northwards. 'The cherry blossoms will be in full bloom by then. I know how much you love cherry blossoms, Pritha.'

She smiled with pleasure at his use of her given birth name. 'I do love cherry blossoms in bloom, it's true. That does sound very tempting. I will have to give it serious consideration.'

'Well, don't consider it for too long,' he said, 'otherwise, my parents might pack me off to Madri to attend a swayamvara.'

She stopped short, hands on her hips and a frown on her face. 'A *swayamvara*? In *Madri*? Whatever for?'

'For the same reason all princes go to swayamvaras, silly. To compete in the contest and try to win the favor of the princess. And if she approve, then to marry her.'

'In Madri, of all places?' Kunti asked scornfully. 'Those Madri princesses are older than the mountains and more wrinkled than old prunes!'

He looked at her with a half-smile on his face. 'Sounds like someone's more than a little jealous of Madri girls.'

'*Jealous*? *Me*, jealous of Madri girls? Why, I–,' she realized he was laughing at her and stopped herself. 'You're teasing me, you scoundrel. You know Bhoja and Madri always compete with each other, so you're just trying to make me angry.'

He shrugged. 'I'm not just teasing. The youngest Madri princess is quite comely, and she will be of age in a few years. I thought–'

She shoved him hard enough to send him sprawling. He was still laughing as she began striding purposefully towards her home.

'Hey,' he called, jumping to his feet and running backwards to keep pace with her, 'I was just teasing about Madri. But I am serious about my parents. They are getting restless, and the invitations to the swayamvaras are starting to pile up. I will have to start attending a few so other kingdoms don't start thinking that the Prince of Mahisha is afraid of competing.'

'You can do as you please,' she said, walking faster. 'What's it to me?'

'Hey,' he said, 'slow down. Now don't go off in one of your foul tempers. I did say that I intended to approach your father and ask for your hand. Not right now, not so casually, of course, but with proper protocol, in a few days.'

She slowed her pace a bit. 'I don't like to be rushed. You know that. I will make up my mind in my own way, at the right time. It could even be this summer, and then you could approach my father in the proper way, and it's even possible we could set a date for late autumn. But it had to be my decision in my own time. I thought you understood that.'

'I do, I do,' he said, 'And I know that it's not done for the boy to want to seem too eager. Marriage is a woman's decision, and it's your right to make that choice when you please. But can I help it if I'm so madly crazy in love with you, Pritha of Mathura, Kunti of Bhoja, apple of my eye, that I can't bear to wait another year, another season, or even another night, to make you my wife?'

She slowed even further, her face beaming with pleasure at his tone and his words. 'I am eager too,' she said softly, almost shyly. 'To make you my husband, Maheev or Mahisha.'

'Then what's there to think about?' He stopped and spread his arms. 'I love you, Pritha of Mathura, Kunti of Bhoja. I love everything about you, from your quick temper to your stubborn will, the way your back arches where it meets your hip, the way you toss your hair when you walk, your strength, your beauty, your love for fried tapioca—'

She giggled. 'Silly!'

'—your prowess at weapons and combat, a true warrior princess and a better fighter than most princes or princesses, your sense of dharma, your refusal to give up on any chore no matter how demanding until it is done to your satisfaction.' He continued in this vein for several moments. She realized with a start: He loves me. He really, truly loves me. This is not mere lust or youthful infatuation. He genuinely loves me and will care for me as long as he lives. This is a man I could spend the rest of my life with and be happy. I need to acknowledge his emotions, reciprocate his expression of love.

She started to go to him, then stopped herself, realizing where they were. The spires of the palace tower were within sight and the rumbling of wagons reminded her that they were within view of the busiest road out of the city. Instead of going to him, she pushed him away playfully. 'Nice speech! Now, go home. I'll see you tomorrow by the lake as usual.'

If he was disappointed by her failure to reciprocate his eloquent declaration, he did not show it.

'I'll be there,' he called out, 'And I'll make sure there aren't any Naga-men stirring up the lake into a frenzy!'

She had already turned and begun running; she waved over her head without looking back. She could imagine the look on his face without seeing it: sweet and wistful and handsome. She laughed to herself as she ran, and allowed herself the freedom to blush deeply and rosily at the thought that she might actually be planning her own wedding in a few weeks.

She reached home a very happy girl. It would be a long time before she felt as happy again.

The royal compound was abuzz with excitement, men and women rushing to and fro on various errands, the guards looking more alert than usual. Even the horses and elephants and dogs felt the excitement, whinnying, stamping their feet, and barking in their kennels.

'Princess! Your father wishes to see you at once. He has a visitor!' said Shatabdi, a round-faced palace staple who ran the royal household like it was her own fiefdom.

Kunti frowned. Her mind was still filled with thoughts of an autumn wedding and she hadn't quite registered the hustle and bustle around. 'What?'

Shatabdi took in Kunti's appearance with a look of horror. 'You can't go before him like that? What have you been *doing*?' She flapped her hands. 'Never mind. Shrutakirti! Mandakini! Take the Princess and get her changed into suitable attire. *Now*!'

The flustered maids hustled Kunti away. She glanced back helplessly at her companions who all wore worried expressions.

'This visitor,' she asked the maids as they dressed her hurriedly but efficiently in her chambers.

'A very important maharishi,' Mandakini sang out as she pulled Kunti's left arm through a sleeve, 'They say he's the same one who cursed Lord Indra for letting his elephant Airavata trample a garland he had gifted him.'

Shrutakirti, who was a mite slower witted, blinked as she fitted the last bracelet on Kunti's wrist. 'He gifted a garland to an elephant?'

'No, silly, he gifted the garland to Lord Indra. That's why he was so angry when Indra gave it to his elephant who trampled it.' Mandakini finished adjusting the garment and began combing Kunti's hair over an urn of smouldering sandalwood, fanning it out to catch the scented smoke.

'What was the curse?' Shrutakirti asked round-eyed. Stories of sages and their curses were a frequent topic of gossip around the palace. Brahmins were known for losing their temper, and for their penchant for spewing curses at those who provoked them.

'That Indra would fall from popularity just as the sage's garland had been allowed to fall, and he would one day become as insignificant as dust.' Kunti spoke the words by rote, recalling her itihasa lessons with the royal guru. 'That led to the great war between the Devas and the Asuras, which in turn led to the Sagar Manthan and the start of the eternal enmity between the two groups.'

Shrutakirti paused in the act of fixing a diamantine necklace around Kunti's throat. 'Devi save us! He is *that* sage? He's supposed to be the worst of them. What if he takes offence with something in Bhoja and curses us all to turn into asses?'

'It wouldn't make the slightest difference to you then, would it?' Mandakini snapped. 'Come on, finish up before *Shatabdi* curses us!'

Kunti saw the younger maid's hands were shaking. She smiled and took the necklace from Shurtakirti's hands, fixing it around her own neck herself. She put a reassuring hand on the maid's arm. 'Whatever you do, don't act nervous or scared around him. That will just make him madder. Be calm and keep your head down, and you'll be fine.'

Shrutakirti nodded but wrung her hands nervously as Kunti turned to leave her apartments

She forgot the maid and everything else as she strode quickly toward the royal hall, wanting to run but knowing it would not be proper for a princess to be seen running in the halls. She reminded herself to take her own advice. *Stay calm, Pritha. However terrifying the stories, he's still just a man.*

A man who had the power to travel through vortexes of air and water and had ruined the King of Gods with a single uttered curse.

|| 5 ||

The royal court of Bhoja was as silent as a tomb.

Even the court jesters, who were paid to keep people amused and entertained at all times, were uncharacteristically silent—because they weren't present at all, she noted. Her father must have ordered them sent away, to avoid causing any offence to the sage. Many brahmins frowned upon court entertainers. On the other hand, some enjoyed a taste of royal entertainment, even expected it. *Especially the apsara and gandharva dances!*

Her father, Raja Kuntibhoja, was seated on his throne, uncharacteristically sombre. That itself was strange: she was so used to hearing either her father's boisterous laughter or his cheerful voice here. His face was composed in a neutral expression, displaying no outward emotion. His ministers, courtiers and nobles all imitated his example, seated around the hall like wax effigies in a display gallery. The only movement came from the servants gently fanning the seat on which the sage was seated, beside the King's own throne.

The sage's long angular face was set in a perpetual scowl. His bush of matted hair, overgrown eyebrows and wild beard looked like they had never seen a comb. *I bet* he *doesn't scent his hair with sandalwood incense!*

He was seated with one leg crossed over the other, staring at nothing in particular. With his stick-thin limbs, bony torso and long neck, he reminded Kunti of a perched grasshopper perched. He continued to stare into the middle distance, contemplating Devi knew what for an endless span of time. Kunti felt sorry for the servants standing by with trays laden with various offerings for the guest's refreshment. She could imagine how terrified they must be, though they stood ramrod straight and barely even blinked.

She wondered why on earth one man, any man, should have the power to terrorize so many. *Just because he is a brahmin? That's not fair!*

The unfairness of it outraged her sense of social justice but she sat as still and patiently as the rest. At last, the visitor raised his head.

'Raja Kuntibhoja,' he said in a voice as harsh and unconcerned with civility as his appearance, 'I shall partake of your hospitality. Kindly ask your first-born to attend me during my stay, as is customary.'

Kunti saw her father's eyes widen.

'Great one,' he replied with unctuous care, 'I have no progeny of my own. However, by the grace of Brahma, my cousin Sura of Mathura saw fit to grant me guardianship of his first-born daughter, Pritha. I have raised her as my own, and she is my sole heir. If it please you, I shall have her attend to your every need during your stay.'

Kunti felt herself flush, knowing that every pair of eyes in the court was turned toward her. Her parentage was no secret. If anything, it gave her a certain status: not only was she sole heir and Princess of Kuntibhoja, but she was also sister to Vasudeva, Prince of Mathura, the capitol of the Yadava nation. That made her a bridge between two nations. But right now, she would have given anything to have an elder sister, a brother, a half-dozen siblings, a hundred even! She sensed the sage's intense scrutiny on her and kept her own gaze demurely downcast.

'So be it,' said the sage Durvasa.

|| 6 ||

It was the only time her foster father appeared nervous and uncomfortable when addressing her.

'I need you to play a more modern role,' he had said, and she had laughed at his choice of words.

'Do you wish me to perform an entertainment for you, father?' she asked playfully.

'Sage Durvasa...' he paused. 'Is notorious for his temper. It would not do to make him irate. He is a powerful sage. A *seer-mage*. Kuntibhoja needs to please him and gain his blessings, not his curses.'

She nodded, matching his serious tone. 'Say what needs to be done and I shall see to it, father.'

'You must stand service on him yourself.'

She raised her eyebrows. 'Myself?'

He rubbed his leathery face. 'I am asking too much of you, daughter. You are a princess, a queen-in-waiting, not a–'

'I can be a serving woman, if that is what the good sage requires. A royal serving woman. I have seen how these sages expect to be treated during such visits. I have heard the stories. Read the itihasas. I know what fury their curses can bring. Besides, I have seen Guru Durvasa's powers at work. He is formidable. I would not want him irate at our good kingdom.'

He looked up at her. 'Our nation's good name and future depends on how well you serve the sage.'

She lowered her chin, all merriment gone. 'You can count on me, pitr. I will make sure he has no cause for complaint.'

She meant every word.

|| 7 ||

The following nights and days were a blur of endless chores. While the entire palace staff was kept on its toes by the presence of the venerated sage, none were worked as hard or as relentlessly as Kunti. Durvasa would demand anything he pleased at any hour he pleased, with no thought for her need for rest, comfort, or nourishment.

In the beginning, his demands were unusual and difficult, but not impossible.

'Go fetch me white marigolds,' he said one night at an unearthly hour.

Kunti bowed her head without hesitation and sent her maids running to go pluck the flowers from her own personal garden. But before the girls had left Kunti's apartments, she was summoned to the guest chambers again.

'They must be plucked by your hands,' the sage added, 'otherwise they are of no use to me.'

Kunti bowed her head without argument and backed out of the guest chambers. Once out, she ran faster than her maids and fetched the choicest white marigolds from her own garden. She ran all the way back to the sage and set them before him, catching her breath.

He did not so much as glance at them. 'I desire sabudana vadas,' he said, using the local term for fried tapioca. Prepare it with your own hands and make sure it is neither too hot nor too cool when you serve it to me.'

Kunti backed out of the chamber and went to the royal kitchen where she prepared the sage's favorite repast. She carried it in a silver dish covered with another silver dish, removing the top only when she laid it before the sage. He took a bite of one of the tapioca balls and ate it without a compliment or a comment.

'I also desire buttermilk flavored with mango,' he said. 'I would like to partake of it the instant I have finished my snack.'

Kunti's eyes widened but she dared not express herself. She backed out and this time she sprinted to the kitchen where she shouted at a cook to fetch her buttermilk at once from the cooling pit, while she ran to the fruit pantry and selected the ripest juiciest mango she could find. She poked open a tiny hole, tasting it to make sure it was in fact ripe and juicy. She didn't bother with slicing, instead she rolled the mango in its skin between her palms until the flesh inside was reduced to a dripping pulp. Motioning to the cook to set the silver bowl before her, she squeezed out the mango pulp through the hole, and stirred it with the handle of a wooden ladle.

A moment to wipe her hands clean on a kitchen cloth, then she raced back to the guest chambers, she slowed to a formal walk as she approached. She entered the chamber just as Durvasa was finishing the last tapioca ball. She proferred him the bowl and waited, heart still pounding, as he sipped of the treacly concoction. He made a sound that could possibly have indicated approval–or it might have just been him clearing his throat.

When he set down the bowl and she saw it was empty, she almost beamed with relief. He, on the other hand, did not indicate in any other manner that he had enjoyed the proferring. It did not matter. The empty bowl was satisfaction enough for her.

|| 8 ||

Over the days and nights, he ran her ragged.

The worst nights were the ones where he would summon her and ask her to prepare one of his favorite items and then, after he was done eating it, sink into one of his meditative trances. She would wait in the expectation of further requests, not knowing if he would summon her again an hour, half a watch, or even a whole watch later. She barely slept the entire time he stayed at the palace. He seemed to spend almost all his time in chambers, either meditating or discoursing with other brahmins and sages on various philosophical matters.

Oftentimes, he would ask her to fetch refreshments for himself and these guests, many of whom seemed discomfited at having the royal princess herself wait on them. Durvasa seemed not to notice or to care for their discomfort.

Once, he asked her to wait awhile. She stood unobtrusively to one side while they continued their discussion of some inscrutable passage in the Vedas, Vedangas or Upanishads. Suddenly, he asked for her opinion on some obscure aspect of the passage in question. 'Which interpretation do you favor?' he would ask.

She blinked rapidly. 'Your own, mahadev.'

'Yes, but why do you favor my reading over the excellent interpretations of these venerated brahmins?'

All eyes in the room were on her.

'Because of the context, mahadev,' she replied. 'It is evident that the reference to storm in this particular instance refers specifically to Lord Indra, personified as a storm.'

'It does not say so at all,' said an elder rishi, looking irate with Kunti. 'The language refers only to thunder, lightning and a flash flood. There is no indication of personification at all.'

'But there is, great one,' she said, inclining her head to show respect for a superior mind. 'In the third line of the second verse of the fourteenth parva, the text specifically uses the masculine when referring to the fury of the storm.'

Everyone stared at her. Even the elder rishi looked gobsmacked. Sage Durvasa leaned back with a gleam in his eye.

'Any reference to a storm would be masculine surely,' he said.

'True, but in this case, the Sanskrit word used to describe the masculine fury of the storm is one that is associated with Lord Indra. 'With what thunderous fury does he strike...'' She quoted the rest of the verse from memory, then quoted three others that clearly named Lord Indra as their subject.

All the white haired heads were nodding by the time she finished the last quote.

'Hmmph,' said the irate sage. 'I concede the point. However, on the matter of the river being Saraswati...' He turned his gaze to Kunti. 'You are Raja Kuntibhoja's daughter? Commend your guru for me.'

She bowed graciously, avoiding mention of the fact that since only male kshatriyas were expected to be educated, she had read and mastered the sacred texts on her own, aided in private by a like-minded group of older women, much older than she for the most part, who believed in the maxim that if women could fight, women should be able to write. Had she enlightened the irate guru on this point, he would likely have choked on his sweet potato savory.

After the guests had departed, she waited patiently for Durvasa to say something, to acknowledge her contribution in some way, if not outright praise her.

He said nothing except to ask her to prepare more fried tapioca, this time with groundnuts.

This familiar pattern continued, with Durvasa frequently calling on her to clarify some point of controversy or to break a deadlock, but never acknowledging her scholarship or memory skills. If anything, he made it a point to always ask her to perform some completely mundane chore immediately after – clean his chambers, wash his garments, fetch him a particularly difficult-to-obtain item from the far end of the city – as if to remind her of her place. Intelligent, well read, endowed with scholarly gifts, yet still a serving girl.

She accepted all this with good grace. She toiled all hours without protest. Endured outbursts without a plaint.

The one thing that galled her was his stubborn refusal to permit her to handle the scrolls.

Durvasa frequently requested a particular text or several texts, often at a most inopportune time. She was tasked with going to the brahmin quarters, which was situated a good five miles outside the city walls, disturbing the bramacharya novices on night rotation – the round-the-clock verbatim *'pad-a-pad'* recitals – and requesting one of them for the text in question, waiting while the novice fetched it, checking that he had fetched the right scroll (more likely than not, he had not), accompanying the novice back to the palace, up to the guest chambers, presenting the sage with the requisitioned scroll, waiting till he had finished with it, then accompanying the novice back to the ashram.

Inbetween, she would of course be asked to perform various of her usual tasks: fetching refreshments for the sage and any guests he may have at the time, or performing other chores he asked of her. The dismissive look that even the most hairless, green-eared novices gave her, asserting their superiority of sex, scholarship, and caste all in a single sneer, irritated her. But she endured even that.

What she could not brook was the fact that she was not permitted, at any time, or for any reason whatsoever, to so much as touch or breathe upon any of these sacred scrolls. The logic being that as a woman, subject to womanly foibles and monthly leakages, she was inherently impure and unfit to partake of the exclusively masculine domain of vidya, the sacred lore of vedic wisdom.

I can be as intelligent as any man, as well read as any

brahmin, as insightful as any scholar, yet because I am a woman, I have no right to be any of those things? Hmmph! Saraswati, grant your daughter patience to endure such absurd bigotry.

On one occasion, the novice insisted (twice) at the ashram that he had sourced the exact text she had named. But when they arrived at the palace and presented the scroll to Durvasa, who immediately fumed and raged at being given the wrong text, the novice immediately pinned the blame on her. He claimed she had asked for this one and so that was the one he had brought; he could hardly be blamed for an ignorant illiterate impure *woman's* fault.

Of those insults, the one that stung the most was the accurate one: *woman's*. Yes, she was a woman and proud of it. Did this young upstart think he had emerged wholly formed out of Brahma's Egg? Did he speak to his own mother and sisters with the same tone? He knew very well that she had requested Parva 231, Canto 89, not Parva 89, Canto 231 which he had brought.

She said none of these things aloud, merely bowed her head and endured the hailstorm of outrage and insults the sage heaped upon her while the novice looked on, smirking, even though her heart raged with the injustice, the unfairness, the sheer *bigotry* of it all.

But none of these or similar incidents were the worst.

Oh, no, that was yet to come.

It was a cold rainy day in the first half of winter. Bhoja did not get snow, but it was far enough North and within blowing range of the Garwhal Himalayas to get bitterly, dangerously cold. Cold enough to freeze water and deliver the occasional shower of hailstones the size of a man's fist. And when the winter winds blew through the city, Shiva help any unfortunate who happened to be out of walls. The daily count of travellers and drunks who froze to death from exposure was in double digits at this time of year.

Durvasa had been in a particularly benign mood these past days. There was a rumor that the sage was planning to take his leave shortly; a rumor perpetrated by herself, based on a conversation in which the sage had been asked by another brahmin if he would be here in the spring. 'Distinctly not,' he replied, 'I must be in Uttarkashi before the winter snows set in.'

This alone had made Kunti want to yell and throw her hands in the air, perform several somersaults and tumbles around the chamber, then dance a very unprincesslike caper, hooting and cheering all the while. She did in fact perform all these antics, but only much later that evening, when she was safely in the privacy of her own chambers, with her friends.

'Finally, we shall be able to see you again daily as we used to,' they said, happily once the initial euphoria had died down. 'We shall go swimming in the lake, picking berries, climb to the top of the rookerie, and do all the happy things we love to do.'

She was about to correct them by saying that since it was winter, they could hardly do any of those things, but she realized it didn't matter. The point was, she would be free soon. Free to resume her girlish ways and indolent, carefree life as a young princess. She would rather dive into a frozen lake than serve the sage Durvasa another season!

So it was with sunshine in her heart that she waited on their honoured guest over the next few days. The passes to Uttarkashi generally snowed in during the third masa of winter. They were already at the start of the second masa. That left less than a fortnight before the sage would have to leave if he meant to reach his destination before snow closed the passes; ideally he should leave within the week.

Kunti was wandering in her mind, day-dreaming about resuming her sword-fighting training again. She had been so consumed with her round-the-clock duties here that her fight guru, a crusty old woman veteran who had served in the Bhoja army and trained three generations of royalty, had squirted a mouthful of betelnut juice with disgust at Kunti's irregular appearances, wiped her mouth with the back of her hand, and told her in the Bhojpuri dialect to come back when she was able to extract her 'head out of the elephant's backside', which required no translation. She missed the physical exertion of swordplay, the world reduced to just the edge of the blade, one's opponent's eyes and the elegant dance of death.

The first time Durvasa spoke, she thought she had misheard.

She stared blankly at the sage, not wanting to commit the sacrilege of asking him to repeat himself, yet not able to believe she had heard correctly.

He gazed up at her patiently. He had been in a relatively less intense mood these past days. Less intense for Duravasa, of course, was like saying a hawk was less intense after he had eaten a full rabbit. It was not something that was easily evident to a casual observer but she had learned to tell a great deal from his most minor gestures, vocal patterns, and body language. One might even say that she could read Durvasa almost as well as she could read Sanskrit. Though Sanskrit rarely lost its temper and flew into a flaming rage if your tapioca cakes were a tad less crisp. Right now, he was calm, and he proved her right by doing something he rarely ever did: he repeated his request without a trace of irritation.

'I require an item fetched from Madri.'

She stared at him without response for several heartbeats. She was too taken aback to simply bow as usual and acquiesce.

'From Madri, Mahadev?' she said.

He named an item. Something so trivial that it could be

found in any marketplace anywhere, or even right here in the palace itself, perhaps in this very guest wing. A paper fan, the kind that visitors from the Far Eastern kingdoms brought with them and traded for local spices or silks, the kind that Eastern women apparently held before their painted faces and smiled coyly behind.

What on earth could a celibate guru want with an Eastern woman's paper fan? Surely not to gift his concubine! Which was what those exotic items were rumoured to be most commonly used for: as gifts from rich men to their concubines. Obviously, the Sage had no women in his life so that could not be its purpose.

She dared not ask the next question, but he read it in her eyes anyway and answered it aloud. Apparently, he had learned to read Kunti almost as well as she had learned to read Durvasa.

'It must be from Madri, specifically,' he said, 'from the shop of the vaisya merchant Gupta. It will be easy enough to find, it is the largest store in the town market, with a substantial stock of baby elephants and lion cubs on display constantly.'

He glanced at the window. 'If you leave right now, you should be back here before the full moon.'

She was dumbstruck. She had no words. Did he realize that Madri lay beyond the hill ranges? That this was winter, and one of the coldest winters in recent memory—the coldest since before she had been born, apparently! Even the royal couriers and courtiers ferrying information to and fro between the two neighboring kingdoms had reduced their biweekly trips to once a fortnight, and then only if the news was urgent. Wars had been postponed to avoid crossing the Madri ranges in winter. Marriages called off. And he expected her to go all the way to Madri now, at the start of the coldest winter in memory, to fetch a *paper fan*?

He was still looking at her, as if reading every thought that passed through her mind.

'Tell Gupta I send my blessings and tell him that he may send his eldest son-in-law to Gajapura next spring, his work will be done. I have spoken to the appropriate authorities.'

She stood there, simply staring at him in utter disbelief.

He added mildly, 'The message must be delivered in person by you alone. No one else must accompany you or he will suspect betrayal. Once you deliver the message successfully, he will give you the fan. Bring it directly to me.'

Delivered in person? By her alone? No one else must accompany? Over the Madri hills in winter, during the season of hailstorms, when the bandit gangs, the bears and the predators virtually ruled those hills? It was insanity. Even the most seasoned courtiers went with a cortege of at least eight armed guards, and no woman, princess or not, went without a full company as well as elephants. He expected her to ride alone, risk death by exposure, by hail, by bandits, by predators, riding day and night without halts for food or shelter, just to fetch him a paper fan? She had suspected it all along but now she knew for certain: he was a torturer. An assassin. A murderer. A ruthless barbaric killer who cared nothing for the lives of the daughters of his hosts. He had probably left a trail of dead princesses and nobleman's daughters in his wake, scattered across the 500 kingdoms like chaff from grain.

And he asked this even though, as she herself had witnessed, he could simply travel from place to place through magical means, the way he had simply appeared from a maelstorm in the lake, a season and a half ago.

She wished that he had drowned in that lake, in that maelstorm of his own creation, drowned and choked and been washed up on the shore of the lake, pale, bloated and half eaten by fishes.

She saw by his face that he read her thoughts, or the general drift of them at least. He read it in her pauses, her stance, her wider eyes, her clasped hands, her slightly furrowed brow. Just as she could read his every change of mood and direction of thought in the way he breathed, inclined his head, or sat.

That was when she thought: *I can't do this anymore. I can't go on.*

But then she remembered her foster-father, Raja Kuntibhoja. How sad and desolate he had been when she first came to live here, broken by the loss of his wife and son in childbirth. How entranced he had been by her every word, gesture, action, not just in those early days which she barely remembered, but as she grew. How he had doted on her every deed. He lived and breathed by her. She could do no wrong.

He had spoiled her more than her real father would ever have spoiled her, or even her real grandparents. King Ugrasena and Queen Padmini were not the most demonstrative of parents, and whatever affection Kunti had received in her father's house had come from her brother Vasudeva. But a brother's love was different. Vasu was kind and gentle, but he was also mischevious and prone to teasing: he was but a boy too back then after all, and she was his sister.

Nothing and nobody came close to providing Kunti with the warmth, affection, lavish helpings of love and care and tenderness that Raja Kuntibhoja doled out on her. She had quickly come to realize how precious she was to him, how much he regarded her as a gift from the gods themselves; a ray of hope in the darkness of his soul. Unlike many kings, he did not seem to care that she was a daughter and that he had no son, that she was no actually of his blood and therefore his line would only continue through her in the most indirect way possible.

He had encouraged her every wish, however unusual, be it learning to master the sword, or learning battle strategy from the most expert general of his kingdom, or playing with friends of all backgrounds, ethnicities and nationalities, without regard for class, caste or social level. Kunti was her own woman, and unlike many fathers, especially rajas and maharajas, he had never sought to clip her wings or make her feel that her freedom was anything less than a natural birthright. For a man, he had been completely accepting of the Arya tradition of matriarchal governance, a tradition that had been mostly abandoned by those whom it ill suited these days. Nobody in Kuntibhoja doubted that it was Rani Kunti who would inherit the throne and kingdom were any ill to befall her adoptive father; nor did anyone doubt her ability to rule as effectively as Kuntibhoja himself.

Except when it came to this one guest. This was the one and only time he had asked her to perform the 'duties' of a modern, fashionable girl of high birth. She did not fear the stories she had heard of Durvasa's legendary temper and terrible curses, or the power he had displayed when emerging from the maelstorm in the lake. She only knew she could not bear to break her foster father's heart, or to cause distress to the people and kingdom she loved so much. She loved them too much to let this awful, self-centred man throw a temper tantrum and use his powerful gifts to cause misery to innocent souls.

It was this love that made her grit her teeth, bite back any reluctance and bow as gracefully as she could manage under the circumstances.

'As you say, gurudev.'

|| 10 ||

People stared at her as she returned three weeks later. Nobody could believe she was Princess Kunti. She looked like a ragged forest hermit, emerging from the deep woods to ask for alms.

When she paused for a moment to catch her breath, relieved to be breathing the spice-scented air of the marketplace again, a passing noble on a horse even tossed her a square stone. She let it lay where it fell and made her way wearily but with growing enthusiasm toward the palace.

Even the gate sentries stared with astonishment as she greeted them and passed through. She went through the kitchen and maids' quarters to avoid causing a scandal among the courtiers. The maids and serving girls who caught sight of her gasped. 'Princess!' one exclaimed. 'How – ?' She broke off, eyes filling with tears as she looked Kunti up and down with knowing eyes. 'My dear, shall I fetch the royal vaid?'

She shook her head, throat filled with an emotion she could not name. 'It is not my blood. I am well.'

That last was not entirely true. She was far from well.

But it was no sickness or ailment she suffered from, nothing that ayurvedic herbs and ointments could cure or treat. It was a fever of the soul. There were things in the world that could affect a young woman in ways more damaging than a physical assault or a disease contracted.

She felt a great deal better once she had bathed, partaken of some nourishment, spent some time drying out and combing her hair over a scented sandalwood brazier. She was humming to herself as she finished, unaware that she was doing so, or that the tune she was humming was the same one her mother Padmini would sing to her and her brother Vasudeva to put them to sleep. It put her in mind of the gentle, comforting caress of her mother, of that warm maternal embrace, the softness of her cheek upon Kunti's own, the scent of her. It was hard living apart from one's family, separated as a child, knowing that every one of those people—father, mother, brother, cousins, uncles, aunts, grandparents—all still existed, that enormous circle of warmth, comfort and filial affection, but that she was now outside the circle, a satellite moon destined to live in her own lonely orbit. What did it mean? Why did such things happen? She had brought comfort, warmth and joy to her foster father Kuntibhoja. But what of her own comfort, warmth and joy? Did she not deserve as much too?

She put these thoughts out of her mind as she finished her toilet, shook them off and breezed out of her apartments and all the way to the guest chambers. Sentries, courtiers, maids, running boys and everyone who passed her by could not help but look twice; some stared, others whispered, but she ignored them all. She walked tall and strong and did not stop for any distraction.

'Gurudev,' she said, bowing to Durvasa.

He looked up absently from the scroll he was perusing. She offered him the paper fan, presented upon her open palms.

He glanced at it with a frown, as if about to ask her what this object might be and why she was troubling him with it. Then he shook his head irritably and said, 'Put it anywhere.'

She placed it beside other items she had fetched for him during his long stay, each of which represented some arduous effort or sacrifice on her part. None of them had been touched or moved from their original position as far as she could tell. She did not dwell on this fact but simply turned back to him and stood politely waiting until he looked up again, questioning.

'Merchant Agarwal of Madri sends his gratitude and says he will surely send his eldest son-in-law to Gajapura next spring as instructed, and will ensure that the boy does not squander this priceless opportunity.'

He had stopped listening halfway through her recitation.

She waited for some acknowledgement, some response. Anything. There was none.

That night, her friends came to see her, eyes wide and hands clasped to their chests with concern.

'Your face!' they said, taking her chin gently and turning

her face this way and that to exclaim in dismay. 'Your arms, your legs, such bruises! These are purple and fresh. How did you come by them?'

She was silent for a long moment, emotion choking her.

'Hailstorm,' she said at last. 'On the road to Madri.' She added after a moment, 'And on the way back.'

They asked her a thousand questions, fussed and fretted about her like mother hens around a solitary chick. She smiled wanly at their fussing, allowed them to redo her hair, attempt to beautify her as best as was possible with a bruise-covered appearance, insisted they bring her favorite savories, invited her to go to the grain minister's son's wedding the next evening. She went along with everything except the last.

'I have to remain here, to serve our guest.'

They made pooh-pooh noises, waving their hands in disgust. They tried their best to convince her to sneak away for a few hours at least. The handsome son of the Jamadgura war minister was expected to attend, stoking gossip about his former steamy romance with the bride-to-be. Scandal and fireworks were to be expected. She heard it all as if from a great distance, viewed her friends as if she were meeting them for the first time, as if all this was strange and faraway, from another time, another Kunti.

She stayed in the palace the next day, making tapioca savories and almond buttermilk for the sage, fetching scrolls, cleaning his muddy wooden cleat slippers, and sundry other chores. The sound of the wedding music was faintly audible from the kitchen floor, plaintive and sad as a dirge to her ears. She wondered how people did such things as dressing up in finery, wearing jewelry, attending weddings, when the world was such a dark and stormy place. What was the point?

She woke up that night and found her pillow soaked; she could not understand how.

It occurred to her as she was drifting off into a restless asleep again: Could I have been crying? But she didn't remember crying. The sage Durvasa left the next day.

‖ 11 ‖

'Memorize this mantra.'

Kunti looked up at the sage. They were at the egress of the guest apartments, the sage about to leave.

Raja Kuntibhoja had come to touch the sage's feet and ask for the customary blessings, which the sage had given. The king had hesitated before asking the traditional host's question: 'I trust everything was to your satisfaction?'

Kunti had felt no trepidation during the long pause before the sage responded. She had passed the point of anxiety a while ago on the trip to Madri. Or perhaps even before. It did not matter. She no longer feared Durvasa's curse or anything he may say now.She was long past all that.

'I have no complaints,' he said finally.

She was looking at her father's face when he heard his guest respond. She saw Raja Kuntibhoja wait, expecting more. Some small words of praise perhaps. A compliment. Maybe even a lavishing of admiration for his daughter's impressive attentiveness and diligence. But of course there was nothing. Sage Durvasa did not praise, compliment or lavish admiration. That single sentence was all he had to say. It was enough. Coming from him, it was the equivalent of a thousand effusive praises. Many of his courtiers, noblemen, brahmins and other seers would say as much to Raja Kuntibhoja in the months and years to come, expressing their admiration for his daughter's extraordinary dedication to the most feared brahmin visitor. There would be plenty of compliments later. But none from Durvasa. Not now, not ever.

Now, Kunti waited at the egress with the customary earthen bowl of yoghurt, which she had offered to the departing guest, and which he had partaken off without comment. He had returned the bowl to her palm and she had thought that he would then begin walking, and continue walking—out of the guest apartments, the palace, the city, the kingdom, her life. He could not walk fast enough.

Instead, he had paused.

And said to her: 'Memorize this mantra.'

Then he recited a very brief couplet. The instruction, and the mantra that followed, were delivered quietly, barely loud enough for Kunti to hear. Nobody else was close enough to hear. The words were intended for her ears alone. He spoke the words and then walked away.

She stood there a moment, expressionless, holding the earthen bowl with the dregs of the yoghurt upon her palm, as the sound of his wooden cleat slippers sounded on the steps leading down from the guest apartments, rang as they crossed the stone floor to the archway, then grew softer, then muffled, then finally faded as the sage left the palace complex and was gone, out of her life forever.

She never saw him again.

Her father came to her and embraced her warmly, releasing an immense sigh of relief.

'Kunti!' he cried out. 'Sweet child, you have done us all proud. All Bhoja thanks you today.'

People crowded around them, smiling, laughing, moving about and talking normally again, abandoning the stiff, sombre attitude they had assumed in the past several months of the sage's visit. She saw her father's gratitude and relief reflected in all their faces. Raja Kuntibhoja was only saying aloud what they all felt.

She knew she should smile at him so she smiled. But there was no mirth in her heart. She did not see what she had done that was so special. She had been given a task, she had done the task to the best of her ability. Whether or not the task had been appreciated and had earned her the recognition of their guest did not matter at all. She had performed her duty, as was the modern custom. It was what any young daughter of a decent noble household ought to do.

|| 12 ||

She went through the rest of that month in a daze, unaware of when she ate or rested or slept or participated in the endless activities her friends involved her in.

She did everything, said all the right words, dressed the right way, but those close to her knew she was not herself, her heart was into anything she did.

Her friends expressed concern for her. Her father showed sympathy for her 'exhaustion' and suggested she might wish to visit her hometown, Mathura, to recover from the ordeal she had been put through.

Everyone was sympathetic, supportive, effusive with praise, admiring, sensitive, caring, but none of this what she wanted.

What did she want then? She did not know.

All she knew was that it was not this, or that, or anything.

Just...something else.

It was a whole season later, in the spring that she woke one night, to a mercifully dry pillow this time, and remembered the sage's parting words.

'Memorize this mantra.'

She had memorized it. Memorizing shlokas by sandhi rote recitation method was something little toddlers were taught to do. It was the way all knowledge was learned, passed on, stored over generations. Memorizing one shloka was like storing a drop in that vast ocean of knowledge.

But for the Guru to call such special attention to it, the timing of his giving it to her, the solemn tone with which he had imparted it, something in his eyes, his manner, his gesture as he stopped her from repeating it back to him, the flaring of his nostrils and widening of his pupils, told her that this was no ordinary shloka.

She mused on the possible purpose of this shloka. She sensed now what she had not realized at the time. This shloka was meant to be, in some way, a reparation for all that she had endured during her long service to the guru. A payment, even. A reward of sorts. She had heard stories of brahmins imparting mantras to hosts who treated them with special grace. Gifts from the gods, they were called. How a simple couplet of rhyming Sanskrit verse could be a gift, a payment, a reward, she did not know. But the stories said that reciting those mantras produced magical results. The results differed from story to story, but all concurred on their being magical. The poor became rich. The sick became healthy. The lovelorn were united with their lost loves.

She stopped herself short.

She had been pacing her chamber, sweeping from end to end endlessly, a practice she had fallen into in the months since the Guru's departure.

It was often the only real exercise she took. Her old habits of running, swimming, racing, horse riding, hunting, archery practice, swordplay, javelin throwing, had all fallen by the wayside.

She had barely seen her friends for a whole season and a half. Two were married, she had heard, the others were betrothed. Girls their age did not stay single long. Girls *your* age, she reminded herself. She knew her father had been showered with requests from Kings and Emperors, asking that she host a swayamvara and permit suitors to vye for her hand as was the custom of the land. She could still refuse them all at the end of the tourney, if none pleased her. But they all wanted a chance at impressing and catching the eye of the legendary Kunti of Bhoja, she who had served the irascible Guru Durvasa and kept her house safe from the ill favor of his cursing tongue. She was the most desirable bride in fifty kingdoms and princes were as restless as princesses— they all wanted to be wed while still young.

Her father had reminded her, gently, that the longer she waited, the more young princes her age would find other brides, less suitable than she but still brides nevertheless. Princes must have wives, just as princesses must have husbands. It was simply the way of the world. But she didn't care about age or availability. The thought of marriage sickened her to the stomach.

He had sensed this, sensed also that somehow, her dislike of the topic of marriage was related to the Sage's visit. 'Did Gurudev say something to you about your future prospects?' he asked her one day after she had staunchly refused yet another request for a swayamvara. 'Did he perhaps foretell your husband-to-be and your life together?'

She frowned at her father. 'He said not a word of such things.'

He blinked. 'Then what is it, my child? What ails you? Do not deny it. I have seen you these past weeks. You take no pleasure in the things that once delighted you. You spend all day sequestered in your palace. You go nowhere, see no one, and have turned in against yourself. You are like a ghost of the laughing, active, happy Kunti you were before he came here. I cannot believe that your change has nothing to do with the Guru's visit. If he said something to you that put fear into your heart, that made you dread marraige or your future husband, tell me now. Men such as he can often make stark pronouncements that terrify us mortals, but their intention is often to caution and help us prevent future calamities, not prevent us from living altogether.'

She shook her head slowly. 'Guru Durvasa said nothing about such things. Or about anything to do with me personally or my future, nothing at all.'

And this was true. Guru Durvasa had barely paid her any heed except as a vehicle to serve his needs. Bring this, fetch that, go there, summon so-and-so. She was nothing more than a glorified servant to him. What did he care about a servant's future prospects? All he cared about was having his needs fulfilled.

'Then what is it, daughter?' King Bhoja asked her, his face lined with anxiety. 'Something ails your heart. I see it in your every aspect. It festers like a sickness in you. It is poisoning your zest for life. Tell me what it is. If it is within my power to give you what it is you desire, I will give it to you, no matter the cost and the effort. Speak but once and you shall have your heart's desire.'

She hung her head in shame, for she heard the concern in her father's voice. She knew he cared greatly for her and could not bear to see her unhappy. But even so, there was nothing he could do. 'I am sorry, father. There is nothing you can do.'

'There must be *something*!' He flailed about mentally, searching for something to appease her. 'Would you wish to go home to your father's house? Would spending some time with your birth mother and father set your heart at ease? Is that your plaint? Does your heart ache for home? Say the word and I shall drive you there myself in my own chariot this very day.'

'No, father,' she said sadly. 'I would love to go home someday, in the summer perhaps, when the orchards of Vrindavan are lush with fruit, and Mathura's markets are bustling with foreign traders after the ships return from western ports. I would love to see my beloved maatr and pitr and my bhraatr Vasudeva again. But that is not what ails me.'

'Then you admit something does ail you?' he said, grasping at it eagerly. 'Tell me then, what is this canker in your heart that robs my beloved Kunti of her happiness and youth day by day? Is it a horse? A place? A song?'

He could not think of anything further to suggest and threw his hands up in the air. '*Speak*!'

She bowed her head for a long time. 'It is nothing within your power to give, father. There is nothing I desire. I am content here in your house. You are a good father and I bless the Devas for delivering me to your house.'

He clenched his fist in frustration. 'There must be *something*.'

She stood up, sighing softly. 'Permit me to leave your presence. I am tired and wish to rest awhile.'

She heard him calling for more wine, irritably. She wished she could tell him everything, but she could not.

|| 13 ||

Now, she paced the floor of her chambers, tracing the same route over and over again, as she went over every detail of the Guru's last instruction to her.

'*Memorize this mantra.*'

But what was the mantra? What did it do? She was certain now that it did something. How to find out what that was without actually using it. From the way the Guru had stopped her from repeating it, she had understood that merely reciting the mantra aloud would achieve some result. But surely there must be a way to know what that result was *before* reciting it?

He must know.

Guru Durvasa would know what the mantra did, of course. But he had not told her, and she had not thought to ask at the time. All she knew was that he had intended the mantra to be some kind of gift to her, that was the tradition after all. Her father had not thought to ask her if the Guru had given her any gift in parting because he had simply been too relieved that Durvasa had not cursed them. The thought that he had actually attempted to reward her for her services had not occurred to Raja Bhoja at all.

The mantra was her secret. She had told nobody about it. She had spoken to nobody about her ordeal, though many had asked. Everyone was curious and awe-struck at how a princess of Bhoja, a presumably spoilt, pampered, self-centered rich powerful beautiful young woman had served a notorious brahmin for so long and so arduously, enduring such hardship and deprivation, without once giving offence. It was the talk of fifty kingdoms, as evidenced by the requests from those fifty for an opportunity to win her hand in marriage. There were stories and tales she had heard snippets of, most resembling the truth not even remotely; she had heard of them from the daiimaas, who had themselves been fishing for the true story. But even then, she had said nothing. The torture of those weeks serving the Guru were locked in her heart and she had thrown away the key. And she did not intend to speak of it to anyone.

Because speaking of it would have meant speaking of the other thing as well, the thing her father had tried so hard to pry from her. The pain of what happened on that fateful journey to Madri. And she could not bear to speak of that to anyone.

But now, she thought that perhaps the mantra was the key. Perhaps the Guru had given her the mantra as a means of appeasing her heart.

Perhaps even, if she dared think it, the mantra would bring her that which she had lost. Now, that would be a true reward. That would be reparation for all the hardship Durvasa had caused her. It would be a gift of the gods, truly. Could it be possible, she wondered? Could he really have been that insightful–and that powerful?

He was a great Guru, after all. She had seen him use his powers with her own eyes, the day he had risen from the lake. Surely he could do much more than simply control nature's elements to travel from one realm to another. He must wield true power.

Perhaps the mantra was magical. Perhaps it could set right what had gone wrong in Madri. Bring back what she had lost. Repair the damage to her shattered heart. Reward her troubled soul. There was only one way to find out. She had to recite the mantra aloud. She paced for hours, trying to decide, to work up the courage to actually do it. It was late that night by the time she arrived at a decision.

The night watch had completed their rounds and even the servants and staff had long gone to sleep. Except for the occasionally restless horse, hound or elephant from the royal stables, the palace complex was quiet.

She stood in her balcony, breathing in the cool bracing air of early autumn, preparing herself, and recited the mantra, once, carefully, enunciating each Sanskrit syllable perfectly, without a single error or repitition.

And then she waited.

‖ 14 ‖

The night blossomed with light.

It began as a slow gloaming, like the soft flush in the eastern sky at dawn, announcing the imminent arrival of the rising sun; except that it was near midnight now, and dawn was a whole watch away. The gloaming grew to a glow, and then suddenly the darkness was dispersed with a flash so bright, Kunti was blinded momentarily. She felt a surge of heat so intense that she cried out, expecting to be seared to death. But the heat receded as suddenly as it arose, reducing to the intensity of a crackling blaze in a fireplace across the room.

Her eyes were still dazzled from the flash of light. She rubbed them and blinked several times, trying to regain her vision.

There was a presence in her chamber.

She took a step back, her hip touching the stone balustrade that enclosed her balcony. There was nowhere else to go. She blinked again, trying to focus her blurred vision. Yes, there was definitely someone there, and he was the source of the heat she felt. Intense, banked heat as powerful as any fire exuded from his body. His face glowed with the heat, making his features hard to see clearly

'Who are you?' she asked, hearing the tremble in her own voice. *Where was her sword?* She scanned the chamber frantically. It was hanging beside her bed, behind the stranger. She looked around for a weapon, edging sideways into the chamber.

You summoned me, he said.

She started. The words had come not from his lips but from his being. Like a thought projected at her. She felt the heat of his mind touch her own and then dissipate at once. It felt like a tiny pinprick of heat had poked her forehead. She forgot her search for a weapon and clutched her forehead, feeling sweat break out at once. She cried out from the pain.

I caused you… discomfort? I did not intend to. I do not often assume mortal form.

The pinprick was more painful this time, the heat more searing. She cried out again, and thrashed around till she found a staff she used for practising stick-fighting. She pointed it at him. 'Stay back. I can call for a hundred guards in a moment.'

It is illogical of you to fear me. You were the one who summoned me. I am merely answering your summons.

She cried out, clutching her head. Sweat was popping out across her face now, rolling down in tracks. 'Stop *doing* that! It *hurts*!'

He was silent a moment, then she sensed the heat

emanating from his presence reduce, banked to a mere warm glow, like a fire that had burned down. When he 'spoke' to her again, the sensation was like an uncomfortable warm prickling in her brain rather than the searing pinpricks of before.

Am I endurable to you now?

She wiped the sweat off her brow with the back of her hand. 'Who are you? How did you appear in my chambers?'

Did you not summon me? I recognize your voice. It was you who recited the mantra.

The mantra. Durvasa's shloka.

'Who are you?' she asked.

He gazed at her steadily. I am known by many names. The most commonly used one is Surya.

She stared at him. The intense, searing heat; the sudden appearance out of thin air and the ability to project thoughts into her mind. Could it really be...? 'Surya *Deva*?' she asked in wonderment. 'The Sun God?'

He inclined his head. At your service.

At my service? *What does he mean.* 'I don't understand. Guru Durvasa did not explain what the mantra does. I recited it expecting... something else.'

What were you expecting?

She hesitated for a second, then blushed.

'A friend,' she replied.

I sense turmoil within you. You were expecting a lover.

Someone dearly beloved to you but now lost... Am I correct?

She said nothing.

I am sorry to have disappointed you. But you did summon me specifically.

She frowned. 'I did *not*! I was thinking of someone completely different.'

The mantra summons any Deva of your choosing. But yet I am here. There is a reason for that: you intended me to be the one.

'I wished for my friend Maheev of Mahisha...' she stopped, her throat choking at the use of his name. She shook her head. 'I was a fool. I should have known my wish would not be fulfilled.'

This Maheev of Mahisha, he was dear to you. A lover perhaps?

She shook her head. 'We never consummated our relationship. Any intimacy between us was only emotional. I was resistant to the idea of a permanent bonding. He wanted marriage. The last time we saw each other, he wanted to vie for my hand in a swayamvara.'

And you did not give him this opportunity. Because you were busy serving the brahmin Durvasa at the time?

'Yes. And in the interim, to uphold tradition and family honor, he was compelled to attend the swayamvara of another princess. In Madri. By chance, I happened to be travelling through at the very time.'

He moved across the room slowly, seeming to glide rather than walk. *Why do you assume it was a matter of chance?*

She had no answer to that. It was a possibility that had never occurred to her, but now that it was suggested, it seemed obvious.

Durvasa was the one who sent you to Madri, was it not? And he sent you at precisely that time?

He was right. It was an odd coincidence that she happened to be despatched to Madri at the very time that Maheev was also there for the swayamvara. In fact, when she heard in the marketplace that the Princess was hosting her swayamvara, the first thing she had thought was: *Maheev must be there.* He could not refuse the invitation because it would reflect badly on his house. And when she went to the tourney grounds, there he was, handsome and resplendent in his golden armor on his gold-panelled chariot, as beautiful and perfect as the first day she had seen him on his visit to her father's palace, two years ago.

'Yes, I see what you mean,' she said slowly, 'it was as if Durvasa sent me on that pointless errand to Madri only so that I could be there in time to watch Maheev...' Again she felt her throat choke and shut her eyes.

To watch him die competing in that chariot challenge. An unfortunate mishap when a stray arrow struck one of his horses and caused his chariot to overturn. You ran to the spot where he fell and cradled his head in your lap and cried as the light passed from his eyes.

She lowered her head. The staff felt like a leaden weight in her hand. She leaned it against the wall and clutched her face in both hands. 'He was broken and bleeding and beyond help. He recognized me and was happy to see me.

He said he had wished to see my face one last time before he died and there I was, a gift from the gods. He told me he loved me...'

And he wished you much happiness in your life ahead. Before he died in your arms.

'Yes,' she said, weeping openly now, 'yes. And I told him I loved him too – but I was too late, he was already gone.' She was overwhelmed and could not go on.

He waited patiently as she cried the tears she had held back since that day, the pain she had banked and hidden from Sage Durvasa, her father, her friends, the daiimaas, everyone, even herself.

Finally, she could cry no more. There would be more tears tomorrow. And the day after. And for many days to come. But for now she was drained. She wiped her face with the hem of her garment.

You mortals have such brief existences. It is always sad to see you fail to achieve your desires and die unfulfilled. Maheev's end was unfortunate. But you have a great and fulfilling life ahead of you. His dying wish is prophetic. You will achieve much happiness in your life – as well as great sorrow. Both are inevitable, I am afraid. Your place in the mortal world is a special one, your life and times extraordinary, and your sons –

'I don't want to know,' she said brusquely. She paused and tempered her tone. 'Please. Do not reveal my future. I know that as a Deva you have sight of all things past and future, seen and unseen. I do not wish to know what lies ahead for me. I want to live my life myself.'

He was silent for so long she thought she had offended him. But when he spoke again, there was no rancor in his voice. *So be it, Pritha of Mathura, Kunti of Bhoja. I will speak of it no more.*

'Is that why you came to me? To show me my future? Is that the purpose of the mantra?'

He smiled. She saw a flash of his teeth, or what appeared to be teeth in a mortal body, but which gleamed with the brightness of a rising sun. Light exuded from his eyes, his body, as he smiled, and she felt warmth emanate from him in a small wave. It passed through her with a stimulating frisson. Such power! Just from a smile.

I am not a fortune teller, Kunti of Bhoja. I do not appear when summoned to show mortals their future. I am Surya, Star of the Sky, Light of the World.

She smiled back despite her emotional state. There was something dangerously charming about him. Like the sun itself, your eyes would always be drawn back to him, even though you knew that staring at him too long would burn your eyes blind. Charismatic yet deadly.

'Then why did the mantra summon you?' she asked.

He took a step towards her. He had mastered his emanations now and she felt none of the searing heat that he had been emitting earlier. Just a genial warmth that was oddly comforting. His features blurred again, and she braced herself, expecting another blast of heat. But instead of the bright flash, his features rearranged themselves to form a new face, a new body, one that was so familiar, so desirable to her that she gasped involuntarily.

He smiled at her now with the face and form of her dead sweetheart, Maheev. Exact to the last detail.

To grant you your wish, Kunti. To give you the wedding night with Maheev that you desired. And the child that would have been produced from that union.

'No!' Kunti cried out, aghast. She backed away, her heel striking something. She heard a clattering sound as the staff fell to the floor. 'I did not ask for this.'

Surya Deva in the form of her dead sweetheart Maheev moved closer to her in the same gliding motion. *Maheev of Mahisha was of the Suryavansha line. A direct descendent of my own lineage. He is the progeny of my own seed. When you used the mantra to attempt to summon him, it was only natural that I, the sire of his bloodline, should appear.*

She shook her head, still backing away from him. 'I did not ask for you, or any Deva. I thought only to use the mantra in order to see Maheev again one last time, if only for a few moments, to speak to him freely, to pour my heart out and say the things I neglected to say while alive.

To feel his touch, to press your lips against his, to hold him close and to melt in his arms...Do you deny that these desires were also in your heart when you uttered the mantra?

She looked down, embarrassed but unable to lie. 'We were to be wed this season, to be husband and wife. I had every right to feel those emotions, those desires.'

As you have every right to live out that desire now, with me.

She was shaking her head before he finished the sentence. 'No. I cannot. It is one thing to desire, quite another to succumb. I am an unwed girl, I am not ready to be wed yet by my own choice. Some day I will find a husband whom I believe I can love as much as I loved Maheev. I am willing to wait until then. What you are proposing is impossible.'

His eyes — Maheev's eyes — glowed brightly for an instant, reacting to her refusal. She felt the heat emanating from him again. *You are mistaken, Pritha-Kunti. I am not proposing. This is inevitable. Once the mantra has been uttered and a Deva is summoned, the summoner will be impregnated. The question of choice does not enter into it. The mantra compels me to instil my seed within your womb and ensures that you will bear a child of that seed. All you can choose is which Deva to summon, and what qualities you wish the child to possess in life.*

She gasped, raising a hand to cover her mouth with her upright palm. 'But I do not wish this! Will you assault me then? Against my will?'

Nay, he said. *Though I can. In your case, I am sympathetic to your situation. Your intelligence and strength of will impress me greatly. I do not wish to possess you by force. If you will not accept my gift in the usual way, through the union of man and woman, then I can impregnate you through the force of brahmaand itself.*

She swallowed. 'What does that mean?'

He raised a hand, the palm beginning to glow at once,

producing a tiny ball of heat and light, a spinning fireball the size of an almond seed. *By passing my seed to you through the medium of my energy. Just as I engender life within the womb of Bhudevi, the goddess of Earth, through the life-giving power my sunlight.*

She hesitated. 'And if I do not want this method either? If I refuse you altogether and bid you leave this instant?'

He sighed. *Do not test the patience of a Deva, Pritha. You will have more interactions with my fellow Devas in your life. And your sons –* He paused, recalling her earlier admonition. *You would do well to keep good relations with any Deva or Devi. You will have need of our aid in your life to come. Do not make this harder than it has to be.*

She reflected on that, her heart racing. Why had she uttered that mantra at all? That Sage Durvasa had brought her nothing but hardship and discomfort. She should have known he would never give her a simple gift. The man cared nothing for anyone. He had given her this mantra out of some patriarchal sense of tradition: men bestowing offspring upon woman as though children were things to be given and taken, rather than mutually created expressions of one human being's love for another. She wished now she had put the mantra out of her mind and never used it. But it was too late now: wishing would do her no good. She was a realistic woman. What had to be, was. All one could do was make the best of the inevitable.

There was also the practical matter of there being no alternative. She could not fight a Deva. And even if she tried and failed, what would that achieve. If what Surya

Deva said was true she would require the aid of the gods in her life ahead. Not just she. *Your sons,* he had said. That tantalizing fragment suggested that her future children would need their aid as well. She could not act now out of pride and wilfulness and endanger her future, unborn children. Besides, she *had* uttered the mantra and desired all the things he had named. Maheev *had* been of the Suryavansha line. She *had* wanted one night with him, if only to give herself the satisfaction of showing him how much she loved him, expressing all that she had failed to express in life. To give him the gift of herself. To give herself the gift of him. She needed it… nay, she *wanted* it.

'I have one last question,' she said, her tone less confrontational now.

He waited, Maheev's handsome face set in that same wistful longing gaze that had always won her heart.

'Will Maheev…wherever he may be now…be able to hear what I say to you?' She hesitated, trying to find the right words. 'I suppose I'm asking if he will, in some way, be able to sense the feelings I express here and now? Is there some way to make that possible?'

He did not answer her immediately. She thought she had finally crossed a line, given offence to a powerful god.

But when he looked at her, it was with Maheev's face, Maheev's eyes, and, she could swear, Maheev's spirit. 'Pritha,' he said, in that same gentle respectful tone she had loved for its contrast to the loud, boisterous voices of most rich young men, 'Marriage is a woman's decision, and it's your right to make that choice when you please. But can

I help it if I'm so madly crazy in love with you, Pritha of Mathura, Kunti of Bhoja, apple of my eye, that I can't bear to wait another year, another season, or even another night, to make you my wife?'

She raised her hand before her chin, shocked speechless. It was not merely a mimicking of Maheev. It *was* Maheev. By the grace of the gods!

He spread his arms. 'I love you, Pritha of Mathura, Kunti of Bhoja. I love everything about you, from your quick temper to your stubborn will, the way your back arches where it meets your hip, the way you toss your hair when you walk, your strength, your beauty, your love for fried tapioca—'

She shook her head in amazement, tears rolling down her face again. She began to walk towards him.

' – your prowess at weapons and combat, a true warrior princess and a better fighter than most princes or princesses, your sense of dharma – '

She put her upright palm over his mouth, cutting off the rest.

'Maheev, oh Maheev,' she said, her heart tearing apart and filling with unspeakable emotion both at once. 'I love you, my beloved. I love you more than anything else in this world. Would that I had told you when I had the chance, that last day we met, after the lake. I wanted to tell you, but I was too proud, too stubborn, too wilful, to admit that I wanted you as much as you wanted me. I was young and arrogant. I thought we had all the time in the world. I thought we had forever. I was wrong. I know now that all we have is the given moment. The here and now. There is nothing else. The future is uncertain, the past unreachable. We only have tonight. I should have told you how I felt, I should have held nothing back. Nothing would have given me more joy than to have taken you as my husband. I wanted to spend my life with you. I want to be with you, my love.'

She paused, then knew she could not stop herself now, 'Tonight.'

He opened his arms and embraced her. She crushed herself against his body. She felt a rushing of emotions, of love, lust, desire, sorrow, joy, as she had never felt before. For once in her life, she stopped trying to be in control, and let herself go completely. She gave in to the given moment. The heat grew within her and took her by storm. She allowed it to consume her. It blazed through her veins like a flood of fire. She let herself catch fire and burn. And he burned with her. Together, they gave themselves over to the blaze.

|| paksha chatur ||

|| 1 ||

The conspirators came from every direction.

    Their individual roads converged in the great raj-marg of madhya desha, where all roads united.

As they travelled farther North, approaching the jagged rises of the mountain ranges, the marg dwindled to a path, and then to a mere line, a fading scar across the stony face of the land. Nothing grew easily here, except small game and predators. There were shapes moving in the gathering shadows as dusk fell, and a peculiar odor in the air. On the tiny scratch of a path, they trundled along together until even that unwelcoming way dwindled to a terrain dotted with rocks large enough to break the hooves of any carriage-horse. A ridge rose steeply from this point, cutting off the view of the mountains that lay beyond.

The irritated travellers dismounted here as they debated how to proceed. Their awkward pleasantries were interrupted by a piercing wolf-whistle from above. Several of them reached for their weapons. They were foreigners here, and the mountain folk were notorious for their distrust of outlanders.

A wizened old woman looked down from the peak of the

ridge.She leaped from her perch, hopping and skipping as agilely as a skipping stone the thirty yards down to where they stood.

Landing with a broken-toothed smile, she rattled off a stream in pahadi. One or two of the travellers understood enough to translate for the others. But it was hardly necessary to know the language to understand her message:

She was to be their guide; they were to follow her.

She instructed them to leave their valets and accompanying guards and disappeared behind a cluster of large boulders nearby, reappearing shortly after with a pack of ugly-faced mules with too-large ears. She handed each one the reins of a mule.

The travellers looked at one another, then at the flea-bitten ragged-eared overbite-faced creatures with open repulsion.

'We are royalty,' one of them pointed out haughtily. 'We expect royal treatment.'

Their guide looked up at him – she was so short that the withers of the shortest mount reached as high as the top of her grey head – and prattled out a line in her tongue. The two or three travellers who knew the language sniggered or laughed in response.

'What did she say?' demanded the pompous one.

'In more polite words, she said you could park your royal ass upon a mule and follow her or you could bugger it royally for all she cared.'

The pompous one glared but said nothing further. There

was much grumbling and some cursing from some of the others as well; the indignity of riding a mule was something few of them had suffered until now. But their own select men and valets advised them that it was in their own best interest to endure this minor suffering. These mountains were notorious for claiming more lives than any enemy they had faced. The mules were the only way to navigate the harsh and dangerous pathway to their destination.

The cursing and grumbling continued. But the wizened old guide led the way and the rest followed, their royal asses mounted uncomfortably on the ugly mules. She cackled in her own tongue, snidely commenting that it was hard to tell which were the bigger asses, the ones riding or the ones being ridden! The pompous one stared at the others who knew what she meant, but they stifled their laughter and said nothing.

As the path wound steeper, the ridge grew more brittle, the chance of falling more likely. Even the protesting died out. It is a peculiarity of mortals that only when confronted by their mortality do they realize its value. A few hours of teetering over sheer falls and the only sound on that knife-edge pathway was the chuffing of the mules. They were the only ones with something to complain about anyway.

Apparently unconcerned with the mortals astride them, they would deign to pause wherever the fancy took them, here to chew on a tiny patch of weeds, there to fart noisily and violently, or a few yards farther, to defecate the well-digested remains of an earlier meal, without any consideration for the royal noses and constitutions being assaulted by these frequent bodily purges.

The wizened guide glanced back from time to time, and chuckled at the discomfort of her unlikely followers. Occasionally, she would pause to stroll back, walking as easily on an inch of dubious ridge as a royal carriage rolling by on the raj-marg of Hastinapura. The travellers could hardly bear to look at her as she went past them, swinging out over a sheer drop without a downward glance. A touch of a saddle here, a stirrup there, a twitching tail further on, and she was by, handing out savories suitable only for mule constituitions. The animals made gleeful chuffing noises at each of these feed stops, and the travellers grew accustomed to a marked increase in the passing of wind and feces for the hour or so following this ritual. She winked at the pompous one as she went by, slapping his mule's rump affectionately. The creature chuffed happily in response; the pompous traveller remained as stony-faced as the cliff face beside him, not with his customary arrogance but with stone-cold fear. He had discovered in the course of the journey that he was terrified of heights but his royal pride prevented him from admitting it. And even if he had confessed, he did not relish the thought of turning back and returning the way he had climbed, alone.

The guide ate with the mules, chewing at regular intervals on the odd-looking odder-smelling contents of her hemp-sack bag. She did not offer a share of her repast to her followers, nor did any ask for it. Accustomed to their every need being met the very instant such a need arose, none had thought to bring any nourishment for the journey.

By the midway point of their journey, around the time the sun began diminishing on the late afternoon of the first day, the grumbling and whinging had ceased altogether.

Only the mules spoke. Eating, breaking wind, doing what they did routinely.

The mortals mounted on their back endured silently. There was absolutely no doubt who was in command. Viewed from a great height, as by one of the floating silhouettes high in the sky above the snow-capped peaks, the procession appeared as nothing more than a worm wriggling its way up the mountain. It proceeded with agonizing slowness, reminding the travellers at every curve in the narrow pathway why the mountain kingdoms had never been successfully invaded by any mortal army.

It took them the better part of a day, a night and the best part of the second day to reach their destination.

On a pathway barely wide enough for a large man to stand facing forward – and only just sufficient for the midget-sized mules to remain afoot with all four hooves pressed close together – there was no room for privacy or modesty. Though the royals protested even more vociferously, they all ended up relieving themselves in like fashion. If you wished to survive the mountain, dignity was an unaffordable luxury, no matter who you might be. They slept on their mounts too, sitting on those high, windy, bone-chilling mountain path ridges, one misstep away from permanent sleep. Most were barely able to doze more than a few moments at a time; for some, it was a harrowing night.

By dawn of the second day, they were almost as indifferent

about falling as about reaching their destination: they just wanted this nightmare-on-hooves to end.

It was with a great sense of relief that they came into sight of their destination. The late morning sun illuminated it as they rounded yet another curve, all but hugging the mountainside with fingernails to aid their mounts, some of whom displayed signs of tiring by now. With bleary, sleep-deprived but irritably curious eyes, they gazed upon the place that they were enduring such hardship to reach.

The remote, desolate snow-capped stony peaks of a place rarely visited and perpetually feared by all who had heard of its terrors, whispered in the dark watches of winter nights. That haunted capital city of a kingdom of mountain fortresses ranging for hundreds of miles in an interweaving maze of stone and rock and black ice.

Pragjyotisha.

‖ 2 ‖

The mountain fortress bore the ravages of a recent siege and assault. Toppled towers, demolished ramparts, great gouges and pits in the sides of the stony slopes themselves all marked the great and terrible conflict that had waged here not long before.

Yet despite these ravages, the great keep was still magnificent. Its rugged rough-hewn beauty, carved from the very rock of the mountain with chiselled artistry, was an achievement to be admired. All of the travellers had heard of the great city. None had had the pleasure, dubious though it might seem at this moment, of having visited here. Its very remoteness and inaccessibility was its greatest strength. But what none of them had expected was its extraordinary beauty. Beauty that rivalled the majesty of the mountains that it stood astride. Not a thing made by mortals that had been set upon this landscape; but a thing drawn by mortals, inch by painfully carved inch, out of the landscape itself. It was organic to the mountain, as much a part of it as these mules were to these impossibly narrow pathways. That was its true beauty.

There were fewer abuses and insults voiced during

the remainder of the journey. As each hooved step took them closer to that vaulting masterpiece of stonecraft, their thoughts turned finally from the discomforts that had plagued them the past day and a half, and toward the invitation that had summoned them here.

When the visitors finally reached the sloping, paved approach to the gate of Pragjyotisha, they heaved a sigh of relief. Some had travelled for the better part of a fortnight to reach this remote keep. Even the closest had been on the road for several days. And then the tortuous path up the mountain path on the backs of the mules, to whom their backsides now felt wedded after all these painful hours.

All swore a silent vow they would never visit this wretched place again. Some swore not-so-silently, not caring if they offended their hosts. The king of Prajyotisha was just a mountain lord, after all. Not true royalty like themselves. None of the Houses they represented would ever think of making a marital alliance with him or his family.

Their guide hand-fed savories to the relieved mules and cackled merrily, shaking her head as she led them beneath the giant draw-gate. One of the travellers was so large that the instant he dismounted, his mule teetered for a moment, then fell over on its left side. The guide crouched over it, fussing briefly. But the unfortunate creature was dead, its heart burst from exhaustion. The old woman remained crouched over it, giving vent to a moan. The pompous one passed her by, grinning down at her and the dead beast as he trundled past heavily. He said something to her that only she heard. She did not look up immediately but after he had passed by, she looked in the direction he had gone and had her gaze been lethal, the pompous one would have dropped dead as suddenly as the mule.

Barely had the last of the travellers passed through when the gate slammed down with a boom that echoed across the mountains.

|| 3 ||

The Lord of the Mountain Kingdoms was no hirsute savage. No doubt, he had ancestors who lived up to the reputation expected of a mountain king: great bearish hulks of men spending their lives carousing and whoring, interrupting these vital activities occasionally to wage war against anyone handy, notorious for their brutish ways and indomitable fortresses.

But Bhagadatta was cut from a different stone.

The current king of Pragjyotisha was a suave, handsome figure clad in a cloak of snow leopard fur that suited his catlike gait and lithe, pantherish movements, as he rose from his seat to welcome his royal guests. He was young, perhaps the youngest of them all, but then again, as they each reflected silently; he had not won his throne by challenge or war, as was the mountain custom.

He had been enthroned by none other than the liberator of Pragjyotisha himself. Lord Krishna Vasudeva. And to have the backing of Krishna was to be untouchable by any and all foes.

Mere knowledge that Krishna's hand was above his head was sufficient to silence any challengers to Bhagadatta's claim. Those few that dared to murmur dissent were pulled back by their own clans and soon grew silent, changing their murmurs to politic praises for the new One King.

The 16,000 mountain clans were too busy repairing and rebuilding their own homesteads and fighting forces after the battle and the debilitating occupation that had preceded it. Even the most cantankerous of them reluctantly agreed that it was no time to be fighting amongst themselves. Perhaps later, much later, when the clans had rebuilt all that had been destroyed to some semblance of its former strength, they would raise the issue again – if the One King lasted that long.

For now, Bhagadatta was, for the first and only time in the citadel's history, the undisputed master of Pragjyotisha. This smooth-cheeked young man – a boy, really, since he was barely within reach of his third decade – was set to rule with an authority that had not been enjoyed by his predecessors for tens of thousands of years.

And because of the consolidated power he represented, the sixteen thousand clans united for the first time in that long history, he was the strongest lord of the citadel that had ever sat the stone throne. Which made him a powerful man by any measure. Even ravaged and debilitated, the mountain state was a force to reckon with, and its unassailable location itself made it impossible for any invading army to threaten – any mortal army. The suscrufa and their asura masters had been a different matter, a shocking interruption to the unassailable dominance of the clans. For other mortal enemies, unaided by supernatural means, the stone citadel was in every sense of the word, *ayodhya*. A city which could not be broken by war. It was this impregnable reputation and might which compelled the presence of the royal travellers at this moment.

He stood at the doorway of his own aerie, greeting the dusty, road-weary, battered-bum arrivals as they strode haughtily in. This took them unawares. No king stood at the doorway of his throne room; it violated every royal protocol. They themselves would have sat on their thrones upon a high dais and loftily acknowledged their guests. To see this young fresh-faced man with the neatly cut beard and charming smile welcoming them at the vaulting doors was disarming. More than one of them returned his warm, cheerful yet respectful greeting with a measure of warmth themselves, caught off guard. Weary though they were from the travails of the road, backs and bottoms aching from the bumpy ride up winding mountain paths, they found themselves responding in like to his charm and graciousness.

Perhaps it was his easy smile, clean-cut good looks, or gentile manners, but even the most hardened among them relented to his hospitality. Within a short time after arrival, they found themselves intrigued, even attracted, to his curious mixture of craggy but handsome mountain features and noblefolk manners.

Bhagadatta apologized for the customary mountain rituals of welcoming, helped them endure the small army of gaily decked women and outlandishly attired men who presented to them a seemingly infinite variety of food, drink and entertainment.

They were washed, bathed, scented, fed, relieved, and otherwise comforted in every way available to royal mortals. They slept that night in luxuriant surroundings. A bit too much fur and stone for some tastes perhaps, but then again this was the high mountain kingdom and there had just been a great occupation and siege. After the backside of a mule, it was Swarga on earth, heaven in every sense of the word. Appetites were indulged, bile was purged, intoxicants consumed, and a very pleasant night was had by all. They were woken the next day at dawn by the gentle pealing of a distant bell.

They were given ample time to see to their individual morning needs, including the ritual sandhyavandana. Purges were consumed to remove the excess intoxicants, over-indulged appetites were appeased by healtheir consumptions, and by the time the sun had leaped the ridge of the eastern horizon to show his full brilliant face to the world, every one of the travellers were eager to meet their host and start the day.

Once again, he surprised them by visiting each one's chambers personally, inviting them to join him in the day feast room for the morning repast. Warmed by the eastern sun streaming in through apertures cut horizontally, they shared a sumptuous banquet of a morning meal that earned even the pompous one's grudging approval. By the time their stomachs were full, their mouths were bursting with the question on all their tongues:

Why had they been brought here?

The handsome young mountain king took them into his

own den. This, again, was unusual and defied protocol. To be welcomed and plied with all manner of comfort, to that they were accustomed. But to be invited to share his most intimate personal space on a first visit – that was unusual.

The One King of Pragjyotisha was an unusual man.

Bhagadatta shut the door of his den himself, the large wooden slab carved with the motifs and totems of his clan booming shut with a heavy finality. The ease with which he did it implied more strength than seemed likely with his compact physique. More than one of his guests reflected that he did it precisely to show off his unexpected strength.

Turning back to the gathering, he invited his guests to seat their battered backsides on furry cushions beside crackling fires and brimming flasks of mulled wine. And it was then, as the high morning light through the vaulting arches illuminated the chamber with brilliant clarity that the gathering came to its true business.

॥ ૪ ॥

Bhagadatta sat comfortably upon a black and red cushion embroidered with the sigil of his clan, a pitcher of wine beside him, as he gazed around at his guests. The flickering light from the large log fire beside his seat highlighted his sharp, strong features. His voice was soft but authoritative, the voice of a young man groomed to rule.

'Thank you for coming,' he said. 'You honor my aerie with your presence.'

'You left us no choice,' said a man with distinctive far eastern features, clad in the garb of the land that lay beyond the redmist mountains of the far northeastern reaches of Jambudwipa.

Bhagadatta acknowledged his guest with a polite nod. 'I ask that we each introduce ourselves. We are somewhat informal here in the high mountains.'

'Informal?' said the pompous one. 'Bloody savages!'

Bhagadatta acknowledged the pompous one with a patient glance but did not retort. He turned back to the first speaker.

'Anga, King of Anga,' said the northeasterner.

'My brother Anga speaks truth,' said a man some years younger but a measure taller than his brother. The resemblance was unmistakable, as was the irritation creasing both their faces. 'I am Vanga, King of Vanga. We are here only because you sent us each a message threatening to reveal our secrets to Bhishma of Hastinapura.'

A tall dark woman with a profile perfect enough it could have been carved from basalt, spoke in a strong voice: 'I am Kaurwa, a daughter of Kalinga. I speak for myself as well as my five brothers. We of Kalinga have no secrets. We are not intimidated by your threats.'

'And yet you are here,' Bhagadatta said, smiling. 'But is it not true that Kalinga is a republic governed by its own people? Yet they send only you, their…queen?'

'We are a free people, unfettered by the yoke of the caste system or dynastic rule. We have no kings or queens, no royalty or commonry, no titles. The People's Republic of Kalinga is ruled by we, the people.'

'And yet, there is only one Kalingan here. Yourself'

'One Kalingan speaks for all, all speak as one.'

Bhagadatta smiled again. 'Then you shall hear for all Kalinga as well.'

A squat bald· man with a flaming red beard made a sound between a snort and a sneeze. 'We of Sumha are not intimidated but we do not take kindly to threats.' He made a grasping motion then closed his empty fist, his knuckles cracking as loudly as dry tinder in a fire. 'Had I my companion Cold Vengeance with me now, its blade would be at your throat, mountain man.'

Bhagadatta leaned forward in his seat, his face sincere and serious. 'King Sumhasana, believe me. We of Pragjyotisha have always respected the long axes of Sumha. We know that to a Sumhasan, his or her axe is a fellow in battle. You will recall that our ancestors have often stood side by side on the same battlefield in the past.' He gestured to the vaulting stone arches and pillars. 'The stone cutters of Sumha cut every stone that built this very keep, a thousand and two score years ago. Even now, we send one in three score of our children to your kingdom to learn the art of cutting from your masters. We would never dream of issuing threats to our old allies. We meant the missive to be an invitation, not a threat.' He raised his gaze and looked at the rest of the gathering. 'To all of you. There was no intent to threaten anyone, merely to extend an invitation.'

'And yet you worded it as a threat,' said an angry tenor voice. Everyone turned to look at the guest who had spoken, a person only slightly taller than Sumhasana but with slightly less facial hair, and a somewhat bulkier torso. 'I am Pundraki, daughter of Pundra, king of Pundar. My father is still crowned King but age and ill health prevent his making this arduous journey. I come in his stead. He was greatly offended by your missive, as am I.'

Bhagadatta inclined his head respectfully, acknowledging her status. 'It grieves me that you too viewed my missive as a threat.'

Pundraki frowned. 'Your message said if we did not attend your invitation, our secrets would be revealed to Bhishma of Hastinapura. Secrets that, if unearthed, would bring the wrath of Hastinapura upon us. Were those not your words, Bhagadatta of Pragjyotisha? Did your courier convey them incorrectly?'

'My courier did his task diligently. However, you have interpreted the words incorrectly.'

'How else can they be interpreted?' Pundraki frowned suspiciously. 'Were you not threatening to reveal our secrets to Hastinapura if we did not attend this...gathering? How else could that be interpreted if not a threat?'

'As a caution from one friend to another.' Bhagadatta said calmly. 'You note the use of the word 'us'. That includes we of the mountain kingdoms as well. Why would I threaten myself?'

The pompous one spluttered around a mouthful of wine, deliberately spitting it out on the luxuriant fur underfoot, right on the snarling head of the white tiger. 'Don't try to dodge us with your petty word-play. That was a threat. You sent it knowing it would force us to come to your godforsaken ass-in-the-sky pile of stone.' He did not bother to introduce himself.

Bhagadatta spread his hands, smiling disarmingly. 'It was never my desire to antagonize any of you. I apologize if the method of my summoning indicated otherwise. It is with friendship and alliance in mind that I have sent for you all.'

'Alliance?' said a lean muscled young man with the metal studdings and piercings of a yoddha, a master warrior – and the arrogance to match. 'I am Vinda, prince of Kekeya. What kind of alliance can the lords of the civilized world, of which Kekaya is the highest in stature, possibly wish to forge with,' he pointed with his sharp jaw, 'a mountain goat?' His almost colorless grey eyes threw Bhagadatta a mocking challenge.

Bhagadatta had no time to respond.

'My neighbor speaks sword-truth,' said a giant of a man, massive as a mountain, with glinting dark eyes that suggested a demeanour as dangerous as his bulk. His mule was the one that had collapsed after arrival. 'Enough dancing on word tops. Admit your ploy was naught but a clever way to ensure our attendance. We civilized people have no patience for your posturing.' Almost as an after-thought he added, 'Vriddhakshatra, king of Sindhudesha.'

Bhagadatta's eyes turned to Vriddhakshatra, locking gazes. 'Would you rather that I have revealed your secrets to Hastinapura? Or perhaps that I reveal them here?'

The Sindhu's face, already a craggy terrain of war scars, remained impassive.

Bhagadatta smiled and spread his arms wide, encompassing the entirely of the group.

'We all have secrets, Pragjyotisha included. The day Bhishma of Hastinapura were to learn what I know about each one of you,' he took his time looking around at each one in turn, meeting their eyes and holding each gaze for a moment before moving on to the next, 'would mark the end of our reigns. And likely the end of our lives.'

'So then it is a threat,' said a man with a flabby belly and unmuscled torso but with curiously long arms. 'At least that much is clear. I am Kartavirya Mara, King of the Haihaiyas of Mahishmati. Now all we have to do is end your life and leave. That would remove this hold you have over us.'

A genial looking man who appeared more like a prosperous merchant than a ruler, but with the leather strappings and purple skin tattoos of the Avantikas, laughed. 'Ripunjaya, King of Avanti, a neighbor of Mahishmati but not an ally. It is rarely that I agree with the Haihaiyas but Kartavirya Mara makes a good point.' He touched the empty scabbard at his waist. 'It also explains why you were so nervous as to divest us of our weapons. But surely you do not intend to use your ill-gotten knowledge to profit from us? You will not live to enjoy it for even a breath.'

Again, Bhagadatta had no time to answer before the next visitor spoke. This was an intense-looking man extraordinarily slight in build. He spoke with the gruff tones of a North-Westerner. 'Madrashya, King of Madra. You will excuse my not partaking of your generosity. During this season, my faith requires me to fast until night has fallen fully.'

The pompous one snorted. 'Fanatics and fundamentalists.'

Bhagadatta smiled at Madrashya. 'We are aware of your fast and have provided the appropriate fast-breaking fruits and nuts. I trust they meet your approval.'

'I have no doubt they shall. As for our presence here, I say to my fellow lieges that we may as well hear what our host has to say at least. That way we will not have made this long journey for nothing.'

Bhagadatta smiled, acknowledging this gracious suggestion.

A menacing looking man dressed all in leather fingered the rough scarring on his throat as he stared in open hatred at his host. 'Druhyu, king of Druhyu. Making us leave our weapons does not render us helpless. There's more than one way to kill a mountain goat.' He picked up a heavy brass ornament from a ledge nearby and hefted it.

A tired elderly man with long flowing grey hair bound in an elaborate manner raised his hands placatingly. 'I am Bahlika Pratipeya, blood kin to Bhishma Pitama. I am willing to take my chances with him. But I am in agreement with Nashya of Madra. At least let's hear what our host has to say. I'm curious. Aren't we all?'

A pert-nosed, flat-faced woman with the squat bow-legged appearance of a rider said curtly, 'Shastra, Chief Rider of the Kambhoja horse clans,' then folded her arms across her chest and leaned back without another word. The Riders were known for being people of action not given to speeches.

The pompous one had held his tongue while the others spoke. Despite his earlier outburst, he appeared to have no compunctions about partaking of his host's fare. This was not surprising considering he was by far the most ample of all present. Wide of girth as well as height, he was only a foot shorter than the King of Sindhudesha, but almost as broad in the torso. The difference was that while Vriddhakshatra was all muscle, with not a gram of flab visible, the pompous one appeared to be all fat, with not a gram of muscle visible.

His entire body jiggled and shivered as he ate ravenously. His large arms, his belly, his neck, his chins, even the flab on his cheeks and the back of his neck shook and trembled as he continued feasting, oblivious to the fact that everyone else had finished slaking their thirsts and satiating their appetites and was staring at him with expressions varying from curiosity to distaste. He glanced up, a meaty chop in one hand and a fistful of fruit in the other, and froze. The realization that they were all waiting for him to speak dawned over his consciousness, warring with the impulse to continue feasting.

Scowling, he gestured with the food in hand, waving the roasted chop-bone at Bhagadatta like a weapon. 'Outrageous. Unacceptable. Your insolence will not go unanswered. You may call yourself King of the Mountain in this godforsaken place, but in the civilized world, we don't treat Arya thus. *Mleccha!*'

Vriddhakshatra made a sound of disapproval. 'Now you go too far, Ushanas of Ushati. To use such a term is not warranted. The Mountain Kings may not marry or commune with other Arya tribes but they are still Arya. Even Lord Krishna of Dwarka blesses their continuance. To call them savage barbarians unschooled in dharma is too much.'

Ushanas tore a mouthful of meat from the chop in hand, glaring over the large haunch bone at Vriddhakshatra. 'Mleccha is too good for him. King of the Mountain indeed! And speaking of that Yadava you call *Lord*, he and his cowardly brother Balarama cowered in their island fortress while Magadha wrought havoc across my kingdom. Far as

I'm concerned, any ally of his is no ally of mine. I intend to leave for home at once as soon as I have refreshed and nourished myself after that wretched journey. Mules!' He spewed a mouthful of obscenities in the Ushati dialect, all apparently directed at his host. Particles of meat and fruit and other edibles spewed with the abuses. Finally he returned to Sanskrit. 'I leave at first light. I need a decent night's rest. Since I am here anyway, go on then, Mleccha. Spin your mountain tale and be done with it!' He resumed his feasting.

Vridddhakshatra muttered something too softly to be heard but said nothing further.

Bhagadatta looked around, giving the others a chance to speak if any still desired. It appeared that every one present had had a chance to speak their minds. He appeared unruffled by the tirade of insults and challenges launched against him.

Smiling at his guests as if all they had done was express how pleased they were to be here, he shrugged. 'I take no offense. All that you have said is reasonable and to be expected. While you have all been disarmed, I too have no weapons here. I show my good faith by shutting out even my royal guard, leaving my person entirely at your mercy.' He indicated the large doors that he had himself shut only moments earlier. 'What I have to say will not take long. Not even as long as your introductions. After you hear what I have to say, if you still wish to take my life, you are most welcome to try.'

He looked around again but was met only with silence.

Even the menacing Druhyu had put down the heavy ornament and was listening with narrowed eyes. Nobody objected or commented.

'Very well then. I will start with a confession.' Bhagadatta spread his arms wide, smiling. 'It was not I who summoned you all here.'

|| 5 ||

Bhagadatta continued in a genial conversation tone as if he were discussing pleasantries with friends.

'Nor was it I who claimed to know your treasonable secrets. That too was the suggestion of my sponsor. This gathering and the proposal that will be made here is all the work of his great mind. I consider him my mentor and spiritual guide. Not only is he an emperor among kings, he is the only yoddha amongst us all who has never been defeated, neither in single combat nor in pitched battle. Only Bhishma Pitama can match that record. The two of them have never confronted one another but were that to occur, I would place my coin squarely on my guru. I introduce him now by his title as God Emperor of Magadha...*Jarasandha.*'

Bhagadatta indicated, not the door, as might be expected, but a blank wall.

Perfectly on cue, a figure stepped out. One moment there was a blank wall, with nothing before it except a richly detailed tapestry depicting some great ancestor of the Mountain King. The next moment, an impossibly thin tall man was standing before the tapestry, his hatchet face as familiar as feared.

Some of the gathering reacted. Almost all displayed shock, consternation, even alarm.

All present had coins in their possession minted with the Magadha lion seal and the profile of this same man. If he could be called a man. Some believed him to be a sorceror only partially of human origin. Others regarded him as a being from another species altogether. Such was his reputation and the legends linked to his name.

His entrance could be easily explained: The tapestry concealed a hidden doorway. Every royal residence had such secret doorways, chambers, passages, stairwells, tunnels, ingresses and egresses.

But his presence was shocking. Whatever the gathering had anticipated or guessed, this was not part of their wildest surmises.

Aware of their shock, revelling in it, relishing every dilated pupil staring at him, every racing heart, each mind leaping, the most dreaded man in all of Jambudwipa looked around at the gathering without smiling or greeting them in any formal way.

'I know what you have done.'

His voice was neither deep nor sonorous, yet it carried to every last ear. His manner was not threatening or aggressive, yet his words, his face, his mere presence, struck fear into the hearts of each and every one present.

Even the pompous Ushanas finally stopped his feasting and dropped the denuded chop bone, wiping his greasy hands on his own anga vastra. Instinctively, he gestured for a servant to bring him fresh apparel to replace the soiled top garment. But of course, none came. He started to call out. It was then that Jarasandha glanced in his direction, a casual almost genial glance. Ushanas choked on his words before they could be formed. He swallowed them with the last morsels of unchewed meat, the food untasted and already turning to acid bile in his belly.

The God Emperor of Magadha met the startled gaze of every person present, his impossibly thin face slashed by a razor-sharp smile. He completed his survey of the visitors and glanced at Bhagadatta, still esconced on his seat. Bhagadatta smiled back at his guest but even those who were farthest from him could see the tightness of his smile, the widened eyes, the fists clenching the wooden armrests of the throne. Still, he smiled and acted as a king would be expected to act. Jarasandha appeared satisfied by his survey. He resumed in the same pitch as before.

'I know you have sought, each in your own way, to separate yourselves from the Kuru empire.'

Again he glanced at each one present in turn, this time lingering a moment longer than before; there was nothing genial about his survey this time. The smile was in his eyes, not on his lips. Each person looked at by Jarasandha felt that the God-Emperor was looking *into* his or her soul, reading its innermost secrets.

Ushanas felt the hastily imbibed contents of his copious belly rumble, a familiar storm warning. Sweat popped on the pores of his wispy top hairs, rolling around the girth of his rounded face to disappear into the folds of his soiled anga vastra. When it was his turn to be looked at and into by Jarasandha, he avoided meeting the God-Emperor's gaze. The gaze lingered a fraction longer on his massive bulk before moving on to the next guest. Sweat-snails raced down Ushanas's flesh, wriggling into the crevices and folds of his abundance.

'Did you think your treason would go unnoticed?' Jarasandha asked. His voice dropped at the end of the question, instead of rising, turning it into a declaration of simple truth. Ushanas quivered. Others in the chamber sat so still, the entire assemblage could be mistaken for a diorama of statuary.

Jarasandha stepped forward, stalking the aerie on silent feet, bridging the distance between himself and the guests of Bhagadatta. There was a jungle-like menace in his motion, the sense of a predator marking his territory.

'Bhishma Pitama sees all, knows all,' he went on. 'What knowledge is not gleaned from hearsay, he gains from simple observation.'

He paused momentarily before each one, addressing them in turn. The first ones were the Northeasterners King Anga and his brother King Vanga. 'Redmist bandits waylaid your tithe due to Hastinapura last summer?' Jarasandha smiled his thin smile. 'Bhishma Pitama knows that the bandits ply their pillage under your protection and would never touch the tithe wagon.'

The brothers glanced at one another, eyes hot with temper, but kept themselves in check. They had the legendary swift rage of the North East, but also the wisdom. They cast their gazes downwards, not meeting the eyes of the God-Emperor who passed on by.

Jarasandha stopped before Kaurwa. The Kalingan displayed no emotion as she gazed coolly back. 'A sea storm delayed the arrival of the Grekos trade ships?' he asked, then tch-tched sympathetically. 'Hastinapura spasas sighted them sailing back homewards. They could hardly have made the 100 day voyage only to have turned back *without* bartering their cargo at Kalinga port.'

The Kalingan's cheeks flushed the shade of rotten fruit beneath her dark skin. She looked away. Jarasandha moved on.

Sumhasana's face was lowered as if to conceal his gaze from the Magadhan. Only his boxy bulk, flaming red beard and bald head were visible: the bald head gleamed with perspiration. Not the flowing rivulets of Ushanas, but a light misting that suggested nervousness.

'Sumhasana,' Jarasandha said. 'Are your fists missing the comfort of Cold Vengeance?' Without waiting for an answer he went on. 'Or are they longing for the cold weight of gold? The rich vein of old gold that Sumha unearthed almost by accident deep within an overworked mine far beneath the bowels of Great Dwarf?'

At the mention of gold, every pair of ears in the chamber pricked up, but none turned to gaze in the direction of the Magadhan and the Sumhasan. A few of them glanced at each other surreptitiously. The rumors of a great cache of ancient gold, the richest and best kind possible, had floated amongst the nations and tribes for years now. But they were just that: rumors. Until now.

Sumhasana's remained downcast, his bald head popping sweat from pores.

Jarasandha all but whispered to the downcast King. 'You dare not use the Old Gold for fear of being discovered by Hastinapura. Your people work the mines and store the gold in deep underground treasuries, hidden in a network of labyrinths so vast and inaccessible, even Sumhasana thieves dare not venture there. It is a vast and rich hoard, and when fully mined, it will be enough to rival the growing wealth of Hastinapura itself. But that is only if Bhishma does not learn of its existence and location. The day he does will mark the end of the hoard and possibly of Sumhasana.'

Now Sumhasana raised his sweating pate to look briefly at Jarasandha. He swallowed, looking away and downward almost at once. But in that brief glance, his terror was clearly visible on his axe-scarred face. 'We pay our tithe in timely fashion, even paying slightly more than is expected, to show our respect for the Elephant Throne.'

'None of that will matter were Bhishma to get wind of your secret cache. For you were obliged to report its existence to the Kuru Empire when it was discovered. The very act of concealing it for so long and of continuing to mine and hoard the gold for these past years marks you and every Sumhasana as violators of the treaty. And you know what Bhishma Pitama does to treaty breakers.'

Jarasandha straightened and looked around. 'You all know.'

Sumhasana dropped his head once again, left with nothing further to say.

Jarasandha paused before the next guest: Pundraki of Pundra. She stared back at him defiantly, not meeting his gaze directly, for Jarasandha's face was so thin, his profile so sharp, it was like looking at a blade with a broadening edge. Even those closest to him could not look directly at him for more than a kshana without experiencing discomfiture.

'You are not the one at fault with Bhishma,' Jarasandha said to the powerfully built daughter of Pundar. 'Your father would be considered the offender in the Pitama's eyes. But that hardly matters. For you love your father dearly and would die in his stead. Which is why it would be tragic if Hastinapura were to receive word of his lapse of judgement when you were away, too distant to be of assistance to him. And as we well know, King Pundra has not strength to lift so much as a dagger in his own defence, leave alone cross swords with one of Bhishma's stature. And we all know, as well, with what contempt Bhishma Pitama would regard your father were that lapse made known.'

Pundraki's dark eyes flashed, her powerful arms bunching to reveal musculature more developed than even the long-axe wielding Sumhasana beside her. But she too dropped her gaze, offering tacit acknowledgement of the truth of Jarasandha's allegation. What was the 'lapse' that the Magadhan spoke of? Why would it offend Bhishma so much? These details hardly mattered. Jarasandha continued his prowl.

'Vinda, prince of Kekaya. Highest of the highest, proudest of the civilized nations. Is that not the way you like to describe yourselves?'

Prince Vinda stared at a point just beyond the tip of Jarasandha's left shoulder, his taut jaw working with what might have been suppressed anger – or fear.

'And yet,' Jarasandha went on, turning his back on Vinda and spreading his thin arms wide to gesture to the gathering at large. 'The proudest and most vain are often the ones with the filthiest, most despicable secrets. For instance, who would think that of all your kingdoms, some of which are quite rough and tumble in their ways, it would be Kekaya who has the most questionable practices in the realm of – ' The Magadhan paused, as if catching himself in the nick of time. The blade-like mouth revealed a pink slice of what might be construed as a smile. 'But to reveal that would be to shock you all, and to destroy that carefully maintained image that Kekaya has successfully built over centuries. Suffice it to say that if that secret were to be revealed, even a family of mountain goats as Vinda here used the term to describe my dear friend Bhagadatta, would not wish to marry his daughters into the Kekaya nation. And Hastinapura?' Jarasandha shook his head and sighed an exaggerated chest heaving sigh. 'Hastinapura would break off ties not only with Kekaya itself but with all other nations who associated with them. It would an ostracizing that would denigrate Kekaya to the status of a 'mlecha' or 'barbaric' nation, and that stigma would haunt its reputation for millennia.'

Jarasandha turned abruptly to the giant of a man, sitting in the next seat. 'Do you not agree, Vriddhakshatra of Sindhudesha? After all, your nation has a tradition of marrying its daughters to Kekaya's sons. Despite knowing of this particular trait. Surely that makes you as 'civilized' a people as the Kekayans?'

Jarasandha moved on without giving the Sindhu a chance to react or respond – neither of which were forthcoming in any case.

'And Kartavirya Mara of the Haihaiyas of Mahishmati? Your so-called feud with your cousins the Haihaiyas of Avanti is legendary. But what if Bhishma Pitama were to know that behind this feud is in fact one of the most startling conspiracies – '

Ripunjaya of Avanti rose suddenly from his seat beside his cousin Kartavirya Mara, as if about to challenge Jarasandha. His cousin turned alarmed, terrified eyes in his direction, and Ripunjaya subsided immediately. Jarasandha did not turn to look at him but the stillness of the Magadhan made it clear that he had noted the reaction of the king of Avanti and was prepared to deal with it in like fashion if required. It was not required. Without completing his sentence, Jarasandha addressed the next in the row.

'Madrashya of Madra, your secret is quite unique from all the others. Yet exposing it would provoke Bhishma's ire no less than any of the others gathered here today. Do you not agree?'

Madryasha's sickly complexion betrayed his reluctant agreement.

'Druhyu of Druhyu, you may have used whatever was at hand to deal with certain persons who obstructed your path to power, and no doubt, you have been careful to bury the bodies deep – or to be more accurate, dispose of them in a manner unlikely to be discovered even by Hastinapura's most vigilant marshals. But the convenient disappearance of rivals or impediments at inconvenient times has not gone unnoticed by Bhishma and if someone were to whisper the locations and details of certain incidents in his receptive ear, he would not hesitate to use whatever weapon was at hand to punish those responsible.'

Druhyu's eyes did not even dare to look in the direction of the ornament he had picked up not long before. The Druhyan seemed to be attempting to merge his person with the seat he occupied, and to avoid Jarasandha's attention at all costs. But Jarasandha had already moved on to the next.

Bahlika Pratipeya was the first to look openly at Jarasandha, or to attempt the feat at least. 'Your threats will not work on me, Jara. I am blood kin to Bhishma Pitama. He will not deal with me as he would with these others. After all, kin is kin.' But his tone was almost apologetic, un-challenging.

Jarasandha matched it with a mocking tone, mimicking the apologetic manner of the Pratipeya. 'Surely, kin is kin. But skin is skin, Bahlika. And yours will not stay long on your flesh if Satyavati were to learn of your illicit transgressions. And if the Dowager Empress gives the order, Prince Regent Bhishma will not hesitate to carry out her command. However great her sense of kinship, Satyavati is not Kuru by blood, only by marriage. She will not care as much for your precious hide as you would.'

Bahlika's stunned expression was response enough.

'Shastra of the Kambhoja,' Jarasandha continued, facing

the pert squat horse chief. 'Your actions speak louder than words. And it is with actions that Bhishma would counter you.'

Neither expression nor word escaped the woman's face, but her flashing eyes and flared nostrils conveyed her sense of alarm, showing that Jarsandha's words had struck their mark.

Finally, Jarasandha stopped before the last guest. The quivering wobbling mountain of a man was already in motion even before the Magadhan turned his attention.

It was remarkable to watch that prodigious bulk move with that speed. In mere kshanas, Ushanas of Ushati had reached the door of the chamber. He threw arms as meaty as the haunch-bone on which he had gnawed earlier, striking the strong timber.

'Let me out, let me out!' he cried in a shrill hysterical voice. 'I wish to leave at once! *Open these doors!*'

The doors remained sealed.

Ushanas turned to Bhagadatta, his several chins quivering with outrage. 'Mountain goat! Oaf! I command you to open these doors at once! How dare you imprison us? Do you know who I am? I am Ushanas of Ushati! I have enough wealth to buy anyone in this room ten times over! I am the wealthiest merchant-king in Jambudwipa. Open these doors at once or I will see to it that nobody trades with the mountain kingdoms for the next thousand years. You inbreeding goats who call yourselves Kings!'

Bhagadatta's face revealed its first trace of displeasure.

The ruler of Pragjyotisha turned to look at Jarasandha who was standing in the center of the chamber, watching the performance with his thin head cocked to one side.

Jarasandha smiled at Bhagadatta who grimaced once, in the semblance of a response. Something passed between them that did not require words to be understood. Bhagadatta nodded once, but kept his eyes lowered and his head averted, studiously ignoring Ushani and everything that transpired thereafter. His aspect made it clear that even though this was his aerie and his kingdom to command, he deferred to Jarasandha. Had anyone of those gathered in that chamber needed any confirmation, that one silent exchange between the Magadhan and the Pragjyotishan made their relationship crystal clear.

Jarasandha began walking with slow deliberate steps towards the Ushati King.

'Ushanas of Ushati.'

The quivering mass that was the 'richest merchant-king in Jambudwipa' turned hesitantly, reluctantly, agonizingly, to look at the approaching Jarasandha.

'Had you chosen to ignore the invitation to come here, and taken your chances with Bhishma Pitama and the might of Hastinapura, that would have been your right.'

Jarasandha was some twenty yards from the doors before which Ushanas stood in quivering fear.

'Had you turned back at any time during your arduous journey up the mountains, that too would have been your choice.'

Ten yards now, and closing.

'Had you paid your respects to your host during the introductions being made, partaken of some refreshment, and started back before the doors were sealed, that too might have been acceptable.'

Jarasandha paused some five yards away, cocked his head, reconsidered.

'Perhaps not then, that might have been too late, but it was still a possibility, if a dim one.'

Jarasandha looked at the Ushati King.

'But to hear our entire plan, to listen to all I had to say, to hear me hint with sufficient detail at the secrets of your fellow conspirators gathered here to provide you with fodder enough to feed the hungry ears of Hastinapura spasas, to eat our host's feast, to guzzle his wine, to partake of his hospitality, and our fine company, and then to act thus. Demanding. Abusing. Insulting.'

Jarasandha shook his head from side to side.

'Unacceptable.'

Ushanas appeared to be melting with terror and sweat. His face shivered as rivulets poured down. Stray morsels of food stuck to his chin and cheeks were dislodged by the streaming perspiration and fell to the floor, a tiny pile of food crumbs in a growing puddle of sweat. 'I heard nothing!' he screeched. 'I know nothing of your plans against Hastinapura! I have no knowledge of your stupid secrets. Let me go. I will not say a word to Bhishma. I am not a fool, you idiots!'

Jarasandha tch-tched, wagging his long index finger from side to side.

'In that case, allow me to enlighten you. We are gathered here today for one reason and one reason only. To discuss our mutual interest in ridding ourselves of the Kuru dynasty and dividing up the wealth and territories of the Kuru empire amongst ourselves. That much was obvious from the time you received the message. Otherwise, why would any of you have come at all? Even an idiot or,' Jarasandha chuckled, 'a mountain goat would know that merely to respond to such an invitation would be regarded as a treasonous act against the Elephant Throne.'

Ushanas shook his head from side to side. 'No. NO! I know nothing of any conspiracy. I am not part of any treason. Let me go. I will never speak of this as long as I live.'

Jarasandha smiled his slash-mouth smile. Even though the others could not see his face now, as he was standing with his back to them all, facing the door, every last one of them shuddered or reacted with something less than pleasure at the thought of that horrible smile.

'At last, you speak the truth,' Jarasandha said. 'You will never speak of this as long as you live. Because you will not live long enough to speak any more.' And before Ushanas could speak another word, Jarasandha moved.

With a flash, his body split into two halves. Like a wood chip struck by a powerful downward axe stroke, Jarasandha's body divided down the middle. The two halves separated from each other with a sticky unguent tearing, producing a sound like that of live flesh being ripped into two. Which, indeed, was what happened. The two halves, still living, stood momentarily, each as steady on its single foot as any man on two.

Had Jarasandha indeed been a man sliced into two halves by a razor-sharp axe stroke, it would have been a feat to rival the tales told by Sumhasana Long-Axe's ancestors. Had he indeed been sliced into two equal halves, the inner part of each half would have oozed and bled, blood and flesh and inner organs visible.

But Jarasandha was no man.

He was in fact, two men that chose to unite and exist as one. If you could call such creatures *men*.Each half, named Jara and Sandha respectively, now stood individually. Not on feet, for these creatures, this *being*, had no feet in the mortal sense. Each stood on a base that was fluid and mutable, coiling and uncoiling as it prepared to make its next move. The effect was not unlike that of two snakes, pythons perhaps, standing upright prior to a strike.

However, it would be a mistake to term these creatures, this being, a snake, or anything allied to the snake family. It was far far older than any serpent that had swam through the primordial ooze on this world. And far deadlier.

The exact features and limbs of each part was not clearly visible to those gathered in the aerie, for Jarasandha had his back to them all, and was facing the door where Ushanas of Ushati still stood, cowering and relieving himself involuntarily of his bodily fluids, the yellow stain spreading under his massive trunk-like feet.

The only one who could see what the two divided beings

looked like from the front was King Bhagadatta, and he was studiously examining at the pattern on the floor of his own aerie. Only the tension in his features and the tautness of his hunched shoulders suggested his own state of...fear?

Terror, more likely.

The two creatures coiled into themselves for a brief kshana, not like any snake anyone had ever seen. Their flesh seemed to grow tighter, condensing, pressing into itself. Like a muscle tightening. Then, with a motion as sudden as a whiplash, each half *flew* across the distance that separated Jarasandha from Ushanas.

Both halves of the Magadhan's body snapped around Ushanas's considerable bulk. There was nothing snakelike about this motion either. It was as sharply executed as the winding of a lash around its target.

Ushanas screamed, entwined by this unthinkable *thing*.

His fat, rolling face was striped diagonally in both directions by the two halves of Jarasandha. The effect was as if two thick pythons had coiled around the man's corpulent body in a criss-cross diagonal pattern. And like two thick pythons, both halves now tightened themselves with unimaginable force.

Parts of Ushanas's flesh bulged from the gaps between the diagonal strips. The Ushati king made one final attempt to scream, but even the last breath had already been squeezed out of his body. Then, with a suddenness that was shocking to all present, despite their familiarity with the many forms in which death acted on a battlefield, the Ushati's body simply...*Exploded*.

It disintegrated into a hundred chunks of bone, flesh, organs, blood. Like the morsels of meat Ushanas himself had been tearing apart earlier. It was all over in a flash of a whipcrack and a breath. What lay on the ground before the doors of the aerie was no longer a man, or even a semblance of a man. It was a scattering of morsels and chunks of raw flesh, in a puddle of gore. The dismantling of the Ushati King took barely a few kshanas.

Bhagadatta still kept his eyes downcast and head averted. Perhaps the mountain king had viewed similar actions by the Magadhan before, and had no desire to view it again. Like a whiplash returning to its wielder, the two sinuous halves flew back through the air to the spot where Jarasandha had been standing.

Each half merged seamlessly with the other, the joining taking place in a single motion. Like clay pressed into clay, merging to form a single piece, seemingly inseparable and unitary.

Jarasandha turned around to face the gathering, his smile slashing his face like a knife-cut. Was it their imagination or were his lips redder than before?

'Now,' Jarasandha said, 'I shall tell you how I intend to destroy the Kuru dynasty and take Hastinapura.' He paused and looked again at each one in turn individually. 'Unless someone else has an objection?'

There were no further objections.

6

Crow sat upon a window.

The window looked out of a chamber.

The chamber was large by mortal standards, but by Crow standards all chambers were small, since Crow's home was the world entire, its roof the endless sky. Crow had no interest in the goings on within the chamber.

She knew there were mortals there, she could see them, arrayed like a murder of crows, keeping distance between them as if in anticipation of a quarrel. Had Crow been curious, Crow might have wondered if there was a pecking order among mortals, and if that mortal sitting on the larger perch at one end of the tiny chamber (tiny to Crow's sky-accustomed eyes) might be the leader. But there was also another mortal standing near the one on the large perch, and all the other mortals seemed to be staring at this standing mortal. Perhaps the standing mortal was the leader. He looked hawkish enough to rip them to shreds should they question his leadership.

None of this actually interested Crow. What did interest Crow was the thing the standing mortal had just done. He had pounced, hawk-like, upon another much fatter mortal. And torn that mortal to shreds.

Crow could not quite understand how the standing mortal had done this: he appeared to have no claws or beak. But Crow had seen the standing mortal split into two sinuous halves, and each half had then *flown* through the air to attack the fatter mortal.

Now that had been a sight worth seeing.

Crow was a bird; birds feared serpents more than anything else, even other birds. Crow had seen serpents kill crows. They moved and killed in a similar manner. Some swallowed their prey whole from the beak, or whatever it was that serpent's mouths were called in their language. But other serpents wound their slimy sinuous bodies *around* their prey and squeezed them to death. Crow had seen this done too, once to a field mouse and twice to rabbits. After the prey was squeezed to death, *then* the squeezing serpents had uncoiled themselves and swallowed them through their beaks/mouths.

But this mortal had not swallowed the prey.

Crow could still see the remains of the fatter mortal, not simply choked and crushed to death like the field mouse and the rabbit had been. The fatter mortal was not merely crushed to death. It was...Torn apart. Shredded. Like the remains after a cat had shredded a pigeon. Destroyed.

Looking at the shredded remains, Crow began salivating. The thought of that tasty feast was what kept her here, on this window. Waiting. Watching.

Just a morsel. Or a chunk. That nice big juicy red chunk right there, with just a bit of white gristle and yellow fat, and oh, my, Lord of Birds, a bit of broken bone with pink marrow peeking out. Crow wanted that chunk.

But Crow was now scared of the standing mortal. The one who had killed the fatter one and turned him from a standing mortal into a mess of shredded chunks.

Oh, my, Lord of Birds, that standing mortal was a scary one. He could split himself into two, turn from a mortal into a kind of serpent – a *pair* of serpents – move like no serpent Crow had seen before, then tear his prey apart like a hawk, or a cat, or some combination of bird-snake-animal that could not possibly exist, and then simply *leave* the prey. Not even eat it or carry it off to eat later.

What arrogance. What waste. What terror. Crow could not comprehend such behavior. Or such a creature. But that did not matter. There were many things in this world Crow did not comprehend. This was not something that kept Crow awake at nights. All that mattered was that juicy chunk.

And how to get it without incurring the wrath of that scary man-animal-bird *thing*.

Crow saw a flock of her fellows fly past in a ragged formation, part of the murder to which she belonged.

She would usually have cawed to attract their attention. The more crows stealing morsels, the better a chance she would have of getting her feast. Always better to steal from another bird, even another Crow, than to steal from animals or mortals. It was a challenge, and if she succeeded, as she often did, it made the food taste better.

So she did not caw. Instead, she waited. Inside the chamber, the standing mortal continued to caw at the other mortals. Or whatever it was that mortals called cawing.

The cawing continued for a while. Crow watched as the day wore on. The sun reached its apex then began its downward slide. Crow waited. Crow watched. Crow did not caw. The afternoon wore on. Crow began to tire.

Crow dozed for a bit, a kind of awake-dozing that only crows did to overcome tiredness. Crow even had a term for it in Crow's language: Crow nap.

Crow watched with semi-interest as pigeons mated on the stone battlements of the mortal structure. The pigeons were vaguely nervous because Crow was watching, but went ahead and did it anyway. Thrice. Shameless. But they were pigeons, what did Crow expect. Not civilized, like crows.

Then, when Crow was starting to feel the pangs of hunger gnaw her belly, the mortals all rose up suddenly and exitted the chamber. In moments, they had all flown the coop. The chamber was empty. Only the remains of the dead mortal lay where they had lain the past few hours.

The blood was congealed, the flesh too, but that didn't matter to Crow. If anything, a little time made food riper, tastier. It was seasoning for the feast.

Crow watched as other mortals began to peer into the chamber, pointing at the remains of the dead mortal and cawing to one another. Crow knew that mortals usually liked to clean up fallen food and cart it away, to be thrown out. Such a criminal waste! But mortal waste was what supplied Crow's feasts. Crow knew that once the mortals carted away the remains of the dead mortal, she might not find them again easily. She would have to search all over again.

Her best chance was to snatch it now and fly. She saw her chance when the mortals left the room, no doubt to bring back objects suitable for carting away fallen remains. Crow hopped down from the window to the stone floor of the chamber.

Crow hopped quickly across the floor, all the way to the remains. My, Lord of Bird, they did smell delicious. Crow looked about quickly, craftily, wary of being seen by a mortal. Or worse – being seen by a cat. Dogs were not a problem, silly funny creatures that cawed loudly but could never catch a crow. But Cats? Oh my, Lord of Bird. Cats were deadly. Not as deadly as hawks, or serpents, or, above all, the standing mortal who could turn into a snake-animal-bird-thing. But still deadly enough.

Crow stood still and waited for several long moments, making certain that no enemy was present and close by. When Crow was certain the coast was clear, Crow pounced.

In a flash, Crow had the morsel in her mouth and was flying across the chamber, through the window, and out, out, out to freedom; away from the mortal house, across the mountains, and as far as she could get from that scary mortal.

The chunk was heavy and usually Crow would have stopped and rested on one of the windows or ledges, shooing away those silly pigeons to make way, perhaps even have tasted a bite or two of the delicious chunk. Easier to carry in Crow's belly than in Crow's beak.

But so scared was Crow of the mortal-animal-bird *thing*, that Crow didn't stop until she had flown clear across the valley and the river that ran through it.

A drop fell from Crow's mouth on the way; it hardly mattered. It was not Crow's job to clean! Crow didn't slow down until she was across the valley and in the safety of a grove she knew well. She had been birthed in this grove and it was always the place she felt safest.

She perched upon a high branch and examined the morsel briefly before tearing into it with great enjoyment.

Oh my, Lord of Bird, mortal flesh was tasty flesh! Where can I get me some of this every day? Oh my. Oh my. Crow raised her head high and cawed happily, not caring if any of her murder heard her now. Crow lowered her black head and feasted.

7

R iver felt a drop.

It was a single drop, fallen from the beak of a passing crow. That was common enough. What was unusual was that the drop was mortal blood.

River disliked mortal blood, or blood of any kind.

River tasted her share of blood, mortal and otherwise, especially during times of mortal war. Which seemed to be almost always. Sometimes, it came in great quantities.

At those times, she avoided tasting it as best as she could manage. Too much pain, anguish, rage still lingering in that blood.

But it had been days — perhaps weeks or even months, for River did not measure time as mortals did — since she had tasted any mortal blood. And a single drop was unusual. So when this drop fell, she couldn't help but taste it idly.

It intrigued her. There was information in this blood, something of import. Something new. Something worrying. She would convey it to her Mother. Not merely *her* mother.

Mother of all Rivers, all water on Earth.

Ganga.

She encased the drop in a bubble and put the bubble into the mouth of a fish. Fish swallowed the bubble which did not burst inside its mouth because River had made it impossible to open except by Ganga. The bubble went into Fish's stomach where it remained as solid as a swallowed pearl. River pushed Fish upto her surface as a flock of cranes flew by. Sure enough, one of them swooped down greedily and snatched up Fish. River caught hold of Crane's tail. Crane gave a cry of alarm, dropping Fish. Fish plopped back into River.

River spoke to Crane, telling him her errand. Crane listened, wide-eyed and did not argue. Crane gathered Fish in his beak and flew away.Over fields and forests and hills and valleys. Until Crane came to another Smaller River, a tributery of Mother River.Crane dropped Fish into Smaller River, passing on River's message.

Smaller River carried Fish dutifully, passing Fish up through several other tributery, streams, rivulets, until Fish was conveyed finally to Mother River herself.

Ganga examined Fish. Removed the bubble from Fish's belly. (A simple burp was sufficient to accomplish this.) Ganga burst the bubble and tasted the drop of mortal blood carefully. Ganga neither liked nor disliked mortal blood. Part of her dharma was to absorb the mortal remains of all those who cast them into her waters. To cleanse and recycle them.

She knew how to read a mortal body and its secrets as well as a saptarishi could read a Sanskrit scroll.

Ganga read the entirety of the information contained in

that drop of mortal blood. When she was done, she knew what she had to do with the information. She had to go to her son and warn him.

|| 8 ||

In the deep forest, Vyasa opened his Third eye. The jungle pulsed crimson. Every tree, trunk, branch, leaf, appeared to be suffused with the opposite of its natural verdancy. It was as if the green blood within their veins had turned red.

A disturbance agitated the forest, coming from nowhere and going no place. It was not produced by wind or any natural force. It was the agitation of the forest itself, expressing its fear.

It shook the high trees, caused the great trunks to shudder, made insects scurry out from their crannies, filling the air with a sense of chaos and terror.

Vyasa's long white beard rippled. He smelled the fear of the forest. It was also the fear of She who birthed all forests. She spoke to him in agitated voices of wind, leaf, insect, animal, all the beings under her protection and in her care. Vyasa listened.

Yes Mother, he said. *I felt it too. The Twice Born is at work.*

She said more to him, which he heard patiently.

He is growing powerful, Vyasa admitted. *And will grow stronger yet as time passes. But it is not time to confront him yet.*

Trees swayed without wind to sway them, branches bent with no hand forcing them, leaves shirred of their own accord. The forest spoke to Vyasa. He listened. But each time his answer was the same.

Not yet, Mother. It is not yet time.

The forest asked one final urgent query. Vyasa mused on it a kshana or two.

When the Five are born, he said. *Until then, we must endure. It is all we can do.*

The Forest stopped its agitation and was still for a moment. Then, with a single keening voice, it sang a song of sorrow and hope.

It was a song not meant for mortal ears. Even Vyasa did not comprehend its entire meaning. But he understood its emotion:

The Great Mother of the Forest, of *all* Forests, of the Earth itself, was crying out for help.

Vyasa listened for a great length of time. Eventually, he gave in reluctantly.

Perhaps there is a way. Perhaps.

The Forest cried out in hopeful excitement. Vyasa sighed.

If Light and Dark unite. It is the only way. But, he cautioned firmly, *it is nigh impossible.*

The Forest waited, shirring, pleading. Vyasa rose to his feet, took up his staff, and draped his anga vastra over his arm.

Very well, Great Mother. I shall make an attempt. I shall go to Hastinapura.

He walked out of the hut, across the clearing, and into the dark woods.

9

Sometimes, Satyavati thought that being a Dowager Queen was easier than being a Mother in Law.

Anything was easier.

Seated on a comfortable cushion in the silk merchant's tent, she tried to get some relief from the heat by sipping on a cooling drink while her attendants fanned her, as she watched her two daughters in law arguing over a length of silk.

Ambika and Ambalika were pretty girls. Beautiful even, if one liked coy petite girls with the bodies of women and the brains of sparrows. Satyavati herself appreciated women who had some substance to them, both physically and mentally. But then, these two were princesses and little more than princesses. What could one expect from the product of entitlement and royal privilege?

Satyavati herself had worked her hands raw as a young girl. First as a fisher, she was treated no differently than the other village children, all of whom were expected to earn their daily meals. It mattered not a whit that her father was the chief of the entire tribe. Fisher King to outsiders, but plain fisherman to his family. He worked hard alongside his people, cutting himself no slack. He believed that work defined a person. Not just fishing, anything one did to ensure one's survival. Anything that made one useful to one's family, one's people, the world in general. To old Chief Guha, doing a job that mattered, doing it as well as it could possibly be done and doing it for as long as one could do it, until the fishes ate your eyes. That was the way of the fisherfolk; and had always been, since Ganga had descended to Earth from Shiva's celestial tresses.

Even when Shantanu, King of Kurujangala, had first met Satyavati, she had been working. Ferrying travellers across the Ganga. The king of the greatest empire in the world, attracted to a fisherman's daughter!

She had once asked Shantanu teasingly, years later, 'Did you want to bed me because of my strong limbs and supple rowing? Because you had never had a fishergirl before?' He had surprised her by replying: 'I wanted you as my wife, because I wanted a wife who was *someone*. More than just a daughter, a sister, a wife. A person in her own right. Watching you work, the pride you took in your ferrying, the way you spoke of your people, of what they did, pointing out the children doing the baiting of the nets as you had once done in younger days, I saw that woman. You had a life, an identity, a job that mattered, not only to you, but a real task, something that affected people, helped people, enabled them, added value to their lives. That was why I fell in love with you.' He then added, teasing now, 'It was only *much* later that I even felt any urge to bed you.' She had exclaimed 'Oh, really!' and slapped away his probing hand – but almost immediately, she had caught the same hand and put it back where it had been.

She sighed now, handing off the half-consumed beverage to an attendant. It was refreshing, but no drink could slake the thirst she felt inside, the parched heart she carried within. She *missed* Shantanu. She missed him as much now as she had the day he had died. Not just his probing hand and sly wit, but his authority, his wisdom, his keen insight, deep knowledge of people and cultures, and above all, his uncanny ability to immediately know what the cause of a problem was, and then to be able to arrive at a solution.

She wished he was here now, so she could ask him whether it would be wiser to banish her two daughters in law into permanent exile, or simply execute them.

She had no ill wish for either of them – well, nothing that she would ever act on at least. But sometimes they could be so, *so* tiresome. Like now, for instance.

Here they were, in a travelling bazaar that set up its tents once every year or two in Khandavaprastha, conditions permitting.

The bazaar was made up of merchants who travelled the length of the Masala Marg from one end to the other, endlessly. That was all they did. A polymorphous collection of men and women of all races, colors, creeds, cultures, they spent their entire existence traversing the rough route along which the civilized world sent its spices – Masala, as it was colloquially known in the capitol of the civilized world – silks, trinkets and salable items of every description. They bought, they sold and traded. Sometimes, they stopped while on their way back from the West, en route to the East.

Other years, they stopped on the way from the East to the West. It depended on what they had to offer, and where they thought those items would fetch the highest prices.

This time they were travelling from West to East. Which was why they were almost out of silk. Silk came from the East and went West, where the lesser civilized kingdoms considered it to be a marvel or a miracle, depending on the culture and belief system. By the time the travelling bazaar returned from the West on its way to the East, all the silks were sold, and sold for small fortunes.

The only reason they had any silk left at all was because Satyavati's daughters-in-law had given standing orders to bring them silk each visit. The merchants complied more out of fear than greed. Any price Satyavati offered could easily be matched by the kings and queens of Western kingdoms. But the might and power of the Kuru empire could not be matched. The problem was: today they had only a single bolt of silk left.

It was exquisite stuff, the red of Eastern seal wax, that deep rich shade that the Easterners achieved so brilliantly. The fabric felt like an apsara's wings between Satyavati's fingers, the individual grains distinguishable. So diaphanous that she could see the whorls of her own fingerpads through the cloth. It was material to be caressed, desired, worn with abandon; the touch of it like a baby's breath on one's skin, the sensation as delicate and ethereal as the first cool touch of the Ganga when young Satyavati had plunged in on a hot afternoon after a long day's work.

It was the most sensuous thing she had ever felt. It

would look beautiful on any woman, and both Ambika and Ambalika should be ecstatic to have it. Instead, they were fighting. Because there was only one bolt of red silk. And each wanted it for herself. Exclusively.

Satyavati had already suggested that they could both make garments out of the material. There was enough, considering these young ones barely used much anyway.

But neither wanted to wear the same thing that her sister would wear, naturally. Satyavati sighed. Her daughters-in-law argued on. The afternoon grew hotterthe bazaar busierthe air dustier and the bickering louder.

And she thought, for the umpteenth time today, and the nth time since the daughters of Kashi had come to her, that being a Dowager Queen was easier than being a Mother-in-Law. Any day and *especially* this day.

Someone came up beside her, awaiting her attention.

She turned and saw the merchant standing beside her. He was a kindly fair-skinned middle-aged man with the high cheekbones and epicanthic folds above his eyes that were characteristic of Far Easterners.

He bowed, speaking softly. She frowned and looked at him. 'Here?' He inclined his head, indicating the rear of the tent.

Satyavati looked back but all she could see was a partition separating the public area of the tent where all the goods were displayed, from the merchant's private space at the back.

She looked at the merchant again, quizzically. He inclined

his head again. Satyavati frowned again. This was quite unusual.

It occurred to her that she was a target for enemies of the Kuru Empire, and that it could well be a ploy.

She glanced at her guards, indicating the rear as the merchant had. They went at once, returning with surprising quickness to bow their heads and indicate that there was no danger.

Satyavati stood and accompanied them to the rear of the tent. One of her attendants held up the fold of the partition so she could pass into the private area. Her guards took up unobtrusive positions to grant her some privacy. She saw the person waiting for her.

Satyavati's face crinkled with a smile that lit up her entire middle aged face, a smile that only appeared for one person in the whole world: her son.

'Maatr.' Vyasa bent his wild-haired head and touched his mother's feet. Satyavati touched her son's head, offering the ritual maternal blessing. She let her hand linger a moment, feeling her heart stir with a long-dormant emotion. In a sense, she had never truly been able to raise Vyasa as a mother usually raised a child. That was because of his supernatural nature: Though born as normal as any mortal babe, he had matured to adulthood within the space of a few hours, before her awe-struck eyes.

She had always been aware of his extraordinary powers and abilities. But somewhere within her heart, there still remained the secret yearning to have nursed her babe, nurtured, guided him on his first steps, gone through all the miraculous stages of growth and maturation. Vyasa was a supernatural being, fathered by a great Rishi and endowed at birth with extraordinary powers, but Satyavati was just a woman. A mother who had never had the satisfaction to watch her own first-born child grow as mortal children grew.

She buried her long-dormant desires, with an expertise born of years of self-control. 'It must be important, for you to leave your meditation and come here thus.'

'It is, maatr. I have a message of great urgency to deliver to you.'

10

B hishma was bored.

The court of Hastinapura was not officially in session. An official session would have required the presence of Dowager Queen. This was simply a conference of the kingdom's ministers regarding various sundry matters. The majority of these matters concerned administrative and procedural issues. The hows and whys of the actual business of political governance. There was a time when Bhishma would have sought an excuse, *any* excuse, to recluse himself from such a conference. Such things bored him at best, infuriated him at worst. What was the point of making up endless rules and byrules for every single thing? Why not simply use one's judgement as each matter arose? He knew the answer: a king overseeing a small kingdom could afford to be autocratic. A large kingdom like Hastinapura could not be ruled by any one man, even a man as omnipresent and sleepless as Bhishma. And an empire like Kurujangala was a hundred times – nay, a hundred times a hundred! – the size of an average-sized kingdom. It required a small army of administrative staff just to keep pace with the endless procedural, diplomatic and trade oversight matters that cropped up on a daily basis. Each of those many departments themselves required oversight, by a competent *honest* minister and each minister had questions, doubts, problems, challenges, that needed to be answered and dealt with on a regular basis. For the entire empire to function smoothly – or as smoothly as any large juggernaut could manage – it required a system. Checks and balances. Protocols. Procedures. Rules. Byrules. Which meant conferences like this one from time to time. Someone had to oversee these overseers, and ensure that nobody amongst them or farther down the line was attempting to get rich at the empire's expense. Or worse.

And because Bhishma was the Prince Regent of the Empire, this onerous responsibility was his burden. Satyavati was an important symbol of the late King Shantanu's rule, especially since Bhishma had sworn a life vow never to sit on the Elephant throne. Her presence authorized every court session as law. Even if she didn't speak a word, as was often the case. The actual burden of governance fell on Bhishma's broad shoulders.

After decades of enduring such sessions he had come to accept it as his lot. It didn't make these conferences any easier, or less boring and tedious. But it helped him restrain himself from reacting to every irritating debate over irrelevant matters of protocol. Like the present debate over whether a feather-hatted emmissary of a foreign kingdom with a title that had no correspondent in Jambudwipa should be met by a minister, a secretary, a clerk, an ambassador, or even, as one bright spark suggested, a *courtesan*.

This last was presumably suggested as a way of

eliminating any possibility of giving offense and provided a warm friendly welcome at the same time. This had given rise to the question of whether the feather-hatted emissary would prefer to be met by a male or a female courtesan, or both at once, or one possessed of both particularities. Then had followed a meticulous discussion on the differences between the services provided by a bisexual courtesan as against a monosexual one. Did these idiots even remember that he was a sworn celibate? Could they be deliberately dragging out the discussion *because* he was a celibate? He dismissed the thought at once. Fools they might be, but not foolish enough to risk angering him.

Bhishma was listening to this bizarre and quite obscene debate with the growing suspicion that his ministers were deliberately prolonging the discussion because of its greater entertainment value rather than because it genuinely meritted such a long discussion, when he felt the change.

It began as a rippling in the air. The scent of lotuses. The cool breath of the glacier that had birthed her. The far wall of the sabha hall, ten times the height of a man, shimmered and dissolved like vapour.

Like a tidal wave, Ganga burst through the high wall and into the great chamber. The great river roared into the heart of Hastinapura, raging torrentially across the throne room, washing over the royal dais and disappearing behind it.

The ministers, the guards, the assorted palace staff and servers, all remained unaffected. This was a sight meant only for Bhishma, not intended for mere mortal eyes.

As Bhishma watched, the cascading water sculpted itself

into the shape of a mortal woman. The shape coalesced into a liquid statue. The statue of living water glistened and gleamed wetly in the afternoon sunshine as it stepped on the royal dais.

Ganga, clad in a garment of shimmering translucent white, touched the back of the Elephant Throne with fingertips formed of water. Droplets coalesced on the gleaming ivory and remained there, a divine blessing.

Bhishma went at once to her, bending to touch his mother's feet. 'Maatr.'

'Devavrata. I have grave news for you.'

‖ 11 ‖

B hishma and Satyavati met shortly before midnight.

They were the only ones present, by mutual decision. Bhishma shut the doors to the throne room behind himself, securing it to ensure that nobody entered, even at this late hour. The torches burned low in their sconces. The rows of empty chairs, the dais with empty thrones, the deserted hall with rows upon row of polished pillars, all served as reminders that they were completely, unquestionably, alone. Whatever decision was made tonight, it would have to be made by the two of them. There was no question of bringing this before the council, the ministers, or even discussing it in open court.

'Do we know who the conspirators are?' Satyavati asked, seating herself not on her throne but upon the nearest convenient seat. Bhishma continued to pace restlessly along the length of the approach to the throne dais.

'Bhagadatta, the one king of the united mountain kingdoms hosted them at his palace in Pragjyotisha. Those in attendance were Anga, King of Anga, Vanga, King of Vanga, Kaurwa, of Kalinga, Sumhasana of Sumha, Pundraki of Pundar, Vinda, prince of Kekeya, Vriddhakshatra, king of

Sindhudesha, Kartavirya Mara of Mahishmati, Ripunjaya of Avanti, Madrashya of Madra, Druhyu of Druhyu, Shastra of Kambhoja, Ushanas of Ushati.' He paused and looked at her with an unusual show of emotion. 'And Bahlika Pratipeya.'

Satyavati sucked in a deep breath. 'But the Bahlikas are—'

'Blood kin to me, yes,' he said. 'Nevertheless, they were present as well.'

'Ushanas of Ushati was killed. That eliminates him from the list.'

'Yes, but his successors, whichever of his sons or daughters it is, will very likely fall into line. The execution of their father and king is a powerful motivator.'

Satyavati shook her head slowly. 'The audacity of these kingdoms! How dare they even contemplate going up against the might of Kurujangala?'

'Contemplation is one thing. I don't care if they contemplate open rebellion or worse from now till the end of time. It is forming an actual alliance against us that rankles. This cannot be allowed to stand, Mother. If word gets out that some of our most powerful kingdoms have allied against us, who knows how many others will join with them. At least a dozen that I can name. And several dozen smaller kingdoms will rush to join in as well, if only to ensure that they back the winning side.'

Satyavati frowned. 'Are you not over-stating the danger? Strong as this alliance seems, these kingdoms you named could not possibly field a host to match our own Kuru armies. Besides, we have many allies that we know we can count on if such a situation arises. Together, we will outnumber the forces of this alliance easily.'

'So you would think,' he said, 'but you are forgetting one more conspirator. The pack leader himself. Jarasandha of Magadha. It was he who summoned these fence sitters to Pragjyotisha. His own Magadhan forces are almost two thirds of our own. Combined with those of the alliance, they would give him an armed force twice the size of our own, and even more than the combined forces of our allies.'

Satyavati clutched the solid band of gold that ringed her throat, as if feeling the metal noose tighten. 'That is a formidable alliance. I cannot deny that. But even so, we can still prevail in an open battle. Kurujangala will always prevail with you leading our armies, Devavrata. No force can withstand you in battle. However strong their armies may be, whatever their numbers, they lack our secret weapon: Bhishma Devavrata. You are an army unto yourself. You balance all numbers and tip the odds in our favor.'

Bhishma shook his head sadly. 'I am flattered by your faith in me, Mother. But even I cannot be in a dozen places at once.'

'What do you mean?'

'I have studied Jarasandha of Magadha's battle strategy for years. He does not engage in pitched battles except on rare occasions, usually when his numbers far outreach those of his enemy and victory is certain. Instead, he divides and conquers. He has not summoned an open council to appeal to these kingdoms. He has summoned them in private, and used force and intimidation – even murder – to press his will upon them. He means to use each one's individual strength against us. He will fight a war of attrition, attacking us on all sides at once, over and over, until the vastra that is the Kuru empire is shredded with holes and rips. Only then, when he sees the opportunity, will he throw all his forces against us in battle, and finish what his allies began.'

Satyavati sat without speaking for several moments, absorbing Bhishma's words. 'Then we will fight him on those terms. We will divide and defend. We will use our allies to counteract his allies, fighting them one on one on as many fronts as he chooses to open up. Better yet, we shall be offensive and attack him as well. We shall rip the fabric of his own empire to shreds. And when we see fit, we shall attack Magadha openly, crushing it without mercy. We are not just one of the 500 kingdoms. We are Kurujangala. We have overcome tyrants and despots, invasions and uprisings by the hundreds. We shall overcome these challenges as well. We shall prevail.'

'Your strategy is shrewd, your spirit indomitable,' Bhishma said, 'But I still fear it will not be enough. There is a risk to being the aggressor. Jarasandha will use our own allies against us as proxies. He will not show his own hand until much later in the game. By throwing our own allies at us, he makes it difficult for us to retaliate or to take the aggressive stance. Each ally we crush is a potential ally lost, and it demoralizes our other allies as well. Our friends will say that we have no sense of dharma; if we crush one of our own allies, the others will point to it as a sign of our tyranny. Already, I am given information that there are rumors spreading across the empire.'

'Rumors of this rebel alliance?'

'No. Rumors of our wrongdoings. Of atrocities committed in the name of Kurujangala. Of tyranny and oppression in Hastinapura. Of slavery. Abuse. Genocide. Assassinations by our hand.'

Satyavati clutched her choker tighter. 'I do not follow. These are all untrue. What purpose does it serve anyone to spread such vile lies?'

Bhishma simply looked at her.

'Ah,' she said, 'I see. Jarasandha is the one fomenting these rumors.'

'He is building an image of us as tyrants. He wants the kingdoms to believe that we are cruel and oppressive, that even our own people want to be free of our tyranny. He paints himself as a liberator of slaves, a friend of the oppressed, benefactor of the disenfranchised. He seeks to turn our own people against us over time, so that he and his allies will be seen to have just cause and we to be in the wrong. He is waging a war of the mind and spirit, as well as of the body.'

'We will fight him on that front as well,' Satyavati replied, undaunted, 'Two can play at that game. We can spread word of his actual atrocities and tyranny. Tales of his cruelties to his own people, his family, his homeland. We will bring him down off his high pedestal.'

Bhishma nodded approvingly. 'These are all sound strategies, Queen Mother. But they are not endgames. Jarasandha does not play for the love of war. He plays to win. He will not stop until he has achieved his endgame.'

'And what is his endgame?'

'To split Kurujangala into pieces, back to the 500 kingdoms that we united and call the Kuru empire. He does not seek to defeat us in open battle, or even to wipe us out to the last Kuru. He merely wishes to destroy our Empire and to take away our ability to hold the coalition of 500 kingdoms that now consider themselves as a single great empire.'

'But what will he gain—?' Satyavati began, then stopped. 'Of course. That will leave Magadha, his own empire, as the largest empire in the subcontinent of Jambudwipa.'

'Indeed. And once he achieves that, he can incorporate all his allies, present and future, into the Magadha Empire, and rule the civilized world undisputed. He means to destroy Kurujangala not by facing us and defeating us in open battle. He means to outdo us by building the larger empire. Once he achieves that, the very fear of his size and power will make kingdoms bow before him and concede his superiority.'

'As they do now to Kurujangala, without even so much as a debate or a fight,' she said. 'He is an evil genius. A demon not to be trifled with. Yet we cannot simply stand by and let him win the day by any means. One way or another, we must prevail. The future of the civilized world is in our hands. Kurujangala stands for dharma, for law and order, for truth and justice. While Magadha stands for slavery, oppression, tyranny, genocide, adharma, chaos and anarchy. The good people, the little people, the kingdoms too small or too foolish to stand up to him, even those allies who have allowed themselves to be seduced by his lies and promises, his intimidation and threats...all of them need our help. We are the only hope humanity has against this demon tyrant. We must stand up to him. We must defeat him. We must find a way.'

Bhishma looked at her. 'I believe there is a way. But it will not please you.'

She looked back at him. 'Speak, son of Ganga.'

He told her.

She blanched. 'But to do such a thing, to thrust such responsibility upon their slender shoulders at this age?! They are mere children!'

'Even so. The war of the mind is always the greater than the war of the body. It is because they are mere chidren that such a step will win us the public sentiment. If he stands against them, everyone will point to Jarasandha and renounce him as an immoral tyrant. No matter the outcome upon the field of battle, we will win the battle of the mind and heart. It will give us the upper hand, and that is all we need.'

'But we will win the literal battle as well, of course,' she said, still pale from the shock of his proposal. 'Upon the literal field of battle.'

He hesitated a moment. 'I will do everything in my power to ensure a victory on all fronts.'

She did not like his answer. She did not like his suggestion. But he was right. Desperate times called for desperate measures. This whole problem had been caused by the perception of their own weakness. The vaccuum left by Shantanu's demise had barely been filled by her sons Chitrangada and Vichitravirya when both had been taken from the world too soon, much too soon. One of them, Chitrangada, had in fact fallen in single combat against Jarasandha himself. That had been a terrible blow against the Kuru dynasty. With the births of Ambika's and Ambalika's sons, the return of honor she had anticipated had not come. Panduranga's skin and sensitivity, Dritarashtra's blindness, these had all but taken both boys out of contention in the game of thrones. It was this weakness in the armor of empire that Jarasandha had exploited. So long as Hastinapura had heirs who were deemed unsuitable, the restless would continue to consider other options. The only way to silence all detractors and doubters was to deal a strong decisive blow, and the only way to do that was through a military victory so great that nobody could doubt the power of Hastinapura.

And right now, that meant sending her two grandsons into war.

If an albino prince and a blind prince, both barely old enough to sit a throne, could confront and defeat the Empire of Magadha in battle, it would silence all their critics. If they could do so and win back the allies that had been lost to Jarasandha through the same use of force, intimidation and seduction that the Demon Emperor had used, it would decisively answer the question of Kurujangala's future. If two boys with such severe physical challenges could achieve such a great victory, then imagine what they could do as grown kings. And their heirs. And the heirs of their heirs.

Unlike a game of thrones, the game of empires was not about merely winning a single seat and crown. It was about proving that you were capable of sustaining your position over a hundred, two hundred or even a thousand years. Empires were built with fear and power. Today, the world perceived Hastinapura as a fading power because its heirs, its true future, appeared incapable of ruling. Bhishma was proposing that they prove once and for all that this was false. That the two princes were not only capable of ruling as ably as any full-bodied man, but of doing far more than most men could. And his plan for doing this was to throw them into battle and launch a swift, decisive strike against the heart of tyranny itself.

It was the boldest, most audacious plan she had ever heard before. If they succeeded, they would remove the strongest argument their rivals and detractors had against them. It was a compelling, brilliant tactic.

'But,' she asked, rising to her feet to face her stepson. 'What if we fail?'

She did not need to spell it out. What if Pandu and Dri prove inadequate to this challenge? What if they are truly weak and inferior to other able-bodied men? What if, being mere boys, they are not ready to take on such a task which would be an immense challenge even for the bravest of kings and generals? What if Jarasandha grabs hold of them, tears them into shreds, and chews up the remains while laughing through bloody teeth?

'If we lose,' he said, 'we will lose knowing that we were doomed to lose anyway.'

She nodded. He was right. If Pandu and Dri could not face Jarasandha and defeat him now, it would likely mean they not be able to do so in future either. A prince could not wait to grow older and wiser to face his enemies in battle; he had to fight when the time came to act. 'That is true,' she said sadly.

'And by acting first, we will have the element of surprise. Jarasandha will not have anticipated this move. Not now, not when he has barely begun his secret alliance. He is unprepared for war with us. We will have the upper hand. We will strike first and hard. We will force him to face us in open battle. And his allies will be too shocked and uncertain to know whether to support him or to continue supporting us. Their indecision, his unpreparedness, the shock of facing young Panduranga and Dritarashtra in battle, of being forced to fight against a blind boy and a challenged boy, these are all factors which are invaluable to us in battle. We only gain these factors if we strike first and strike now. Either that or we stay on the defensive afterwards.'

'And yet,' she said, 'if we lose...' She looked away for a moment. 'We lose not only the empire, the reputation of the Kuru dynasty, but also the future of both. Pandu and Dri are all we have, Devavrata. Would you sacrifice them for the sake of victory?'

'No,' he replied. 'I would prove their ability to lead our empire, our dynasty, to victory. I would silence their critics once and for all. I would ensure that everyone in the civilized world believes beyond the shadow of a doubt that Kurujangala is the greatest empire in the history of humankind.'

She was silent a long time. She knew now that he had already made his decision. He intended to go through with this. All that remained was for her to agree, or to oppose. Even in opposition, he might still proceed. He had the authority as Prince Regent and Military Commander of the empire. He had every right. But she could still oppose on principle alone. As a Dowager Queen. As the reigning Matriarch of the dynasty. As a grandmother.

'They are just boys, Devavrata,' she said at last, unable to find any other argument to counter his implacable logic. 'Just boys.'

He shook his head slowly, his proud craggy face betraying an empathy he rarely displayed and in that moment she understood that he felt as deeply as she did, cared as much as she did, loved them no less than she did. And yet, this was the only way. 'They are Kuru.'

She had no argument to counter those three words.

She put her hands on his broad, powerful shoulders, looking up at his face.

'May the gods forgive us,' she said.

He bent and touched her feet, taking her blessings, which she gave with a heavy heart.

He rose upright again, his face betraying the same heaviness of heart that she herself felt.

'If there were another way,' he said.

She touched his cheek gently, reassuring him. 'But there is none. What must be done, must be done.'

He put his own hand over her hand, pressing it to his

cheek. He held it there a moment longer, then released her hand. He stood there a moment, looking around at the throne dais, at the proud throne, the banners, the carved motifs of empire and dynasty, the great portraits and frescos– all the symbols and trappings of a great lineage. All of it was now in the hands of two young boys who probably slept the sleep of the innocent in their distant forest ashram even at this moment.

'My mother once told me,' he said, 'that like all noble dynasties, the Kuru line is touched with both tragedy and greatness. She said that where there is great power, there is always great tragedy as well. She said this was proven by the fact that all the children of the Kuru line had been born in the darkest watch of night.'

She nodded, acknowledging the wisdom in his words. 'This is true. They have all been born at night.'

He released a long breath. 'The children of midnight are fated to face the worst terrors of the dark and the arcane. While all mankind sleeps, we awaken and put on our armor and go forth to battle the forces of darkness. It is our dharma. We fight evil by night that the world may awaken to see the dawn tomorrow. That is the dharma that awaits young Pandu and young Dri. They must do this not because I decree it or you approve it. They do this because it is their destiny. They are the swords of dharma. It is their duty to go forth and battle it. Whatever the outcome, victory or tragedy, or some of both, they must act. That is their dharma. The outcome is not theirs to anticipate or expect.'

He looked at her. Their eyes met and she nodded once,

giving him her complete and unconditional permission. He nodded, acknowledging and accepting her support.

Then, without another word, he turned and strode to the doors, flung them open, and left.

She knew that he would go directly to the stables, board his chariot and ride for Guru Kripacharya's ashrama that very minute.That was Bhishma's way. Do now what must be done, without hesitation or delay. It was what made him indomitable.

She prayed that the same indomitable spirit would serve her grandsons as well.

She clasped her hands together and knelt on the cold stone floor, praying for hope, victory and a miracle for herself, her family, her dynasty, her empire, for the children of midnight.

|| paksha pancham ||

How did we get here?

Is this really happening?

It's not too late – we can still stop this now, can't we?

Three questions that seethe up in the gullet like hot stomach acid when you first confront the armed forces of your enemy. The sight of that great host, thousands upon thousands of armed soldiers, horses, chariots, war elephants, lancers, spear throwers, archers, all gathered in this field for the sole purpose of your destruction – to kill you, in other words – will strike fear into the heart of even the bravest of the brave.

For young Pandu and young Dri, it was the most terrifying sight of their lives.

For Dri, who couldn't actually see the field of battle or the armies arrayed upon it, it was even more terrifying. However terrible the reality of a situation, imagination can always find a way to make it seem worse. To him, the strange sounds and smells of the enemy forces, the raw animal stench and peculiar noises, the very theatricality of the entire enterprise, all merged into one contiguous nightmare following on from the horror of his weeks in the forest ashram. He had thought that was the nadir of his short life. This was worse, much worse.

For him, the three questions that rose in his gullet like acid were desperate pleas to escape this situation. The inevitable panic that strikes every warrior head on when faced with the stark reality of war.

How did we get here?

By grandfather Bhishma Pitama's chariot, yes, but how did *we* get *here*? All of us – Kurus and enemies – on this field, in this situation, facing assured mutual destruction?

Is this really happening?

Denial. The refusal to believe that anyone could be foolhardy enough to actually go to war. That I could actually be here today, on this field, spending this fine summer day trying to stab, puncture, hack and otherwise injure other warriors while they attempt to do the same to me and my fellows. Surely it's just a bad dream. Or a hallucination. Or... Sacred Devi, it isn't really real, is it?

It's not too late – we can still stop this now, can't we?

Bargaining. There must be some way out of this that doesn't involve me killing or being killed? There has to be. Because, I just... I can't. Stop it. Somebody, please, stop it.

But of course, it was already too late. The three questions were moot. The field was set. The armies were aligned. The blades were out. And blood would be spilled.

All the three questions really did was force you to confront the ugly truth of your situation. After that, you really had only three choices: Panic and run. Die. Or Deal.

Pandu dealt.

Dri...struggled, but he managed to deal too.

They were crown princes of Hastinapura. They were the future kings of Kurujangala. Their entire army was looking to them for leadership. They couldn't run. Dying was not a preferable option. They had no choice but to deal.

|| 2 ||

The leaders of the enemy forces were neither boys nor blind, yet they were facing some doubts and questions of their own.

Jarasandha of Magadha was a terrifying being. What he had done to Ushanas of Ushati was horrific enough, but the tales of his atrocities were legendary. Every one who had gathered that fateful day in Bhagadatta's aerie in Pragjyotisha knew the tales; many had witnessed first-hand the results of those atrocities and none dared to risk incurring the Magadhan God-Emperor's wrath.

But that was then and this was now.

And today, here and now, upon this field, they were not facing Jarasandha the Atrocious, they were facing Bhishma the Terrible. Bhishma, whose name called up countless tales of awe-inspiring battle feats. In his own way, the Prince Regent of Kurujangala was as terrifying if not more so than the God-Emperor of Magadha. And it was he they would have to face today on this field, in a few moments. This was causing some consternation among the enemies of Kurujangala.

The allies sat upon their horses and chariots upon a hill

overlooking the field, close enough to converse with one another. The same group that had met at Pragjyotisha were present here, every last one.

Anga and Vanga, kings of eponymous neighboring kingdoms, were dressed as per the custom of the redmist mountains. Stripped down to loincloths girded with diagonal leather harnesses to carry their weapons, their bodies were shaven of all hair, oiled and painted with red, black and yellow dyes that made them resemble vanars more than mortal men. This was precisely the intended effect: the vanars of the Redmist mountains were a formidable force, dominating the region with their enormous numbers. While they did not go out of their way to attack mortal inhabitations or cities, the converse was not true: the marauders of Anga and Vanga were notoriously aggressive. They would pick a fight with anyone just to prove their prowess. This competitive attitude had led over time to their copying the appearance of their vanar neighbors when going to battle: contributing to the legends of their vanar-like ferocity in combat.

'What are we waiting for?' Anga demanded, flexing his painted biceps. 'Let's kill some Kurus!'

'Aye, brother,' said his sibling Vanga, 'I have my heart set on killing a Kuru prince today.'

Both raised their hooked spears, designed to pluck down vanars from overhanging branches, and brandished them aggressively, ulullating the Anga-Vanga war cry.

Kaurwa of Kalinga looked down upon this display of machismo from astride her Macedonian mare, a magnificent white beast some 24 hands high. In the Kalingan style, the mare was unsaddled; Kaurwa rode her bareback, contrasting her mount's absence of accoutrement with a swaddling of tightly wound fabric that encased every part of her lithe body, revealing not one inch of her dusky skin. Even her face and head were wrapped in strips of cloth, only her eyes peering out hotly from a visor-like gap. She made no comment on the display of testosterone from the northeasterner brothers but her attitude of haughty disdain spoke for itself.

Beside her, the short squat form of Sumhasana of Sumha openly grimaced through his flaming red beard. 'We of the cave cities believe in showing respect for one's foes. Kill them we must, it is our dharma. But crow about it, we need not. It is ill luck to behave thus before the start of battle.' He hefted his longaxe, its shaft and blade carved with a fine filigree of symbols; this was the legendary weapon Cold Vengeance, forged and hammered over three hundred years earlier and responsible for the deaths of many hundreds, thousands even, in the hands of his father and forefathers. With his free hand, he wiped the top of his bald pate of the fine sheen of perspiration that seemed omni present.

The powerful arms of Pundraki of Pundar flexed as they swung twin longswords, each a gleaming length of scintillating steel and gold inlaid handles. With smooth fluid actions, she sheathed both weapons crosswise on her back. Her back, torso, thighs, calves and even her neck all bulged with massive slabs and ropes of muscle, exposed by her lack of garments. At a glance, she appeared to be a naked mass of muscle, leather and metal, the crossed sheaths upon her back extending in similar strips of leather inlaid with

metal around her limbs and body. In contrast to her bulk
and musculature, even the two northeasterners appeared
slender.

'You expect too much of those two, if you expect civilized
behavior,' she said. 'The men of Anga and Vanga are not
known for their intelligence or their sense of dharma. But
even so, in a brawl, I would rather have them on our side
than against us. They can fight dirty, and that may come in
useful when facing that old stick-in-the-mud Bhishma.'

Vinda of Kekeya's cold grey eyes took in Pundraki's
appearance and garb, lingering a moment longer than
necessary upon her feminine areas. His face and body were
shaven clean like the Kings of Anga and Vanga, but his lean
muscled body was only oiled for battle, not painted. Metal
studdings and piercings decorated a substantial portion
of his body and face, adding an odd contrast to his sharp
jaw and clean handsome features. There was a sense of
menace and suppressed intensity to his seemingly slow, cool
exterior; the metal decorations inserted in his skin echoed
that sense of threat. He wore a number of blades around his
waist, a broadsword, a shortsword, a thin needle-pointed
dagger, and several others of varying sizes, thicknesses and
curvatures.

'If this were a brawl, you would be right. But for a
pitched battle against the likes of Bhishma of Kurujangala,
their bravado will be short-lived. I wager they will not last
the morning. If they do, it will only be by scuttling from the
field with their tails between their painted arses the instant
they see Pitama's ivory chariot racing towards them.'

Pundraki considered this for a moment, returning Vinda's lingering gaze with a like appraisal of her own, openly viewing the Kekayan's masculine parts with sexual curiosity. 'I will accept that wager,' she said casually, 'the winner earning the right to bed the other.'

Vinda returned her gaze with a matching look. 'A very equitable wager,' he replied. 'I accept.'

Vriddhakshatra of Sindhudesha snorted in amusement but made no comment on either the wager or anything else. A giant of a man, he sat astride a young bull elephant with eyes which had eyes dancing with madness. His face which was a map of battle scars, his severed left ear, and two missing fingers on his right hand, all testified to his veteran experience in the business of warfare. The enormous weapon he carried, a lance-like object with an end shaped like a butcher's chopping blade, looked like it needed an elephant of its own to ride into battle. Both Vinda on one side and Kartavya Mara on the other gave the Sindhu and his elephant plenty of space.

Kartavirya Mara was the most unusually mounted of them all. He sat upon a wooden litter of unusual size and dimensions. It spanned about a yard in width, some three yards in length, and was over a yard thick. None of the other leaders of nations had ever seen or heard of such an unusual litter before. Even more unusual were the number of litter bearers. Some two dozen Haihaiyas stood beneath the litter, bearing its weight upon their shoulders, with another two dozen standing on either side of them. Six dozen men and women to carry one man? There was more to the contraption than met the eye but nobody wanted to ask Kartavyava Mara and he was not the sort to chat pleasantly about such things. He sat comfortably upon a cushioned sedan seat, his flabby belly and gelid torso shivering with every movement. His arms, unnaturally long for his height, hung down by either side of his chair, reaching the sides of the litter.

'Where is the Magadhan and his sycophant, the Mountain King?' he asked of no one in particular. He was chewing on a plug of some intoxicant-laced betelnut preparation and from time to time leaned his head to spit a wad of blackish red effuvial, not caring if it splattered his own litter bearers. 'It is almost time for the battle conches to sound and they are not here yet. What is our strategy to be? In what formation and order are we to attack and defend? What tactics will we use to outmaneuver the great Bhishma?' He ended his litany with a hawk and purge that coated the back and neck of a litter bearer who stood stoically.

Kaurwa shook her head, visibly disgusted at the display of arrogance. To a Kalingan, such overbearing behavior was intolerable. This was why Kalinga had dissolved its monarchy and become a republic, so that rulers like Kartavya Mara could not assume the mantle of entitlement.

Ripunjaya of Avanti chuckled genially. 'It would be a fine thing if they were to leave us in the lurch here. Why, it would even make one suspect that perhaps this whole exercise is the connivance of Bhishma himself, designed to lure us out into showing our hostility and justifying him quashing Kurujangala's enemies in one sweep.' He slapped his leather gloved hand against his trousered thigh, his purple neck and face tattoos quivering as he laughed at the thought. 'That would be quite brilliant, tactically speaking.'

Madrashya of Madra made a sound of despair, grimacing at Ripunjaya of Avanti. 'Speak of auspicious things, liege of Avanti. Our leaders will arrive at any moment. My stomach is already churning from fasting for the past three days and nights, I cannot bear to contemplate on such inauspicious thoughts.'

The next person, Druhyu of the eponymous kingdom, fingered the ugly web of scars across his throat, glaring with inexpicable fury at everyone around, contributing not word to the conversation. His compact two-horse chariot was as ugly as himself, cruel rusty spokes and barbs poking out at every angle, threatening to rip open anyone, man or beast, unfortunate enough to come in its path.

It was Bahlika Pratipeya who spoke next, tossing back his flowing grey hair. 'Bhishma Pitama needs no stratagems or undharmic tactics. If he desired to punish us for our transgressions against Kurujangala, he would simply have mounted his chariot and come to our front gates, meting out the harshest penalties under the law. My blood kin does not resort to trickery or subterfuge to achieve his ends. He is a man of dharma.'

Pert-nosed, flat-faced Shastra, Chief Rider of the Kambhoja horse clans, nodded in agreement without saying a word to her fellow allies, but bent her head to the twitching ear of her sleek muscular stallion and whispered continually to him. The stallion shuddered with pleasure and anticipation, pawing the firm earth to show his eagerness to carry his mistress into battle.

The last of the allies was the only person who had not been present at the gathering in Pragjyotisha. Her squat, broad physique and wide features revealed a strong resemblance to her father, Ushanas of Ushati. But Usha betrayed neither of her father's loquaiciousness nor his gluttony. While broadly built, she was more solid than fat and the way she stood upon her four-horse chariot suggested practice and experience belying her youth. She was clad in oddly festive colors and accoutrements, rainbow-hued shawls and robes swirling around her stocky form. The clutch of javelins standing in the well beside her was similarly colorful and bejewelled. Clearly, though she had inherited her father's genetic makeup and was now queen of his kingdom, she was very much her own woman.

There was no time for further discussion amongst this motley group upon the hilltop. The sound of cloven hooves from behind them caused them all to turn their heads just as Bhagadatta and Jarasandha appeared from over the rise. The One King of Pragjyotisha and his mentor the God-Emperor of Magadha were dressed much as they had been that first day in the aerie, which was to say, they were dressed for court, not for battle. This fact did not go unnoticed by any of the allies but none remarked on it. Whatever questions or doubts anyone had until this moment were dispelled by the appearance of the two men responsible for this military campaign. It was with their ears rather than their mouths that they paid service to the new arrivals.

Jarasandha and Bhagadatta both drew up their mounts at an angle that afforded them a view of all the allies.

Bhagadatta smiled casually at each of them in turn, unfazed by the scowls, grimaces and even outright hostility (from Druhyu) that met his attempts at friendly greeting. He said not a word.

Jarasandha sat silently, his back to the enemy lines, staring down at the reins clutched in his thin bony fist. Several moments passed. The first gloaming appeared on the Eastern horizon. The Kuru lines straightened up into picture perfect formation, not a man out of place, and then fell completely silent, ready for the imminent battle. Several of the allies' mounts dropped the inevitable loads of manure and steaming hot streams of pungent urine, filling the brisk morning air with two of the many odors of battle. The stench of human urine, offal, blood, vomit, intestines, bowels, and other bodily parts would join it as the day progressed, but for now, these were the strongest smells. A flock of kraunchya birds flew by from west to east, calling out mournfully. Higher in the sky, carrion birds had begun to gather in anticipation of the feast to come.

'You fear Bhishma.'

Jarasandha spoke without raising his head, his voice barely loud enough to be heard. But even the horses pricked up their ears and tilted their heads in his direction. He had everyone's complete attention. There was no grumbling now, or wayward comments. Even the perpetually angry Druhyu lowered his flaming eyes and listened.

'But it is not Bhishma you will fight today.'

Slowly, after another long pause, the God Emperor of Magadha raised his head. He swivelled his skull, taking in every one of the allies. Even though he did not linger on any one; each man, woman and beast felt his gaze sear their minds. Pupils widened. A horse whinnied nervously and was restrained by its rider.

'It is the crown princes of Hastinapura whom you face on this field today. Dritarashtra and Panduranga. One blind since birth and the other crippled by his inability to withstand direct sunlight or bright light. Both boys, barely on the cusp of manhood, extracted from their guru's ashram before they could complete even a full season of learning.'

Jarasandha raised an arm and held it an impossible angle, pointing behind himself at the Kuru frontline across the field. 'There they stand, about to enter their first battle of their lives. No experience in single combat, armed or unarmed combat, horseback, chariot, foot or melee. No experience at all, in truth. Only a few score practice rounds, mostly with each other, with virtually no supervision or expert guidance. Why is that? When even a little boy or girl born in the Kuru line is an expert at all varieties of combat by the age of 9? Because Dritarashtra and Panduranga were born crippled, and deemed incapable of achieving the high standards demanded of their lineage. Yet, because they are Kuru, and because they are the crown princes, tradition demands that they lead today's battle.'

Jarasandha lowered his hand and moved his horse, riding along the line of allies slowly, looking each one in the face as he passed. Each one felt an uneasy prickling in the back of their head, at the base of the skull, as if the Magadhan's gaze penetrated through their eyes into their brains all the way to the command center of their bodies.

'Bhishma believes he is achieving several things with this ruse. By bringing the crown princes to lead this battle, he creates the illusion that they are capable of ruling someday. Naturally, he intends to lead the actual fighting himself, using his mastery of warcraft and his own prowess as an unsurpassed yodha to crush our rebellion. He intends to win the battle almost single-handedly, then credit the victory to young Dritarashtra and Panduranga, thus ending our uprising, crippling our armies, and proving beyond a doubt that the two crippled grandsons of the late Emperor Shantanu are true heirs to the Kuru dynasty. It is a brilliant plan but it is this very plan itself that will be the Kurus' undoing today.'

On the field, the conchbearers on both fronts raised their white conches to their mouths, lifting their heads to prepare to issue the first call. Jarasandha glanced in their direction but did not react. He continued speaking as calmly as if they had all day to discuss the matter at hand.

'Bhishma's plan depends on the two boys merely being

figureheads, seen by all, present in action, perhaps even tossing a spear or loosing a few arrows, drawing swords for effect mayhaps, but not actually engaging in full combat. Our plan is simple: Engage the boys. Focus our entire attention upon them. Attack them with every cader and weapon at our disposal. Assault them relentlessly, ruthlessly, and do not stop until both boys are lying dead and maimed beyond recognition upon that field today.'

The conch bearers sounded the first call, a short sharp burst that filled the early morning sky as the first rays of sunlight crested the Eastern mountains. The allies responded with quickened breath, flared nostrils, and quickened pulses. But in their eyes was a spark of hope that had not been there before. In some eyes, there was even...excitement. In one pair of eyes, there was malevolent glee. Druhyu grinned broadly, rising to his toes and peering down at the field as if to mark out the two young lives he looked forward to ending this day.

'Bhishma has anticipated this stratagem, of course. He anticipates everything, knows everything. But he will have no choice. While every last one of you attacks the two Kuru boys, he will be forced to leave them to fend for themselves. Because he will be preoccupied with a more pressing threat, locked in a fight which he will neither be able to win nor end quickly. Because he will be facing me personally in a fight to the death, and if you think Bhishma is a warrior to be feared, then know now that Jarasandha am no milk-sipping calf of the fold either.'

The second call sounded, the mournful lowing of the

conches lingering longer than the first time, but breaking off just as abruptly.

Jarasandha stopped. He was now in the same place he had been when he had begun. He scanned the allies once more with the same intense gaze. More than one shivered as if the warm summer day had turned unexpectedly chill.

'When we win the day – and win we shall – I shall ask each of you for something. Nothing too precious. Yet not trivial either. You will give it freely of course, without hesitation or question. And in case you need reminding, our pact remains in effect even in the unlikely event that one or more of you should fail to survive the battle.' Jarasandha's gaze paused upon Usha of Ushati. 'Your successor will inherit your part in this alliance. We are bound together now, not merely until death do us apart, but until Bhishma and the Kuru dynasty are completely destroyed.'

Jarasandha looked at the assembly in one wide sweeping glance and smiled, showing thin long teeth divided clearly at both the top and the bottom. '*Cry vengeance now, and let loose the wardogs!*'

Jarasandha turned his horse to face the battlefield, girding the reins in a preparatory stance as the third and final call began to sound.

As the conches finally faded away to a grim silence, the Magadhan spurred his horse onward and galloped down the hill at a blistering pace, blazing a trail down the hillside, aimed as straight as an arrow at the legendary white chariot of the War Marshall of the Kuru forces: Bhishma.

The battle had begun.

|| 4 ||

Bhishma saw the lone rider galloping straight towards him and narrowed his eyes. The gesture was not to enable him to see more clearly: the son of Ganga could view the individual hairs in each feather of a crow from a hundred yards away. He was reacting to the tactic. At the pace the Magadhan was setting, he would be at Bhishma's chariot momentarily.

'Dri! Pandu!'

At the sound of their names, both boys turned their heads. Their young faces were drawn and taut, raw with anticipation and a heightened state of awareness close to panic.

'Do as I said, and all will be well,' Bhishma said. He had unslung his longbow and gripping it in one hand; an oddly shaped missile was clasped in the other hand. 'In my absence, protect each other. Remember, you are sons of Kuru. Fight bravely and tirelessly. No retreat, no parley, no surrender. Those who rise against Kurujangala must be taught a lesson.'

Bhishma raised his longbow above his head and roared: '*Jai Ganga Maata!*'

His chariot lurched forward, the reins wrapped around his waist and controlled by deft movements of his torso. Picking up speed with lightning swiftness, the fabled white chariot raced ahead of the Kuru frontline, heading not directly at the oncoming rider, but at an angle designed to draw him away from the two princes.

Dri and Pandu swallowed nervously, throats thick with terror, hearts pounding in their bony chests. Pandu wiped an errant drop of sweat from his forehead and glanced at his brother. Dri was standing with that odd stiff stance that meant he was scared and frozen into inaction.

'Dri,' Pandu said softly. 'I am here with you, through thick and thin. We will stand and fight together.'

Dritarashtra's throat worked. He turned his sightless eyes toward his brother. His voice was gruff and unlike his usual speaking tones. 'I can take care of myself.'

Pandu blinked. 'Bhishma Pitama said we are to protect each other.'

Dri sucked in a deep breath and released it. 'Protect yourself. I will protect myself.'

Before Pandu could say another word, Dri slapped the back of his charioteer who obeyed the command and urged the chariot's horse team forward.

Pandu watched in dismay as his brother's chariot rode away from him, toward the frontline of Kuru chariots, preparing to make their first charge. Pitama's instructions had been for them to remain here in an observer position until he said otherwise. But Dri's action left him no choice.

He could hardly remain here while Dri rode into battle. Besides, Bhishma Pitama's last instruction had been to protect one another, and whatever Dri may say, Pandu intended to ensure his brother's well-being no matter what. 'Forward,' he instructed, and his charioteer chased Dri's chariot, catching up easily.

Satyavati watched from the high platform off the field. A select guard and entourage surrounded her and the other ministers and courtiers who enjoyed the privilege of viewing the battle from this vantage point. The platform itself was no less than a throne podium, bedecked with embroidered carpets, comfortable seating, attendants with food and drink, and all the luxuries that royalty commanded. The courtiers and ministers feasted and drank as they discussed the battle formations, odds and tactics as if viewing nothing more than a sport. Which, in a sense, was true: War was indeed a sport. A sport of kings and queens. Only Satyavati was not entertained. Those were her beloved grandsons down there, riding their chariots to the frontline despite Bhishma's assurances to her that they would only observe from the sidelines and not engage in actual combat. As for Bhishma himself, he was already halfway across the field, racing to meet one of the enemy riders who seemed a madman galloping as if in a race – a race to the death, she hoped.

'Who is that?' she asked.

The ministers closest to her broke off their discussion

of tactics at once. 'Why, Maharani, that is the wretched Magadhan who has plagued the world so much of late. The two-faced Jarasandha. The mleccha who considers himself an Emperor and a God, both at once. Such hubris deserves a most painful death at the hands of Pitama!'

Satyavati leaned forward, gripping the cushioned arms of her royal seat. Jarasandha himself. And it looked like he was racing to challenge Bhishma himself. Forcing Bhishma to leave both Dri and Pandu unprotected. This was not an auspicious beginning. Not at all.

|| 6 ||

When Bhishma estimated the distance between his racing chariot and the oncoming chariot of Jarasandha to be seven hundred yards, he raised his bow and loosed his first volley. The arrows he used were bunched tightly together in a packed sheaf; each long arrow was segmented. The full sheaf of one hundred and eight arrows rose into the sky. As they reached the zenith of their arc, the hundred and eight split into ten times that number, each yard-and-a-half long arrow separating into ten darts with pointed metal tips. As they fell, the natural force of the easterly blowing wind and the angle and trajectory used by Bhishma caused them to spread in an umbrella like formation, except an umbrella protects those beneath its shade. This umbrella consisted of one thousand and eighty pointed metal-tipped darts of six inches each, each now falling with a velocity and force sufficient to punch through metal armor and bone and pierce the vital organs of the human body. The formation was so precisely aimed that no two darts were more than a few inches apart. The entire umbrella had a diameter of three hundred yards, and was aimed to fall with Jarasandha's chariot precisely at its center at the time of groundfall.

Both armies and their leaders saw the volley and drew in breath. Those who had enjoyed the privilege of witnessing Bhishma deploy this same missile before knew that such a volley was capable of bringing an entire company of a thousand foot soldiers to a painful halt, killing a tenth of them instantly, wounding most of the others.

The person for whom the volley was intended did not even look up at the descending umbrella of death. Instead, he pointed a finger at Bhishma and grinned, displaying his divided teeth. Even across the six hundred yards that now separated them, that skull head grin was easily visible to all the thousands of watchers.

Then Jarasandha disappeared from sight.

The volley made groundfall with a metal shirring. Darts embedded themselves into the hard, packed dirt of the field, the shafts almost disappearing into the ground from the force of impact; they embedded themselves into the wood and metal parts of Jarasandha's chariot; they pierced the flesh of Jarasandha's unfortunate horse team, penetrating their innocent hearts. The horses stumbled, broke their forelegs and collapsed in a cloud of dust, the chariot upending and somersaulting over their broken dart-pierced bodies to crash and tumble over and over on the field, coming to rest almost a hundred yards further on. During this chaos, of Jarasandha himself there was no sign.

Only Bhishma's demi-god eyes saw what actually happened. At the moment when he raised his finger to point at Bhishma, Jarasandha split himself into two. His two halves separated as precisely as a wood chip cut by the sharpest axe and stood independently for barely a fraction of a shana. Then, in a movement so fast it was a blur to the mortal watchers, the Magadhan divided himself again–and again–and yet again. A hundred fold.

Each segment of himself was so thin, it was barely a sliver. Yet every portion of his body, organs, hair, skin, bone, vein, blood, bodily fluid, remained perfectly intact and functional. Each sliver of his body existed and survived independently, an organism unto itself.

As the volley of darts fell, the slivers easily avoided being struck - not a single dart so much as nicked any one of Jarasandha's parts. As the horses died and the chariot upended, the hundred slivers of Jarasandha flew up into the air, as slender as gossamer wings. In midair they conjoined once more, assembling themselves into a perfect whole.

To the watchers, it seemed Jarasandha disappeared a moment before the volley struck, then reappeared in midair, miraculously. Jarasandha landed on bent knees, lithe and easy, his slender, axe-like face still retaining the same grin, his finger still outstretched, his eyes winking at Bhishma. Bhishma, now less than five hundred yards away and bearing down fast. The watchers gasped in astonishment.

Never had anyone present seen an assault by Bhishma so successfully thwarted. Even without knowing how Jarasandha had survived the volley, it was clear that he had indeed survived it. And that had never happened before, to anyone's knowledge.

Bhishma pursed his lips and acknowledged his enemy's hardiness. So Jarasandha was every bit as difficult to kill as his legend claimed. Very well then. He would use harsher tactics. It was a long time since the son of Ganga had faced an adversary with supermortal abilities. But it would take a lot more than such tricks to survive Bhishma.

He raised his bow to loose his next assault. But before he could attack again, Jarasandha made his move.

|| 7 ||

Satyavati was dismayed as she watched Jarasandha survived the deadly volley. Everyone around her expressed shock as well. The war minister, a curmudgeonly old man who had spent more time in the drinking taverns of Hastinapura than on battlefields, was the only one who expressed admiration for the Magadhan's survival. 'It looks like Pitama finally has a fight on his hands. About time too.' The old minister had been allowed little say in a kingdom where the War Marshall, Bhishma himself, was a one-man army undefeated in his entire lifetime. Satyavati dismissed his smug comment as the frustrated bitterness of a once-famous warrior overshadowed by the greatest yodha of all time, but she couldn't help wondering if there was even the slightest truth to his words. *If Bhishma has a fight on his hands, then what of Dri and Pandu? Who will look out for them?*

She turned her head to look at the place where Dritarashtra's and Pandu's chariots had been stationed moments earlier. Distances being so vast on the field of battle, she had to search to spot them amongst the endless rows and columns of different caders. There they were, their bone-white chariots and purple-black flags standing out amidst the red ochre chariots and leaf green flags of the other charioteers. They had moved from the sidelines to the frontlines and that was worrying enough. But at least they appeared to be standing in one place, not entering the fray. And perhaps being with the rest of the chariot lines was safer than being isolated on the sidelines. Satyavati knew very little about warcraft and battle tactics; unlike most queens, she did not come from a warrior-royal background. Her father was a fisher chief, not a warrior-king. But as Emperor Shantanu's queen and later as the Dowager Empress of Kurujangala, she had seen enough battles and heard enough war campaigns planned to have picked up some basic knowledge about the ugly business. However many rules and warrior codes everyone talked about, the brutal truth was that the entire purpose of war was to kill, maim, wound and destroy. It was all very well for Bhishma to assure her beforehand that so long as the princes did not engage any enemy on the field, kshatriya dharma prohibited from anyone attacking them. In the heat of battle, with persons such as Jarasandha and Druhyu and some of those other rebels involved, she would not put it past the enemy to bend the rules – or even break them.

She raised her gaze to the enemy lines and saw her worst misgiving realized. 'Ganga, mother of rivers,' she said, clasping her hand to her chest as she rose to her feet.

The alliance of enemies of Kurujangala was descending from their hilltop vantage point, charging downhill at the Kuru frontlines. Elephants, chariots, cavalry, foot soldiers, they appeared to be making a concerted assault on her army. There was no attempt at any formation or finesse:

they were simply pouring everything they had in a full-frontal assault.

And their intended target was clearly the chariot lines where the two young princes of Hastinapura were stationed.

Satyavati pointed at them, raising her voice. 'They are violating the code of battle. They have no right to attack our princes unprovoked. Someone, send word to Bhishma Pitama at once. They must be stopped!'

But nobody heard her, no one paid heed to her voice or noticed her shock and alarm. Everyone was too busy gaping and gasping at what was happening at the other side of the field.

‖ 8 ‖

Pandu had watched with amazement as Bhishma Pitama loosed his first volley; then with shocked disbelief as Jarasandha survived the volley.

Now, he watched gobsmacked as Jarasandha pointed a finger at Bhishma Pitama, then disappeared into the earth.

Not disappeared exactly.

Pandu could see a flurry of movement just before Jarasandha vanished: a blurring of the man's outline and shape, as if his body had...disintegrated? Not quite but it was close enough. The fragments or pieces or whatever they might be, then burrowed into the earth not unlike worms burying themselves in the ground. The speed with which they burrowed raised a hundred tiny puffs of dust.

How was that possible?

Pandu had heard a story about Jarasandha, the person telling the tale implied that the God Emperor of Magadha was not human but some kind of demon. Pandu had laughed at the time. He had been raised to think rationally and scientifically. He had studied the Vedas and the Vedangas. There were no more asuras or rakshasas or any of the demon races left on earth. They had all been exterminated long,

long ago. This was not the age of Rama, or the age of Shiva. This was the modern age. The time of the Kurus. Jarasandha could not be a demon. It was probably a superstition spread by those he had defeated rather than admit their own failure, Pitama had told him and Dri. At the ashram, only a few weeks ago, Dri had asked one of their guru, Acharya Vishwesh, the teacher of hand to hand combat, if there were still asuras in the world. The Acharya had told them to focus on their assignment at hand and put all irrelevant thoughts out of their minds.

But the question was very relevant now. For how could a mortal man disintegrate into pieces and burrow into the ground like a nest of worms?

Pandu watched as Bhishma Pitama's chariot slowed its forward advance. Even at this distance, he could see Pitama lowering his raised bow to point at the ground, then fitting a new set of arrows to the weapon. That meant Pitama also had seen Jarasandha burrow into the earth! So Pandu had not been seeing some cheap illusion. Jarasandha had disintegrated himself and buried down through the ground.

As Pandu watched, Pitama loosed the clutch of arrows, releasing his second volley down at the ground itself! Imagine! Firing arrows at the earth! But his heart felt a thrill of anticipation: Pitama was the greatest warrior who had ever lived. He would outsmart and outfight the Magadhan, just see now.

The volley of arrows struck the ground with an impact that exploded like a thunderclap. The sound and the vibrations caused by the impact rippled through the air and rolled across the field, reaching Pandu a moment later.

His chariot lurched. The entire line of chariots shuddered. Horses neighed in alarm, elephants trumpeted, soldiers cried out. Pandu reeled, gripping the side of the well of his chariot to retain his balance. His charioteer reached out a hand to help him but Pandu managed on his own.

He turned to the chariot beside him, concerned for his brother. Dri was standing upright, his charioteer's hand on his shoulder to steady him.

'Dri! You should have seen it. Pitama—.'

Dri turned his head in that way he had when he was listening to something approaching. Suddenly, Dri cried out and raised his hand, pointing to the west.

'Bhraatr!' he cried.

Pandu turned to see what Dri was pointing at.

His heart thudded. The entirety of the enemy forces were charging straight at them. Tens upon tens of thousands of foot soldiers, horse caders, elephants, chariots, all in their own akshohinis, all heading directly for this part of the field. They would be here in mere moments.

And the only person who could help defend them against such an assault was a whole mile away, far across the field.

Bhishma watched as his second volley struck the ground and burrowed deep within. The tremors and thunderclap of the impact were deafeningly loud this close but he did not need to brace himself. The son of Ganga was capable of standing upon still water without causing a ripple. This was solid earth. He remained unmoved. His horses whinnied in distress and he spoke to them gently, reassuring them.

He watched the ground carefully. It was impossible to tell exactly where Jarasandha had burrowed to. The speed with which the Magadhan had achieved that feat was impressive. In a mere blink of an eye, he had split himself again into segments, this time burrowing down instead of flying up. But Bhishma had countered the move with that second volley. The snake arrows he had used had penetrated the surface and were now crisscrossing the ground beneath the field in a wide spreading pattern impossible to predict or to avoid. This time, no matter how thinly Jarasandha divided himself, or how cleverly and quickly he wriggled, he would not escape harm. The snake arrows would turn even the smallest pebbles underground into grains of sand. No living thing could avoid being destroyed by their progress.

They would burrow fifty yards deep then be still. By now, Jarasandha was probably reduced to a million infinitesimal parts. Bhishma allowed himself a grim twist of his lips to show his satisfaction.

The ground beneath his chariot erupted. A wave of wetness drenched his entire form. Metal shards exploded through the air, flying in every direction. He was thrown up, up into the air forty, fifty, sixty...a hundred yards high, savaged by a series of ripping, bone-deep cuts and stabs and punctures, spurting blood and precious fluids from a hundred wounds all at once, pain coursing through his entire being.

|| 10 ||

'Devavrata!'

Satyavati's anguished cry silenced the entire royal assembly. Everyone turned to stare at her, their own eyes wide with shock and terror, before returning to the horrific scene unfolding upon the battlefield.

Bhishma was under assault, his chariot and horses shattered to fragments by the force of Jarasandha's attack from beneath the earth. Jarasandha's hundred slivers had emerged with the intensity of a horde of rampaging elephants, smashing up through the surface of the field, shattering Pitama's chariot, cutting his unfortunate horses to shreds, and flinging Bhishma himself up into the air a hundred yards like a hollow doll. Now, as Satyavati's cry faded away, they watched Bhishma's punctured body spatter blood from a hundred wounds, the snake like segments of Jarasandha's divided body attacking him from every angle, sinuously winding around his limbs, his torso, even wrapping around his face and neck, cutting, slicing, stabbing. The level of damage being inflicted upon Bhisma's body was beyond human tolerance. No human male could survive such an assault. And still Jarasandha continued to attack and inflict more and more damage to the Prince Regent's horribly disfigured and abused body. They hung in the air above the field, the spurts and spray of blood vividly visible against the clear blue sky. The writhing snakes and worms that were Jarasandha's body worked their vicious assault relentlessly, both attacking Bhishma while carrying him higher and higher. Two hundred yards, three hundred... Bhishma's writhing body resembled a rabbit attacked by an entire nest of vicious serpents. It was a horrific sight to behold for even the hardiest war veteran. Even if Bhishma somehow broke free of that deadly assault, he would fall to certain destruction. Five hundred yards above the spinning, writhing mass continued its relentless assault unabated. How much longer could the son of Ganga survive – if he was still alive at all?

Another cry burst from Satyavati's throat.

'Dri! Pandu!'

A turn of the head, a glimpse of the scene unfolding on the eastern side of the field, and everyone gasped and blanched again, reacting to an equally horrific sight.

The entire enemy army had encircled and engulfed the chariot company of the Kuru forces.

A thousand Kuru chariots were a formidable force, when in motion, charging at an enemy, loosing arrows by the thousands, flinging deadly aimed javelins and spears, wreaking havoc in the ranks of the enemy army.

But caught thus unawares, stationary in a lowland position, boxed in on all sides by enemy forces, not only enemy chariots as the rules of war specified, but even elephant, cavalry and foot caders, there was very little the Kuru charioteers could do. They could and were fighting back, using their arrows, javelins, spears, defending themselves with everything at their disposal. But deprived of the ability to move, to maneuver, to fight in motion, they were like a hobbled blinded horse. A chariot is not meant for defense: it is an assault vehicle. By attacking the Kuru chariots en masse, by breaking the rule that specified that only like caders could challenge like caders – chariots versus chariots, horse versus horse, foot versus foot, elephant versus elephant – the Rebels had gained the upper hand. And by throwing the entire might of their army, all their akshohinis against a single chariot company, they were ensured not merely a victory but a massacre.

This was no more a battle.

It was a massacre.

Vulture hung motionless in the sky.

She looked down upon the beautiful carnage below.

What a feast! What a spread! What a cornucopia of carnal delights!

Her sons and daughters, brothers and sisters continued to arrive from all points of the compass, now in the hundreds, soon in thousands. There would be no infighting amongst their own today. Today, there was plenty for all. Everyone would feast and satisfy their most gluttonous appetites. Eat all you can! Carry what you will! Come back for second and third and even tenth helpings. Eat till you cannot fly. Sit and digest and then eat some more.

Ah, it was heavenly.

Vulture loved battles.

If only the humans could host a battle every day, vultures would feast all their lives.

Not only their kind, even the other scavengers, both winged and on foot, would have ample repast. Even those who did not usually scavenge could not resist such a festival of savories.

She could spy them gathered at the edges of the battlefield. Hyenas, rats, wolves, even lazy lions and panthers and leopards and wild dogs...in the sky there were crows and jackdaws and even a few gulls who had somehow come this far inland and stayed to feast.

But what was this now?

Rising up in the sky like a pack of squabbling birds, a mortal fighting a nest of snakes?

No.

Those were not snakes.

Vulture knew snakes well. She loved snakes. They were a fine delicacy and one of her main sources of nourishment. She could spot a snake from a mile high.

These furiously writhing things were shaped more or less like snakes, but they were something else entirely. She smelled a peculiar odor from them. Somewhat mortal, yet something other than mortal too. Asura then? Naga? Pisacha? One of the other snake like demon races? She had thought they were mostly extinct but who knew what lurked in the far corners of the earth. Those rabid monsters had a way of coming back when least expected.

She could not tell precisely what manner of demon this creature was, but it was a demon, no doubt. And yet it smelled of mortal blood too. A crossbreed then. Vulture had eaten a few of those in her time. They did not taste good. She cried out to his flock, cautioning them to avoid the crossbreed that flew like a bird and moved like a snake. There was plenty of better fare to enjoy without spoiling one's appetite on asura flesh.

But what was this now?

Clearly, the crossbreed was winning the unequal fight. He had picked up the mortal male from the surface of the earth and carried him high above, much as a carrion bird woul do with prey. Using his unnatural crossbreed abilities, he was raking and cutting and puncturing the prey with furious energy in mid air. Already, from the smell and sight of the mortal blood spilled, Vulture could see that the mortal could not possibly survive this assault. It was an unequal battle whose outcome was a foregone conclusion.

But there was something unusual happening now.

For one thing, the mortal blood that Vulture smelled was not only mortal.

It was something else.

What then? Was the mortal also a crossbreed like his attacker?

Yes. But not a demon-mortal crossbreed. This was a different species of being.

A demi-god.

Part god, part mortal.

And he was not succumbing as any mortal would have succumbed long before now.

He was fighting back.

And he was doing it in a very unusual way.

‖ 12 ‖

'Protect the princes!'

The call went out from the captains of the chariot cader, across the ranks of the chariot company, repeated and carried forward a thousandfold. Dri heard it even above the rising thunder of the oncoming army. The unexpectedness of the enemy tactic had caught everyone by surprise, but being blind gave Dri one advantage: he relied on his other senses more than the sighted, and his ears had warned him of the approach of the enemy long before anyone had fully comprehended what was happening. Perhaps the chariot captains had assumed the enemy forces would change direction at some point, moving into different formations or positions across the field. But Dri had sensed the single direction and unity of those thundering hooves, wheels, and sandaled feet. They were all headed here: directly here. Every last elephant, chariot, horse and foot soldier. Not just intending to attack in a full frontal assault, but to circumbulate this position and surround it completely. By the time the Kuru chariot captains had realized what was happening, it was too late to escape—they could have retreated but how would it appear if the leaders of the Kuru army began the battle by turning around and running away? That was unacceptable. So they had done the best they could, moving line upon line of chariot in a circuitous action, ringing the two white chariots occupied by himself and his brother, protecting them by multiple ranks of Kuru chariots. By the time the first lines of the Rebel forces struck their frontlines, Pandu and he were buried fifty chariots deep in an island of over a thousand Kuru vehicles.

But that island was fast being eroded by the ocean of enemy forces.

The Rebels were not merely deploying a tactic here. Dri could tell from the mayhem and screams and shattering of wood, screaming of metal, howls of agony from animals and humans alike, that the assault was a final endgame with no intention of giving quarter or allowing retreat. They meant to get him and Pandu today, here on this field within the next few hours. And to smash their lives out like an elephant pounding a skull of an unfortunate Kuru charioteer fifty yards away.

Because he could not see, Dri could hear everything. And hearing was but a form of seeing. His preternaturally alert senses, already honed by the time in the jungle, were sharpened and heightened by the mortal peril of battle. He could make out individual sounds and events in the cacophonous melee that enabled him to know things that no sighted person could observe through vision alone.

About seven hundred yards to his right: A horde of armored elephants smashing through a line of Kuru chariots, demolishing chariots and horses and charioteers altogether. The elephants were wounded, impaled, pierced and killed, their screams provoking their fellow *gaja* to panic and stampede with even greater ferocity.

Five hundred yards over his left shoulder: Several dozen wooden wagons were ramming into the Kuru chariots. The wagons were laden with pots of oil. As they smashed against the wall of Kuru chariots, the pots broke open, spilling oil everywhere. From the far side of the hill, Rebel archers loosed burning arrows that went high, arched and fell, igniting the oil. Kuru charioteers and horses went up in a blaze of fiery torture. Barely had the fires died down, and a company of Rebel chariots were already rolling down hill to smash through the smoking debris and finish the job.

In the other direction, behind his right shoulder, four hundred yards diagonally out that way: An entire battalion of cavalry attacking the chariot wall on that side with every weapon at their disposal. The brave Kuru charioteers were fighting back furiously, but the sheer weight of numbers worked against them. Their numbers were reducing by the hundredfold while the enemy could afford to lose twice as many and still have enough left to keep attacking all day.

All around him, swirling like a miasma, the screaming chaos of an unequal battle.

Kuru forces all across the Kuru lines were converging here, attempting to support their besieged chariot company and rescue the princes. But the enemy's action had been too swift and unlawful to have predicted or countered in time. Even now, to engage the enemy, the Kuru army too would have to forego the rules of war. That was not possible. The Rebels were already at fault by defying the might of the

Kuru empire. If Kuru armies also started breaking the law, then the empire would lose all respect in the eyes of other allies. No matter how the battle proceeded, Kurujangala had to abide by dharma and restrict their actions to the permissible limits. That meant pitting like against like. Which was a tall order since the Rebels had smartly spread their foot soldiers around the periphery of their circle. This meant that Kuru elephants and cavalry could not attack that outer circle directly. Kuru foot soldiers were battling the Rebel foot soldiers, trying to break through, and by concentrating on driving wedges through certain points, the Kuru generals were succeeding in making inroads. But that outer circle was almost a mile away and by the time they broke through and sent the heavier caders into the fray, it would be much too late.

Dri estimated that it would perhaps eight or ten hours for the Rebels to reach him and Pandu and engage them directly. His lack of experience made him assume that he could be wrong by several hours. They could break through in as few as four or five hours then. This battle could easily be over before the sun reached its zenith.

He was surprised to find that he himself was not as panicked or scared as he ought to have been. If anything, the sheer odds confronting him and his fellow Kurus made him feel angry. A surge of self-righteous rage was building inside him. Who were these Rebels to resort to such low tactics? How dare they stoop to such means? Even if they succeeded, did they really think the world would cheer their victory?

He was, of course, too young to understand that history favors only the victors of war. Once the Rebels won the day, they would be joined by other disgruntled allies of Kurujangala. The Rebellion would grow into a nationwide, perhaps even worldwide, phenomenon. With Bhishma Pitama gone, and the only two heirs to the empire dead, there would be no line of succession left in Hastinapura. Chaos would erupt across the length and breadth of the empire. Pocket rebellions would occur. Allies would fight allies. Everyone would tear the Kuru empire to shreds, and feast on the remains. And in a hundred years, the Kuru dynasty, Bhishma Pitama, Pandu, Dri himself, all would be half-forgotten names, tragic footnotes in the history of Bharata.

Dri could not see that far. He could only view the events of the present hour. And those events were terrifying and soul-crushing, but also so desperate that anything, any action, seemed preferable to merely standing here in a chariot and waiting to die.

'Pandu,' he said.

He had to repeat himself twice more, raising his voice the third time to be heard. Pandu was enraptured by the horror of the battle raging around them, visible only in violent glimpses but shocking enough to have hypnotized him into rapt fascination. Dri could sense Pandu's own fear and rising anger, the suppressed frustration and outrage he shared with Dri. Neither of them had actually expected to have to fight today. Both had feared the prospect but had not seriously believed they would be in any real threat.

That situation had changed abruptly and shockingly. The person they had assumed would lead and win the battle on his own was no longer here by their side to protect or advise them. They were left to their own means, with only each other to turn to. Dri turned to Pandu.

'Bhraatr,' he cried out, his deep tenor voice loud and commanding.

Pandu turned to gape at his brother. 'Dri?'

Dri held out his hand, reaching towards Pandu. 'Bhraatr, are we Kurus or are we cowards?'

Dri heard Pandu's sharp intake of breath, the moment of stunned silence, then the slow release of breath that told him Pandu was smiling.

He felt Pandu's hand grasp his own, squeezing it tightl in response.

'We are Kurus!' Pandu shouted back in answer.

'Good,' Dri said in a normal voice. He smiled in Pandu's direction. 'Then let's show them how Kurus fight.'

|| 13 ||

Satyavati clutched the sides of the railing. She had left her comfortable cushioned seat and fan-turning attendants and rushed to the railing to view the horrific events more effectively. Those were her family out there, facing terrible, shameful deaths upon that field. She loved them dearly and could not endure the thought of losing them. But that was only part of her anguish. To lose them was terrible enough; to lose them like this was unbearable. The great Kuru line could not end thus, driven down to its knees in the dust of a nameless field, overcome by treacherous allies and illegitimate tactics. This could not be the end of her beloved Shantanu's legacy. She would not have it.

She was a breath away from rushing down from the pavilion and taking to a horse herself to join the battle. She would rather die here today than stand here watching the destruction of her line. A fisherwoman she may have been born, but she was a Kuru by marriage and by inheritance, and she would fight even if only for a few desperate shanas rather than let this travesty stand.

But just when all seemed lost, something happened upon that field.

|| 14 ||

Jarasandha and Bhishma were almost a thousand yards high.

Jarasandha's assault continued unabated, his hundred segments attacking Bhishma's body without respite, constantly chopping, cutting, hacking, stabbing and piercing. Bhishma's body was covered with so many wounds that it now appeared entirely red. There was not an inch of whole skin left upon his frame. His limbs were brutalized, his torso cut to shreds, his muscles and tendons hanging like frayed ropes, skin dangling in patches and flaps and face a single mass of bloody pulp. He was no longer recognizably human or male or even a living organism in any sense of the term.

Yet he was alive. His greviously punctured lungs still wheezed and hissed, drawing agonizing gasps. His battered and stabbed heart still pumped blood, though most of its contents fell through the air to patter down, wasted, upon the dusty field far below. His organs still struggled to perform some fraction of their given tasks. He was alive only in the sense that he was not yet completely dead. But to call him a living being, let alone a man, would be to abuse language itself.

And still he struggled, feebly now, for there was barely enough blood left in his body to carry energy enough to work his limbs. His arms and legs flailed and his back spasmed. His eyes and ears struggled to observe. His brain functioned.

Two bloody limbs that vaguely resembled hands, with a few appendages that might once have been fingers, grasped one of Jarasandha's snaking segments and attempted to twist it like a rope, seeking to tear it. But the strength that had once brought mighty warriors to their knees was fading fast; and the body that had won a thousand battles and challenges was decrepit and damaged, and Jarasandha slipped out of his grip easily, slicing open the last tendons that enabled Bhishma to use his hands. Now, those two once formidable limbs hung limply down, useless as the skinless limbs of a butchered beast at a feast.

With every attempt at taking a breath, he still fought, as he would continue to fight, to the very end. But it was a lost battle now – Bhishma had nothing left to fight with, and Jarasandha was still powerful, ferocious and had every advantage left.

Jarasandha sensed the imminent end of his prey and his frenzied movements slowed until his various segments were wrapped around Bhishma's body like ribbons. He allowed himself and Pitama to hang suspended in midair for a moment, then began to squeeze his separate parts. The Rebels on the field below, those not wholly engaged in pushing home their own certain victory at this moment, glanced up and knew what was about to come next. As he had done to Ushanas of Ushati at Pragjyotisha, Jarasandha would now squeeze the last vestige of life out of Bhishma's body as easily as two fingers squeeze a ripe grape.

But before he could accomplish this end, rain began to rise up. Strictly speaking, if it was rain, it should be described as falling. But this rain fell upwards, not downwards, rising from the ground to the sky.

The rain came out of the earth itself, from the groundwater beneath the earth, from great water table that lay like a vast oceanic lake under the surface of the land. It burst out of the pores of the field and rose like rain drops, falling upwards as rapidly as a heavy rainshower.

It gathered speed as it rose, rising faster and faster, and converging upon the place where Bhishma lay entrapped by Jarasandha, a thousand yards high. The sound it made was like a hiss. It gained speed until, by the time it reached Bhishma and Jarasandha, it was moving as a blur. Enough water to fill a sizable lake gathered from miles around to converge upon a space barely seven feet long and three feet wide—and crashed into the two battling enemies with the force of a cloudburst.

The sound caused everyone on the battlefield below to pause a moment and stare upwards at an incredible sight.

A cloudburst of water, large enough to drown a village, exploding on impact with the body of Bhishma a thousand yards high.

The brunt of the impact was borne by Jarasandha. For by wrapping himself around his prey's body, he had encased Bhishma in a protective layer of his own flesh. The force of the water striking his thinly spread form was so intense that it caused Jarasandha to lose bodily cohesion completely. His flesh was smashed into a thousand tiny droplets. He exploded like a cloud of spray in mid air. The cloud of spray drifted down like red mist, carried eastwards by a current from the southwest.

As the cloud was carried away by the wind, those below watched to see what had happened to Bhishma.

Bhishma's body remained floating in midair, no longer entwined by Jarasandha, but now entirely encased in water. The water was several yards deep, forming a giant block roughly rectangular in shape. The edges of this rectangle were not smooth or perfect, they were wavering and fluid, rippling in the current of wind, but the water cohered into this shape and remained thus. In the center of this rough rectangle was the Pitama's body, now only blurrily visible but still intact.

As everyone watched, the block of water began to harden and grow bluer in hue. The water was lowering its own temperature, despite the morning sun shining down. In moments, the block had frozen solid. This solid block of ice remained where it was in midair, a thousand yards high above the field.

|| 15 ||

'*K*auravas!'

The battle cry tore loose from two young throats. It applied equally to children of Kuru of both sexes but in this particular case, it was used to mean, literally, 'Sons of Kuru!' Shouted by both Pandu and Dri together, at first it was noted only by the Kuru charioteers. They turned their astonished heads to see the two young princes raising their voices—and their swords.

It was a miserable morning for the charioteers of Hastinapura. What should have been a battle with a foregone conclusion had turned out instead to be an unwinnable fight. The enemy's unlawful violation of the rules of war and their cowardly tactic had turned the balance against the Kurus. The sheer mass and speed with which the Rebels had attacked the Kuru chariot lines was unheard of. Nobody could have anticipated such a move. To start a battle by cheating! What dastardly behavior. But any outrage had swiftly been replaced by dismay, then alarm, and now outright panic as the odds mounted against the charioteers. Now, barely an hour into the battle, the sun only a hand's breadth above the eastern horizon, the brave charioteers were already facing not just their own imminent death, but also imminent defeat. That the enemy would prevail was inevitable now. That they were outnumbered, surrounded and facing certain death was a certainty too. Both these ignominious outcomes were galling. But the knowledge that the heirs of Kurujangala would be killed was unbearable. They might not be able to prevent that from happening, given the odds and circumstances. But they would not stop trying. So long as there was even a single Kuru charioteer alive and standing, they would fight and give the enemy as hard a time as possible. The Rebels would win today, but they would pay a price for that victory. The captains sent out the word: ten for one. That meant simply, Kill ten enemies for every single Kuru felled.

And that was what they were doing now: Selling their lives dearly. Fighting with whatever they could, using every means at their disposal, against impossible odds, to make the enemy pay an expensive price to achieve their goal. The charioteers of Kuru had fallen into a fighting spell, a hypnotic state wherein all they saw was the enemy and all they sought was the means to kill that enemy. The world reduced to that narrow purpose. Even the fantastic battle raging in the sky between Bhishma Pitama and the Magadhan Jarasandha was only an occasional distraction. They could do nothing to help their Prince Regent. And for once, Bhishma Pitama could do nothing to help them. They were each fighting a separate battle.

The sound of that battle cry had started them out of their reverie, waking up a part of their minds that had shut down in anticipation of the looming defeat.

'Kauravas!'

Prince Pandu and Prince Dri shouted again, their eager young voices a stark contrast to the gruff older voices of the other charioteers.

The charioteers turned and paid heed to their princes.

Prince Dri and Prince Pandu were standing on the rims of the wells of their chariots, each with a hand on the flagpole that carried their house colors. They were waving to attract their fellow Kurus' attention.

Now that they had that attention, they delivered their message. It was a single word order, yelled with the same furious youthful intensity as the battle cry.

'Break through!'

Both boys pointed in the same direction. The charioteers turned their heads to look in that direction. They saw the opportunity at once.

Every charioteer's nightmare is to be stuck and rendered immobile, whether by an obstruction, a broken wheel, a dead horse, or by the worst of all calamities—a chakra. A ring of enemies so dense that even the most skilled of Kuru charioteers could not find a way to break through.

They were in the worst chakra imaginable right now. Ringed in on every side by layers upon layers of enemy forces, not merely chariots, but cavalry, foot, and even elephants, blast it! It was impossible to break through such a chakra, and even if they could break through, they had had their hands full until now merely surviving and protecting their princes, which meant creating a chakra of their own, circling their own chariots to prevent enemies from reaching their princes, but also preventing themselves from breaking out.

But now Pandu and Dri were pointing to something that every charioteer recognized instantly.

A weak spot.

The place where the wagons had breached the Kuru wall of chariots, was a scorched patch. Because of the fire and hot ashes, the enemy had sent only chariots through that breach. Elephants and mounted horses might panic at the smell of fire and cause havoc. Foot soldiers would be useless too. Only chariot teams could go through that fiery breach and attack the Kuru lines. So they had sent chariots through, many of whom were still here, fighting and killing more Kurus on every side.

But chariots moved. Which left a gap in the wall. And because of the fire, the enemy was not throwing elephants and cavalry and foot soldiers at that spot as it was doing everywhere else.

There was a weak spot in the chakra at that place. Not a very great weakness, and one that the enemy could fill in a few moments once the leader in charge of that side filled the breach with more chariots. But for the moment, the spot was weak and the opportunity there for the taking. And the two princes had spotted it and were calling to their army to act.

The charioteers of Kuru answered the call.

|| 16 ||

Satyavati clapped her hands together and drew in breath.

She had been watching; as above the field, the cloud of red mist that had been Jarasandha dissipated, blown away by the wind. The block of ice that remained marked Bhishma Pitama. Though he lay still as death within the block, she could not believe he was dead. He could not be.

She knew that the water that had finally defeated their enemy and saved Bhishma's life was no ordinary water. It was Bhishma's mother herself.

Ganga had come to save her son.

Devavrata, whom the world knew as Bhishma Pitama had been born of the mortal Emperor Shantanu and the Goddess of The River That Nourished the World.

Ganga had felt her son's life blood, pattering down through the ground, soaking into the dirt of the field, and had risen up to come to his defense. She had destroyed Jarasandha. And saved her son.

Even now, Satyavati knew, within that block of ice, Bhishma was being healed by the powerful and magical Gangajal, the precious sacred water of Ganga herself, descended directly from heaven to earth, purest of the pure, most blessed of all fluids, the water of life itself.

She had clapped her hands together and shouted '*Jai Ganga Maata!*' and had heard herself echoed by everyone on the royal platform.

Then she had turned her attention to her grandsons. And that was what had caused her to clap her hands together and draw in a breath. Dri and Pandu were leading a charge!

The two brave boys had somehow managed to rally their Kuru chariot cader and ordered them to change tactics. The defensive wall the charioteers had built to protect the two boys would not last long. It made sense for them to change from a defensive to an offensive approach. In the absence of Bhishma Pitama or another senior leader they could not undertake such a change of tactic, but the Princes of Hastinapura could. Ordering the chariots to attack, they were now leading them through a very narrow breach in the enemy lines, barely wide enough for a single chariot to pass through at a time, and now, even as Satyavati watched, they were approaching that breach.

She watched with rapt attention and hands clasped in silent prayer.

Jai Ganga Maata.

Jai to all the Gods and Goddesses in Swargaloka.

Protect my grandsons and bring them home safe and sound.

She watched and she prayed.

'*K*auravas!'

K Dri's heightened senses informed him that the breach he was seeking lay directly ahead. It was he who had found the breach and informed Pandu of its existence.

Even though Pandu had eyes as sharp as an eagle's, he had not been looking for it, while Dri, not needing to look with his eyes, had heard the absence of sound in that one particular spot that meant an empty space – a small but vital empty space.

Dri was using the same heightened sense to drive his chariot towards that breach.

Even Dri's charioteer could not see the breach himself – there was too much debris and smoke still in the air to see the narrow gap. It was only Dri's blindness and acute hearing sensitivity that enabled him to guide his charioteer through taps and touches on his back and shoulders, indicating which way to turn and drive.

For several agonizing moments, they drove through dense smoke, so thick and foul smelling that even Dri suffered a moment of self-doubt. If they drove through this and found a line of Rebel chariots waiting with drawn bows beyond the smoke, this would be his first and last battle tactic ever executed.

And then, with a sudden thrill, he sensed that the smoke had cleared and they were on the other side – and most importantly, that there were no enemy chariots waiting to greet them with arrows.

Dri heard his charioteer shout, 'We are through, my prince!'

And then he heard Pandu shout from behind.

'Break through!'

And the message was passed on from mouth to ear to mouth as the Kuru charioteers followed their princes lead and drove their vehicles through the breach.

Moments later, they were spotted.

Dri heard the sounds of enemy captains shouting at their forces, ordering them to close the breach. In another moment, he knew, the enemy would realize that the Kurus breaking through the breach were none other than the princes themselves, their main target. And then, the entire might of the Rebel forces would descend upon this part of the field. They would be assaulted on all sides by insurmountable forces and would go down in a hail of arrows, spears, javelins, elephants, cavalry, and god knew what else.

But for now, they were heroes. They were princes. They were brothers in arms. They were Kuru.

'*Kauravas*!' Dri yelled forcefully, drawing his bow and taking aim. He let loose, directing his arrow by sound at the thickest cluster of enemy he could sense.

He heard the *thwa-thump* of the arrow punching through armor and piercing flesh and bone, heard the startled cry of the man, and heard him fall to the ground, crushed under the wheels of the chariot behind him.

My first kill.

'*Kauravas*!' he cried again, and loosed a second arrow.

He heard Pandu echo the battle cry and loose an arrow too, at the same instant as his second arrow found a home in the throat of another Rebel charioteer. The man let loose a gurgle, and fell back in the well of his own chariot, spasming as his heels drummed out the rhythm of death. Dri was already loosing a third arrow before he died, then a fourth, and a fifth, as Rebel charioteers converged on him from all sides.

Then he was in the thick of battle, being shot at and attacked and fighting back and loosing arrows and yelling till he was hoarse and his fingers bled from the string and his hand found only an empty quiver as it reached over and over, instinctively, for the next arrow that was no longer there.

‖ 18 ‖

'*K*auravas!'

Pandu loosed arrows in rapid succession, feeling a thrill of satisfaction each time he saw an arrow find its mark and an enemy fall. His gurus had taught him that the taking of life was a serious matter not to be glorified or gloated over. But to him right now, it was not the satisfaction of killing that thrilled him; it was the surviving and succeeding. His first battle, his first actual experience of mortal combat. Surrounded and overwhelmed by enemies more numerous than any yoddha could ever hope to overcome, unsupervised and with his ward unable to protect him, and yet here he was, not only surviving this calamitous turn of events, but actually fighting back, eliminating enemy charioteers by the fistfuls – and succeeding. He had loosed almost his entire quiver already, close to three score arrows, and he had counted more than half as many strikes. It was impossible to tell if those thirty had been killed instantly or merely wounded, but even so, those were thirty Rebel warriors he, Panduranga, had put out of the fight. What had the charioteer captain said earlier to his cader? 'Ten to one?' Pandu had already done the work of three charioteers, and if he only had more arrows, he could continue to bring down many more yet.

Even as he thought this, his arrows ran out. His hand continued to reach into the empty quiver, feeling the rim of the container, desiring just one more arrow. But there were none.

'More arrows?' he called out to his charioteer.

The man glanced back, noting Pandu's empty quiver. His eyes flashed up at Pandu, and in that look, Pandu saw respect, admiration and pride.

'I'm sorry, yuvraj,' he said. 'I did not expect you or Prince Dritarashtra to engage the enemy or I would have stocked more. But we have those.' He jerked his head at the back of the chariot as he maneuvered the chariot past a Rebel chariot turned on its side, wheel spinning. The Rebel charioteer lay half-crushed beneath the chariot, an arrow through his throat.

My arrow, Pandu thought proudly. He felt a twinge of remorse for having taken the man's life but in battle, there was no time for such humane consideration. Kill or be killed. Besides, the enemy had violated the rules of war. Pandu was only doing what he had to in order to survive.

He looked in the direction his charioteer had indicated. At the back of the chariot, hooked to the well rim, were a clutch of spears and javelins. Pandu unhooked a spear and hefted it.

Around him, the chaos of battle reeled and screamed.

Chariots of both sides were driving every which way, the Rebel forces tripped by their own ingenuity. Their attempt to ring in the Kuru forces had left their numbers relatively thin at the outer ends of the chakra. Pandu saw that he was barely two or three hundred yards from clear ground. If he could fight his way through the last lines of enemy chariots, it might be possible to break the chakra altogether, enabling his chariots to turn back and attack the enemy from the outside, forcing them to fight on two fronts at once, inside and outside. There might yet be a way to turn this battle around.

'Dhruv,' he said to his charioteer, 'Do you see that flag yonder?' He pointed with the spear.

'Aye,' his charioteer replied, turning the heads of his horse team to dodge a volley of arrows from a cluster of chariots racing towards their position from the east.

Pandu ducked down behind the well of his chariot, feeling the *thwack-thwack-thud* of the volley striking the outer wall of his chariot. One arrow fell into the well itself, skimming his shoulder and drawing a tiny spurt of blood. He ignored it. 'Make for that flag, but don't let the enemy see that we're making for it.'

The charioteer, a middle aged man with a bristling red beard with flecks of grey, furrowed his lined brow. Abruptly, his battle experienced brain glimpsed the tactical significance of Pandu's order. He grinned, displaying yellow teeth with a double gap in the lower line. 'Yuvraj, you are a born warrior. A brilliant maneuver! I will pass the word along to the rest of the company.'

'Do that,' Pandu said as he sought and found a target for his first spear. A Rebel chariot cutting out of line and racing towards them at a sharp angle, the man aiming a longbow straight at Pandu. There was an instant when Pandu was taking aim at the same time as the enemy charioteer, and their eyes met across the distance. Pandu saw that the arrow was aimed directly for his throat and from the intense calm of the archer, he sensed it would hit its mark. He heaved the spear a shana before the archer loosed the arrow and watched his missile fly through the air, quivering and shuddering as all spears do when thrown with force, as the arrow shot towards him. In that intense concentration of arrow time, he felt himself move, twisting his head and neck just a few inches to the right, and saw and heard the arrow whicker past with deadly accuracy, passing through the empty space which his Adam's apple had occupied an instant ago. Still bent to the right, he saw his spear strike the chest of the archer, punching through his breastplate and driving the man back against the well of his own chariot. The mortally injured archer gazed across the distance at Pandu, and Pandu saw the look in those eyes, a look that acknowledged that the better warrior had won the bout, before he tumbled backwards, falling out of his own chariot and into the dust of the field, dead where he lay.

Pandu heard the pounding of the blood in his own head and heart as he reached for another throwing spear, felt the awe and humility that came from knowing he had just killed yet another man, a veteran from the looks of it, a man who had trained and fought and survived several battles before this, yet who now lay dead on this very field, less than seventy yards away, felled by the very first spear thrown by the hand of a young boy in his very first battle.

He felt humbled by the knowledge of what he had just done, saddened by the thought that he had taken yet another life, and also proud that he had survived yet another brush with death – not by hiding behind adult protectors or walls of soldiers dedicated to protecting his life, but by looking another man in the eye and matching his weapon with his own throw, by fighting and winning the right to live. What a privilege it was, this life, to breathe, to walk the earth freely, simply to exist here and now. Freedom was a privilege dearly won by the brave and the unbowed. Pandu had paid a fraction of the price of his own freedom and right to live. He vowed then and there that he would earn the right to the rest of his life himself, by fighting for it every minute of every day. Himself. Not by having others fight for him.

He aimed the second spear at a chariot racing alongside him, the archer aiming a shortbow at him and loosing arrows in quick succession. Pandu dodged the arrows easily – the archer's aim was wide and his speed too desperate – but saw the man's true intent was not to hit him but to distract him while two other chariots came at Pandu from the other direction. Pandu nodded to himself, acknowledging the ingenuity of the tactic. Now he had three enemies racing at him from different directions, all loosing arrows, and closing in fast. Pandu contemplated the situation for a kshana, ignoring the whistling arrows flying past, the cacophony of battle all around, the dust and heat of the field, and focussed on the problem. He saw himself and the other chariots as if from a height, three dimensional miniatures moving on a table top field. Everything else faded away to a white drone.

Without thinking or analysing, he picked up another spear and a javelin and kept them in his right hand as he hefted the first spear in his left hand. He aimed and threw the first spear. Without waiting to see it strike, he turned and threw the second spear and finally the javelin, both in quick succession. As the javelin left his hand, he heard the sound of his first hit and turned to view the result.

The first spear struck the wheel of the first of the two chariots coming at him from behind. The chariot upended and tumbled end over end, causing the chariot behind it to crash into it. Both vehicles went crashing in a jumble of screaming horses and wood and men, the driver and archer of the first chariot lost in the crush, the driver of the second chariot also killed instantly. But the archer of the second chariot had time to see the disaster coming and leaped off his chariot, rolling with the expertise of a veteran and returning to his feet, shortbow and arrow ready to loose. The javelin struck him through the belly – not the chest as Pandu had intended, but then, the man was shorter than he had appeared when standing in the chariot – and the archer crumpled with a shocked look on his face. He had seen the spear and the crash and anticipated it; he had not anticipated the javelin to come so soon after, nor the accuracy with which it was thrown.

The second spear had been aimed at the archer of the other chariot, the one trying to distract Pandu. That bowman lay slumped over the rim of the well of his vehicle, Pandu's spear through his chest, as his charioteer raced pointlessly alongside Pandu's vehicle. He registered the death of his officer and veered away, useless without his archer.

Pandu was reaching for another spear when he felt a piercing agony in his eyes. He moaned and crouched down in the well of his chariot, shielding himself. He had been so caught up in the success of his first combat, he had completely forgotten his primacy weakness: light. Until now, he had been able to fight without any restriction because the day was young and the early morning sunlight was soft and slanted, but now, as the sun rose a hand higher in the east, the light was growing stronger, brighter, too strong and bright for Pandu's sensitive colorless eyes. He realized now that his skin was also feeling the effect of the stronger sunlight. Soon, the heat and light would be too much for him to function at all. In the ashram he had been shielded by the dense jungle. Here on the open battlefield, he was naked and unprotected.

'Yuvraj,' Dhruv asked with concern, glancing back at him. 'Is all well? Are you struck?'

Yes, I am crippled by infirmity, and wounded by light, Pandu wanted to tell him. But he held his tongue. Pandu's weakness was a closely guarded secret in the Kuru house. Mother Satyavati had cautioned him against talking about it openly to anyone. *Anyone.* '*Let your enemies and detractors say what they will. Never acknowledge or comment on it yourself.*'

'I will be fine,' he replied, 'continue with the maneuver.'

The charioteer did as he was told, glancing back only occasionally to check on the wellbeing of his prince.

Pandu suddenly realized that in the excitement of his own first combat he had completely forgotten not only about his condition, but also about his brother. It was as if, for the past half hour, his entire world had been reduced to himself and the enemies trying to kil him. He had not even thought of Dri for that entire half hour.

He stood up in the well, ignoring the shooting pain from the gaudy rays of sunlight that struck him in the face. He raised a hand to shield his face from the direct light. 'Where is my brother? Where is Yuvraj Dritarashtra?' he asked.

|| 19 ||

Dritarashtra listened for the sound of his javelin hitting its mark: not the charioteer nor the archer, but the ground immediately before the rolling wheel of the enemy chariot. The javelin bit the ground at a sharp angle, obstructing the oncoming wheel just enough to force the vehicle itself to veer sharply. That brought it into the path of the half dozen other Rebel chariots coming at Dri's chariot. The charioteers all struggled desperately to control their teams and avoid a collision, as Dri's charioteer urged his team and drove them forward through the final outermost gap. Dri felt a thrill of excitement as his senses told him that they had done it, they had broken through the last line, they were now outside the enemy chakra!

'Break through!' his charioteer shouted.

Dri heard other voices taking up the cry and passing it on. 'Yuvraj Dri has broken through!'

He felt a sensation of deep pride. Today, he had shown the world as well as himself what he could do. Not merely something that a blind man could do just as well as any *normal* person, but that he, Dritarashtra, Prince of Hastinapura, heir to the Kuru empire, could accomplish, even in the heat of battle, fighting an overwhelming enemy, against impossible odds. He had shown them that he did not need to be compared to other boys his age who were sighted. If you wanted to compare Dritarashtra, then compare him to the warriors lying dead on this field, the ones killed by his arrows, spears, javelins, and his tactics. Match that, if you can!

'Yuvraj.'

His charioteer's voice was suddenly anxious. Gone was the joy of a moment ago.

'Yes, Atharva?' Dri did not share the man's concern. Whatever the situation, he was ready to deal with it. He was Dritarashtra, the Kuru prince who had led the Kuru chariot cader to what now seemed likely to be a miraculous comeback, if not outright victory. And the day was yet young. The sun barely two hands above the eastern horizon. There was much left to be done today, and he, Dritarashtra, was ready and able to accomplish it.

'From the north and west, my lord,' said the charioteer, his voice deathly serious. 'We cannot outrun them and we are out of weapons. I was not given to expect that you would be required to engage in actual combat, my prince. I only stocked a single supply of arrows and missiles.'

Dri tuned out the man's voice and focused instead on the approaching rumble of vehicles from the north and west. Yes, there was indeed a small force approaching from that direction. Two chariots. The rest on horseback. Why did they concern Atharva so?

He listened carefully to the sound of the men and women in that group. From the sounds they made, the displacement of the air that passed over their bodies, the impact of their horses's hooves in the dirt, the sounds of their grunts and their voices when they spoke, by interpreting the complex interaction of sounds and effects in and around the actual persons, he could form a picture of the men and women themselves.

There were only five of them. Just five. What was there to be so concerned about?

Then he felt it. It was a quality not merely in the sounds themselves, but also in the spaces between the sounds. These were not ordinary soldiers, or even officers. They were master warriors, yoddhas, kings and queens, princes and princesses, or champions of royalty. Master artists in the art of war.

And they were all approaching with the sole intention of killing him, Dritarashtra.

And he had no weapons left.

Suddenly, the bravado of the past hour left him as rapidly as water from a sieve.

The pride at all his kills, the joy at his arrows, spears, javelins hitting their mark, the exultation of his first tactical victory, all of it faded away, leaving only a stark realization.

He was weaponless, alone and about to be attacked by the real enemy.

Not the soldiers, captains, generals, or even the champions

of the enemy army. The rulers who had united in the alliance against Kurujangala.

And from the grimness he felt in their hearts even at this distance, he knew that they meant to kill him by any means using whatever it took.

Suddenly, in a single moment, he was little Dri again, blind, lost and lonely in his dark cold world, grasping and groping for someone, anyone, spurned by his own mother, laughed at by his play companions, sneered at by his peers. Alone in a jungle of frightening beasts who would rip his flesh apart without a second thought.

'Pandu?' he cried out, suddenly afraid. 'Pandu, where are you, bhraatr? I need you, Pandu!'

‖ 20 ‖

'Pandu!'

He heard his brother calling and tried to peer over the rim of the well. Another shaft of sunlight struck him directly in the eyes, causing him to cry out with pain. To his sensitive eyes, it seemed like the entire world had caught ablaze, the field burning with white hot sunlight. Even to peer at it through half-lidded eyes, through the gaps in his fingers, was agonizing. Spears of pain shot into his eyes, piercing his brain. He could not think, move, act. Breathing was an effort. His skin was afire. His insides burning. Gone was the Pandu who had stood and loosed an entire quiver of arrows, flung spear after spear and javelin after javelin. Here was Pandu, a little albino boy who could not stand direct sunlight for even a moment without experiencing a subsequent day and a night of acute head-splitting agony.

Even through the agony, he could hear his brother's voice, calling. Even through his pain, he knew that he ought to do something. Dri was in trouble. Dri needed his help. He should go to Dri. He should help his bhraatr. But how would he do that? He had no weapons left. He could not even stand up in the well of his own chariot. He could not open his eyes or see for the intensity of the sunlight beating down upon the field. He was blinder than Dri right now. His skin was on fire, his insides were ablaze. He was in terrible agony. He crouched down in the well of the chariot, hugging his own knees, trying to get through the pain and the sense of utter helplessness.

He could not help Dri now. He needed help himself. Who was there to help him? Not his mother, who would not even hug him as a child, who was repulsed by his white skin and pale eyelashes and colorless eyes. She regarded him as a freak of nature, a curse upon her life. A blight upon her own life. Even the other children looked at him differently, treated him differently. Other adults too. Speaking with extra care around him as if he was not merely albino but retarded of mind too. Everyone treated him like he was different, damaged, undesirable. Nobody came to help him when he needed help or comfortor, like now, protection.

He was alone. And so was Dri. *We are each alone in our own private hell. We must live through this. If we can.*

|| 21 ||

In the block of ice floating a thousand yards above the field, the body of Bhishma lay suspended. The miracle waters of the Ganga had worked their magic, healing the many hundreds of wounds inflicted by Jarasandha. Repairing the damage and destruction to muscle and sinew, bone and gristle. The process was not yet complete. Almost, but not quite.

A little while longer, perhaps another hour or two, and the reparation would be complete. Bhishma would be restored to his perfect self. But the voices of his nephews were audible to him, even inside his coccoon of ice. He could hear their agony, their suffering, their terror.

They needed help.

The enemy was bearing down upon them. They were weaponless and isolated, exposed and helpless. The enemy was strong and ruthless. Druhyu of Druhyu was eagerly racing towards them, grinning at the thought of driving his blade through that young flesh, maiming and butchering the young princes of Kurujangala. The others were not as savagely inclined towards killing young ones as Druhyu was, but they were equally motivated to kill the princes.

Killing them would end the battle, win the day, and secure a triumph for the Rebellion. The world would rise up against Kurujangala and tear the empire apart, sharing the spoils. And they, the first to defy the might of Hastinapura, would enjoy the lion's share. They would be emperors and empresses in their own right. Everyone would fear and be in awe of them forever after.

All they had to do was kill two frightened young boys and show their chopped heads to the world, displaying them like prizes of victory.

Inside the coccoon of ice, Bhishma knew all this and more. He had to act now, before it was too late. It was not merely his responsibility, it was his dharma. And Bhishma always fulfilled his dharma.

With a sudden explosion, the giant block of ice burst apart, shattering to fragments in mid air. They fell to the field below as a shower of tiny chips, none large enough to hurt anyone, already melting on contact with the late morning sun, the baking field and the hot earth.

Bhishma hung in midair, his skin still scarred and bruised, the reparation incomplete, not entirely restored to his former strength. But still Bhishma.

He fell from the sky, falling to earth with blistering speed, like Garuda bearing down upon the army of Nagas, and landed upon the field with an impact that shook every last mortal and beast for miles around. The dust from his impact rose fifty yards. When it cleared, he stood there on bent knee, powerful shoulders hunched and head lowered.

Slowly, he raised his great head, his mane of grey-white

hair fell back over those mighty shoulders and arms.

He raised his eyes to stare at the oncoming chariots and horses of the Allies who were racing towards the chariots of Dri and Pandu. Bhishma rose to his full height, standing astride the field, naked and weaponless, body still oozing blood from a dozen unhealed wounds. He faced the oncoming Allies who slowed, awe struck at his astonishing appearance and the sheer majesty of his presence.

Behind him, Pandu and Dri still cowered in their chariots, aware that their guardian and protector had arrived, but still suffering from their respective conditions. Bhishma spread his arms wide, gesturing to the Allies confronting him.

'You wish to kill the Princes of Kurujangala? Then you must kill me first. If you can.'

And he folded his arms and stood, waiting.

‖ 22 ‖

Satyavati wept.

She fell back into her chair and sobbed tears of joy and relief. She did not need to watch the battlefield any more. There was nothing left to see now. Bhishma was back. No harm could befall her grandchildren now.

The House of Kuru was safe once more.

|| samaptam ||

R adha frowned.

From the looks of it, the basket had drifted into the shallows, got caught in the rushes, and remained there. Someone must have dropped it into the river and it had floated downstream. She put her bundle of clothing down and stepped into the shallow water. She waded out to the rushes, stretching to reach the edge of the basket. She snagged it with her forefinger and pulled it towards herself. My, but this thing was heavy. What was in it?

She turned and pulled it behind herself with one outstretched hand, all the way back to the bank, where she climbed up again, turned, and lifted the basket with both hands, setting it down upon the bank.

At first glance it looked like there was nothing in the basket but an old blanket. She frowned again and loosened a corner of the blanket which appeared to be pinned to the side of the basket. She lifted the loosened corner, peeling it back to reveal what lay beneath. She gasped.

'Deva!'

There was a baby under the blanket.

He lay there happily content, wide awake and alert,

staring up at her, his arms and legs moving slowly beneath the blanket which securely pinned him in place.

Deva, but he's a beautiful child. What is he doing in a basket on the river?

As she stared down, the baby pushed hard with his arms and legs, freeing himself from the blanket that secured him and probably kept him from capsizing the basket on his trip downriver.

Radha stared down, seeing the strange shell-like covering that grew naturally over the chest and abdomen of the baby. There were similar growths on his ears as well. They appeared to be natural extensions of his flesh but rather than appearing gross and abnormal, they looked quite fitting somehow. As natural as hair on the head, or nails at the tips of one's fingers and toes.

The growth resembled a warrior's chest armour. Like a breastplate. But unlike a brass or iron breastplate, this was golden in hue, like a perfect golden coat of armour over his naked skin. Like a *karna*, a natural kernel of protection.

The baby gurgled and kicked again, waving his hands at her. He was aware of her and responding to her presence.

He is so beautiful, in his plate of golden armour. What a beautiful boy. Surely he is a gift from the gods! Why else would I find him here and now, floating in the river. Me, an ordinary charioteer's wife?

She reached down and offered the baby her finger.

He grasped it at once, pressing with a grip and strength that astonished her.

'My, but you're a strong one, you are, Karna.'

She came to a decision then, bending over and picking up the handle of the basket.

'You're coming home with me,' she said quietly. 'Any mother who would abandon you on a river does not deserve to have a boy as beautiful as you as her son.'

He kicked and waved wildly again, then, with a forcefulness as strong as his grip, he began to wail desolately. It was the most painful cry she had ever heard, as if he had understood her words and could not accept the cruelty of his situation.

Yet it was only the truth. What mother would abandon such a child in such a fashion? How did she live with herself? Surely this abandonment would come back to haunt her some day, till the end of her days.

Radha picked up the basket and started for home. She would do her laundry tomorrow. Laundry could wait.

The Mahabharata continues in
another epic action-packed instalment

The Darkness Before Dawn

Coming Soon from Jaico Books